THE ACCIDENTAL SENATOR

Volume One
The Accidental President Trilogy
A Political Fable for Our Time

by

Dixie Swanson

Copyright © 2011 Dixie Swanson
All Rights Reserved

Back cover photo: ©Olga Bogatyrenko/Dreamstime.com

ISBN: 0983329303
ISBN-13: 9780983329305

Library of Congress Control Number: 2011923028
Prose Publishing, Houston, Texas

This is a work of fiction. Names, characters, places, and incidents either are the product of the author's imagination or are used fictitiously. Any resemblance to actual persons, living or dead, business establishments, events, or locales is entirely coincidental.

For A.D. and D.H.
The Muse and the Midwife

CHAPTER ONE

THE PATCHWORK FAMILY

February 23, Washington, D.C.

Theirs was a patchwork family, stitched together over nearly forty years. The group was two white sisters, an African-American aunt, and her nephew. Who knew why this family worked? Maybe it was because it was a mix of genetics and choice. They were very happy, at least up until the previous year when one began a slow dance to the death with cancer.

Texas Senator Priscilla Adams Logan, fifty-two, the older of the two sisters, was dying of breast cancer. At diagnosis, it was already on the loose. Now it was everywhere.

To save her, oncologists poisoned her, surgeons lopped off pieces of her, and radiologists burned her, all to no avail. She did everything medically possible. Now she was living out her last days with her family around her.

Her sister, Abigail Adams, thirty-six, a doctor from Houston, specialized in Pediatric Emergency Medicine. She worked at the sprawling Texas Medical Center, handling calmly and quickly whatever rolled through the door. In the fourth largest city in the nation, everything rolled through the door, sometimes at the same time. Children in car crashes or with burns or unpronounceable illnesses were just a day's work for her.

As soon as her sister was diagnosed, she worked double shifts so she could spend three days a week in Washington. Since she was never home, she threw out her futon and moved back to the family's house in Tanglewood, a leafy enclave in Houston.

When it was time for hospice care, Abby told the hospital she was leaving to care for her sister. If her job was there when she went back, fine. If not, she would find another. She would never find another sister.

If these two women were at all remarkable, it was because of the third woman in the family, Regina Temple. Regina, the "queen" of their family, was a formidable African-American woman in her later years who had once been the family housekeeper. She stepped up to guardian when the girls' parents died in a car accident. She had raised them, and had done it on her "lucky" nickel. Sometime along the way, she added her nephew, Duke Temple, to the little family. He was now a second-year student at Georgetown Law School.

Priscilla's penthouse at the Franklin Towers looked like a cross between *Architectural Digest* and *Hospital Supply Weekly*. The celadon greens, peaches, and creams of the furnishings clashed with the acid green of the oxygen cylinder in the corner. The French antiques looked right at home with the soft landscapes, but the battered bedside commode screamed at them. The folding walker and wheelchair mocked the elegance of the otherwise serene room. The BlackBerry and Kindle on the bedside table were mixed in with a few half-full crystal glasses with bendy straws in them. The wastebasket held crumpled tissues.

In the middle of the amply appointed bed, Priscilla was getting harder to find. She had shrunk to almost nothing except a bald head with a nasal oxygen cannula, a caved-in chest with a central intravenous line into her heart, and a belly swollen with fluid and metastases to the liver. Her arms and legs were stick-like and seemed to be just wrinkles in the expensive sheets. Her once-blonde hair was gone, as were her eyelashes and eyebrows. Her skin, once peachy, was a dull bronze from her liver failure.

It was a frigid Saturday near the end of February, and Duke was visiting his "Auntie Pris." He was six-five and the color of warm mahogany. He often inspired fear, especially on the football field for Harvard. Now he was wheedling.

"C'mon, Auntie Pris," he said, holding the silver spoon to her mouth. "Reege'll be hurt if you don't eat more cheese grits. They're your favorite."

"No, not hungry," she said softly. She didn't tell him everything tasted like cardboard and felt like shredded razor blades going down. Her esophagus was raw from fungal infection. She patted his big warm hand with her small bony one. He squeezed it ever so gently.

Pris remembered him as a baby. If she held him and patted him, he patted her back. He was still gentle at the age of twenty-five.

"Maybe a root beer float would taste good?" he asked.

"Maybe."

He rocketed out of the chair and went into the kitchen.

"Do we have root beer and vanilla ice cream?" he asked Regina, who was polishing silver. She did that when she was stressed. If she was really stressed, she made everyone join in.

"Does this look like July to you?"

"No, ma'am. I'll be back in a few minutes."

He bundled up in the black cashmere watch cap and muffler Priscilla gave him for Christmas, zipped himself into his shearling jacket, and headed into the frigid February wind. Tran's Store was half a block away and served the impulse needs of the Franklin residents at a fraction of the price of in-building stores. Mr. Tran knew rich people hold onto money tighter than a stamp hangs onto an envelope.

The bell tinkled as Duke pushed the door open. Cold air flooded in with him. Usually Tran smiled at a customer. But he'd been robbed three times, each time by an African-American man, and he feared them. He kept a loaded handgun below the register.

Duke was used to Tran's hostility. He took off his cap and instinctively held it out with both hands to show he was unarmed. Even though he'd been in the store a number of times, Mr. Tran showed no sign of recognizing Duke. Secretly, Duke was hoping the daughter, Kim, a petite and pretty young woman, would be there.

Duke got his purchases, paid, and left. Tran was glad to see him go.

Once back at the penthouse, Regina greeted him at the door.

"You went out for nothing. She's back asleep again."

"Well, it's here if she wants it later."

"Abby will be back soon. You want to wait and see her?"

"Love to, but I've got a piece due for Law Review on Monday."

"What's her name?"

Duke kissed his Auntie Regina's cheek and said, "You're my best girl, you know that."

Then he was gone.

The day was dying and soon it would be time to get Pris ready for bed. Regina and Abby had a system. Regina took care of the house and food, supplying a steady stream of bland nutrition Priscilla labeled "nursery food." Abby did all the medical and nursing care. Together, they bathed her and changed the sheets. Sometimes Pris sweated through three sets of sheets a day. No blankets were necessary, even in the dead of winter. The tumor in her belly was huge and hot, Abby explained, sort of like having a heating pad inside you.

Regina was getting out a fresh set of sheets when Abby came in from her walk. A tall strawberry blonde, Abby had curly hair that was a riot of static in the winter air.

"Hey, where's my baby?" Abby asked about Duke upon entering the apartment.

"He said he had a Law Review article to work on. On Saturday night," Regina huffed.

"Reege, you are too hard on him," Abby said.

"And you think he hung the moon," Regina countered.

"Well, he did. Don't you remember the time he saved Mr. Burleson? The geezer was wandering into traffic, and Duke grabbed him by his belt before he became road kill. Duke was only twelve."

"Anyway, I still think there's a woman someplace in all this."

"And what if there is?"

"He's got grades to keep up if he's going to get a good job."

Abby held Regina's shoulders and looked her square in the eye.

"Reege, he's a Phi Beta Kappa from Harvard. Georgetown Law Review. Relax. You're just worried about Pris and putting it off on Duke."

"You might be right," was as far as Regina would ever go. "Let's get Pris put to bed."

Abigail ran the sickroom like an ICU. Before entering her sister's room, everyone washed his hands. The simplest of germs would carry Pris away. Regina brought in a pile of fresh linens, and Abby brought in a big trash bag. First, while Pris was still asleep, they threw away the day's sickroom debris. They cracked the sliding door to the balcony to freshen the room.

Half of Washington sent flowers daily, and Abby threw them all out the next day. The water was a breeding ground for lethal germs. Tonight Abby threw out white peonies and Casablanca lilies from a man named John Lafferty. *Who finds peonies in February?*

Pris awoke in time for her bath. First Abby did her mouth care with a foam swab and special rinse. A toothbrush, even a baby one, would feel like steel wool on her raw gums, and toothpaste would burn them.

Abby gave Pris her dose of medicine for the yeast in her mouth and esophagus.

"Reege, tell us the story of how you got us," Abby said as they worked on a bed bath. The gentle contralto of Regina's voice, combined with her storytelling ability, usually soothed Pris as much as any medicine. Abigail turned up the oxygen. Just getting a bed bath and clean sheets was exhausting Pris these days.

"Pris here remembers. She was in high school, but Abby, you were just a baby and fat as a tick.

"My mama, Empress, wanted me to be an LVN. But I fainted at the sight of blood. So I did housework and saved my money to go to teacher's college. I'd worked for your parents for nearly ten years and almost had enough money saved.

"The oil business was always boom or bust. And your daddy paid cash for everything, even the house. Your parents were real good to me. They never asked me to work holidays, and the money was regular. I got bonuses when a well hit. One time I used a bonus to fix our roof; the rest went into my college fund. Once, when a well hit, your dad bought both of them matching Cadillacs. Your mom got a fur coat one July when another well hit."

Abby gave Pris a dose of morphine. Moving her for the bath and changing the sheets was excruciating. Her bones were riddled with cancer, and there is no pain like bone pain.

Abby checked Priscilla's skin carefully for signs of bedsores and saw nothing. She turned Pris every two hours, even at night.

"One Friday, your daddy said, 'Regina, I am ashamed I don't have money for your wages this week.'

"I'd heard him talking oil talk, so outa my big mouth pops, 'Well, I'll just take a sixteenth of the well you're working on.' Your daddy looked like I slapped him.

"'Okay. A thirty-second,' I said. I figured I could come down a little." She chuckled.

"'And what do I get?' he asked.

"'I'll work for you for six months, whether it hits or not.'

"So we signed papers and shook hands. If the well hit, I would share the profits with thirty-one other people until the well ran dry."

Reege and Abby slipped Pris into a clean gown. To change the sheets, they rolled Pris to one side of the bed, taking off the old sheets behind her and putting down new ones. Then they rolled her onto the clean sheets and did the same thing on the other side of the bed. The scent of death was in the dirty sheets.

Tonight, Pris wanted to be on her right side, so Abby put a down boudoir pillow between her withered knees, and a larger one behind her back.

"When I told Mama Empress what happened, she threw a conniption fit," Regina continued with the story.

"'Girl, I got bills to pay,'" Regina said in her mother's high-pitched little girl voice. "She even hit me upside the head with the light bill, like some paper flapping was going to hurt me."

"Powder or lotion tonight?" Abby asked her sister.

"Powder," she said.

They sprinkled Pris with scented dusting powder and rubbed gently. Everyone needs the human touch, especially people in pain.

"After about three weeks, I was getting seriously scared. But a deal is a deal. I was looking at five more months of nothing coming in. Your dad called me into the back room. He handed me a check with the most numbers I'd ever seen after my name, except for my Social Security number."

Pris was sleeping by then. Abby shut the balcony door, and they tiptoed out, each with an armload of laundry and trash.

Abby wrote a thank-you note to Mr. Lafferty and got ready for bed.

Abby insisted on sleeping in Pris's room on a rented rollaway bed. Its middle steel support was a thorn in her side, but it woke her every few hours to reposition Pris.

As Abby fell asleep, she remembered the rest of the story. She'd heard it many a night as a bedtime story.

Regina told no one about her money. "I'd have to pay for every funeral in the Third Ward."

And she saved every penny to pay for a real college. Just before her six months' deal was up, the girls' parents didn't come home one night. There had been a car accident. Regina got a call at two in the morning from Miss Penny next door and came right away.

"I was some kind of scared being out in the middle of the night in a taxi. I just thought your parents were in the hospital. But the Lord had taken them home."

Once the distant relatives learned the dad had plowed his money back into a dry hole, no one was interested in the penniless girls. That was just fine with Regina. She was thirty, and two girls she loved needed her. She hired a lawyer, became the girls' guardian, and moved into the house. She kept the remaining Cadillac and bought a clunker for Pris, who was just learning to drive. Each Sunday, she thanked the Lord for the pumping well and prayed it would continue. Nevertheless, she put money aside, and she pinched a penny till it squealed.

When Pris was in law school and Abby was almost a teenager, Regina's baby sister, Duchess, died of a brain aneurysm during labor. They got the baby out alive, but Empress was too old to take on a newborn. Regina asked the girls about taking on Duke. The girls were all for it. So the three became four.

CHAPTER TWO

THE GOVERNOR

"Aw, Prissy Lou, I get to pick," the big man whined. "We agreed I'd get your Senate seat if you moved…up to…Vice President."

The governor of Texas, Lawson Gray, realized his gaffe. Priscilla wasn't going anywhere except down into a grave.

"Too tired to fight," Pris whispered.

If Texas politics was a brawl, Priscilla Logan had been one of the best brawlers ever. If she was too tired to fight, the end must surely be near.

Priscilla was holding on for two wishes, and Lawson Gray was the man to grant her the first. She wanted her sister to fill her seat in the U.S. Senate until the November election. Gray wanted to put in a rich donor placeholder, someone content to be called "Senator" for life. It galled him to give this plum to a nobody.

Priscilla paused for breath. "I could…tell your wife…a few…things."

Pris needed four breaths from the oxygen, but she smiled with a hint of her old mischief. Lawson wondered how Priscilla always knew what he was doing, especially the sex stuff. *She must have sexual radar.*

Priscilla patted his hand. Her touch felt like bones in crepe paper. Cancer was gnawing the life right out of her.

She wore her wig and a thin gown in the dead of winter. She wasn't vain around Lawson Gray, whom she'd known since college. They'd seen each other naked more times than either could count. She was beyond vanity.

"Okay, then," Gray replied. "But she's got to promise not to run. I mean swear on a stack of Bibles higher than the Capitol Dome."

After three terms as governor of Texas, he was not about to ruin his own chances for the Senate. A deathbed favor was one thing. Political suicide was something else entirely.

"She...won't...run."

"Then I'll appoint her. Now you get some rest, girlie." He kissed her forehead. She no longer even smelled like herself.

Governor Gray clenched his jaw tighter as he returned to the living room. If he thought about Priscilla dying, about their passionate romance in college or their years in Texas politics, he'd blubber like a boy who's lost his puppy. He'd think about the sister instead. What was her name? Anna? Amanda?

Regina, whom he regarded as the family's Chief Domestic Officer, appeared from the kitchen, bringing him a bourbon and water in a crystal tumbler. Her skin was just the color of the bourbon. She innately carried herself like royalty.

"Here's your 'iced tea,'" she said. "Fresh brewed. Just like you like it."

"Regina, will you marry me?" he asked his usual question.

"I've made one altar call for Jesus," she replied with a scowl. "I'm not making one for a man the likes of you."

"Why not?"

"Well, aside from your perfectly good wife, you'd want me to start cooking again."

"What man wouldn't want your fried chicken or collard greens?"

"I'm over that. I have things sent in." She was lying, and she hated lying. She'd made all of that and more over the last month, trying to tempt Priscilla to eat. That very morning, she'd cooked oatmeal with real cream. Pris ate two bites.

Their usual teasing made it easier on them both. He downed his drink in two gulps, and Regina got his topcoat from the closet.

"How long will you be in town, Governor?" Regina asked, helping him on with his coat. People in politics are overly fond of their titles, so she always used them.

"I'm going back tonight. I was hoping to meet the sister." He craned his neck, looking down the long hall. "Help me with her name?"

"Abby? I sent her out to get some air. She's wearing herself out," Regina replied.

"Abby. But she's not Logan, I know. What's her last name?"

"Adams. Abigail Adams. I thought you knew that."

Aw, she-ut, there goes the election.

CHAPTER THREE

THE PRESIDENT

No matter what, Regina got out for a walk daily and ordered Abby take one too. Arguing with Regina was like pushing string. It was easier just to take the walk.

Abby endured two circuits around Franklin Towers. The world was gray and frigid. Gray snow piled up on curbs. Exhaust from cars frosted it black. Most of the cars were muddy gray with winter grime. Only car service Town Cars were clean, their taillights satanically red in the gloom.

Abby had taken her walk and could go inside. Franklin Towers had a warm golden interior scheme like the New York building. It did brighten the day. The water wall and a huge stand of bamboo lifted her spirits, even if they screamed "Mere Mortals Unwelcome."

Abby pulled off her red knit cap, and her curls sprang forth. She unwound her muffler, stuffed gloves into her pockets, and unzipped the red down parka. *I feel like Santa Claus. Oh, well, beggars can't be choosers.* Most of her outerwear was from Priscilla's closet. In her hurry to get here in the fall, she'd only brought a single leather jacket and her boots for bad weather. Those were all she needed in Houston.

Though she and her sister were built differently, they could usually wear the same size. Abigail was taller and bigger on top, while Priscilla was a little shorter and wider. Now Pris had wasted away almost to nothing.

In the elevator, Abby entered her keycard in the penthouse slot. A well-upholstered matron silently sniffed her disapproval. *Who on earth could be going to Senator Logan's penthouse with such unkempt hair? Was she wearing cowboy boots with baggy sweatpants, and a red down parka? Dear Lord, what was the world coming to? Surely Senator Logan could afford decent-looking help.*

Regina was rushing around, straightening things when Abby walked in.

"Oooh, Abby, the White House called. President and Mrs. Harrington are coming at six, and this place looks like a bunch of farmhands live here." Regina scooped up a sofa cushion and gave it a good thump.

When Regina had a cleaning tantrum, it was a sight to behold. She once threw out the day's mail. All complaints merited the same response, "Keep it put away, or I throw it away. I never apologize for clean."

"Regina, the house is spotless," Abby said, removing a needlepoint pillow from Regina's warpath. "You had the cleaners here yesterday. Besides, the President puts on his pants one leg at a time, just like anybody else."

"You can act like he's just folks, Little Missy, but no one in my family has ever met the man. I wonder if I have batteries in my camera. I think I'll wear my purple wool dress. Ooh, I hope I remember how to use the camera." Regina headed down the hall.

Abigail could just imagine Regina in full church attire, complete with matching hat and bag. Her hair might be graying, but her smile was still a thing of beauty. Her body was ample, but tidy. No molecule of dirt, evil, or unkindness ever dared show its face around Regina Temple. It was a rare fool who didn't see Regina's worth at first glance.

An oversized bowl of rare fragrant orchids sent yesterday couldn't hide the ever-increasing scent of death on the way. She turned up the air purifier, cracked the door to the balcony, and sprayed some air freshener.

Priscilla was barely visible in the mound of pillows and mussed sheets. She was disappearing a little more each day.

"Nice of him to come," Priscilla said, her lashless eyes fluttering open.

"How's your pain?" Abby asked, washing her hands.

"Six of ten," Priscilla said.

"I'll give you some morphine."

Even though Abby was a physician, at first she was nervous giving her own sister morphine. Priscilla wasn't a patient, she was her sister. As accustomed as she was to all the hardware of medicine, the central line suddenly became a direct route to her sister's heart. It was also a highway for pain relief. Abby said many prayers of thanks for its existence.

Abby drew up the morphine, cleaned off the port with a special antiseptic pad, and slid the morphine slowly into the central line. Within a heartbeat or two, it blocked the brain's ability to understand pain. Pris's look changed to one of peace.

Abby knew Priscilla's increasing need for morphine was rolling out the red carpet into the Hereafter, but she couldn't stand to see her sister hurt. If the morphine shortened her sister's life, so be it. *Prolonging death is not the same as prolonging life.*

"Want to freshen up?" Abby asked.

"Um, yes," Priscilla said. Abby went into the bathroom and got a warm washcloth and some baby wash. She increased the oxygen flow while she gently sponged away the day's sweat. Priscilla drifted in and out of sleep as Abby put her into a peach and lace bed jacket, and added her custom-made, human hair wig. She dusted Pris's cheeks with a little blush and put a dab of lip gloss on her sister.

Then she turned the oxygen back to normal. Oxygen was tricky. Too much, and the patient forgot to breathe and died. Too little, he suffocated. In terminal illness, there's no right way.

She carped at residents about keeping hospital rooms clean, so Abby kept everything as tidy as possible. For the President's visit, there was nothing she could do about the huge oxygen cylinder. However, she stuffed the folding wheelchair and battered folding walker into a smaller closet. The latter barely fit. The rollaway bed fit easily into the huge dressing room. The commode went into the bathroom.

She put clean, ironed monogrammed pillowcases on the pillows and added a lightweight cotton blanket for modesty.

"I'll take it off as soon as he leaves," Abby said.

"Change clothes," Priscilla said to Abby.

"Okay," Abby said.

A swarm of Secret Service agents in suits and ties arrived well before the President. They mumbled their standard speech, "Ignore us. Just carry on." They searched the apartment thoroughly, even going out onto the frigid balcony. They wanded Regina and Abby.

Two agents tried to enter Priscilla's bedroom. Abigail, by now in black pants and a white shirt, greeted them with a bottle of hand sanitizer.

"No one comes in here with dirty hands." This was not a request.

The female agent, who looked barely old enough to babysit, stuck out her hands and quickly complied. The man, a Clint Eastwood clone in his fifties, looked suspicious.

"I'm a doctor," she said, cocking her chin to one side. "Use it or your boss doesn't come in here." He gingerly rubbed it on his hands.

"See? That didn't hurt a bit." Abby gave him the briefest of smiles.

The pair looked in the bathroom, behind drawn drapes, and even under the bed. The female agent opened the closet. The folded walker seemed to jump out at her. By reflex, she put her hand to her weapon as she recoiled away. Abigail couldn't help but chuckle when the young redhead composed herself, stifled a tiny smile, and stuffed the would-be assassin back into the closet.

When Abby overheard the agents say the President was five minutes out, she sent the male agent out of the room. She awakened her sister, helped her take a few sips of water, and turned up the oxygen.

"Sit me up," Pris said.

Abigail could only imagine how much that must hurt bones riddled with cancer. She propped her up against the bulwark of pillows.

"There," Abigail said, "The senior senator from Texas is ready to greet the leader of the free world."

"Put on a scarf," Pris said, gesturing vaguely to the closet.

The stacked orange boxes went almost to the ceiling. An Hermés scarf was the default gift for Washington women. Abby grabbed one, fuchsia flowers strewn across a black field. *This'll do.*

"Lipstick," Priscilla said. "You're my sister and heir, not nurse."

That was the longest sentence Pris had said in weeks. Abby was distressed at the word "heir" but said nothing. *Must be the morphine talking.*

Abby didn't care about her appearance. Harrington wouldn't notice her anyway. She used a little of one of her sister's lip glosses, then she threw it away. It was, in hospital jargon, dirty.

Abby wanted the President to use hand sanitizer. The doorbell chimed from the service entrance at precisely six o'clock. *Punctual, at least.*

Regina used to joke the previous President would be late for his own funeral, but not Walter "Schusss" Harrington. He ran his life with a stopwatch.

An agent opened the door. Others entered before and after the President and Mrs. Harrington. Abby led everyone through the kitchen and into the living room.

Even in the spacious living room, he loomed large. Abby was five-nine, and she felt dwarfed. He must be at least six-four, and with an upright bearing, he seemed taller. He was the President from central casting: handsome, graying, with a scar above an eyebrow.

Harrington's scar had served him well. In politics, it saved him from being "too pretty." Harrington got the scar in high school football. A sophomore benchwarmer, he stepped in for an injured quarterback and was bloodied scoring the winning touchdown at Homecoming. The head cheerleader, a senior girl with a glorious body, had relieved him of his virginity, as well as his pain, later that evening. He still smiled every time he saw the scar in the mirror.

Skiing was his testosterone sport now, and at sixty, he was still fit for it. He loved his nickname, even if it referred to a skiing wipeout forty years earlier. His wife, Evangeline, joked she called him "Shush" because, like many politicians, he loved the sound of his own voice.

He reached out and shook Abby's hand.

"Hello, Dr. Adams, I'm Walter Harrington."

Abigail was stunned as his warm hands enfolded her cool one. He was laser focused on her. She realized, too late, that she was blushing.

"Uh, hello," Abby replied. *How lame is that? Introduce Regina. And don't forget the hand sanitizer.* "I'd like you to meet Regina Temple, the 'queen' of our family." Abigail was relieved when he dropped her hand and turned to Regina.

"I'm so excited, Mr. Harrington, I mean President Walter," she said. "Oh, goodness. You know who you are. And you, Mrs. Harrington, don't you look lovely. Just seeing you will cheer up the Senator. That's such a 'happy red' dress you've got on."

"I like 'happy red,' Ms. Temple. No wonder you are a Washington legend," the short, dumpling-like woman said to Regina. She was lucky her husband was President. Any CEO would've turned her in for a trophy wife long ago. Walter Harrington was smarter than that. Half the voters were women, and few liked skinny blondes with fake breasts. He was also faithful, something that let him sleep well at night.

Mrs. Harrington brought a small bouquet of violets as a nosegay for Priscilla's pillow. Pris would love them.

When the President and his wife were in with Priscilla, Abby and Regina were both a little shaken. Regina, usually unfazed by the rich and powerful, was almost giddy. Abby was confused. Charm wafted off the Harringtons in just the right amount. Any more would be cloying, and less, cold or haughty. It must be the political nature. Priscilla had it.

Not Abby. Hospitals don't leave much time for pleasantries. On a busy night in the emergency room, sometimes she had only ninety seconds of sympathy for a grieving family.

Speaking of families, how did he know her name?

In a few minutes, the couple reappeared in the living room. Both had red-rimmed eyes and were holding hands. *Damn, I forgot the hand sanitizer.*

"I had to drag him out," the First Lady said with a conspiratorial air. "Captive audience."

"The slightest thing tires her," Abigail said.

"Oh. Would it be okay to get a picture?" Regina interrupted.

"For you, Regina?" the President replied. "Anything." Regina almost swooned but grabbed her camera from behind a sofa cushion. The Secret Service agent winced. He should have caught that earlier. Regina made him take the picture, twice, "Just to be sure."

"If you'll excuse me," Abigail muttered toward the three as she slipped into Priscilla's room.

"Infants First…he'll sign…and…fund." Priscilla's eyes were bright and she wore a smug smile. It was her pet piece of legislation and had been Abigail's idea. It mandated infants be enrolled at the local elementary school at birth. There the parents would have monthly parenting classes, infant stimulation sessions, learn basic safety for each age. Preschool would start at three. Babies would be monitored, and early intervention started for developmental problems. Harrington liked everything except the price tag.

"Wonderful," Abby said, taking off her sister's wig and removing the light blanket.

"Who says no to a dying woman?" Priscilla said with her eyes closed, a smile on her face.

"No one in his right mind disobeys you," Abby said, helping her off with the bed jacket. "The violets must smell sweet pinned to your pillowcase."

"Trust Poppy," Priscilla said softly as she sank into her pillows.

As Abigail prepared another dose of morphine, she wondered what Priscilla's Chief of Staff had to do with anything. It had been a tiring day, and there were so few days left.

"'Specially at first. Trust her." Priscilla was slurring her words. She turned her head toward the violets and sighed.

"What do you mean?" Abby asked, full syringe in hand.

There was no reply.

CHAPTER FOUR
GONE

So. It was over.

Instinctively Abby wanted to do CPR, but that was not Priscilla's wish. In repose, Pris's face was without pain. Her eyelids, lips, and nail beds were rapidly turning a purple-blue. Trillions of cells were dying, some faster than others. Abby knelt at the side of the bed.

"I love you, my sweet sister," Abby held Pricilla's hand and whispered into her ear. Maybe her words and touch would soothe a brain that was blinkering out. "I love you so much." She talked of sweet things for a few minutes, even if it was useless.

Then Abby put her stethoscope to Priscilla's ravaged chest and listened for a full minute. She heard nary a heartbeat.

She checked her watch. Time of death: 6:58 p.m.

She straightened the sheet and put back the blanket, folding them back as if Pris were asleep. She took off the nasal oxygen cannula and turned off the tank. Its gentle hissing stopped.

Death was indeed quiet.

She knew to phone the hospice people, and they would send the funeral home. There was no need to call the police for hospice patients. She made the call from Pris's room. The funeral home would come up the service elevator.

She went into the kitchen to the smell of frying bacon. Regina's back was to her. She was making them a BLT. Abby put her arms around Regina's waist and laid her head on Regina's broad shoulders.

"Reege?"

"Ummm," Regina said, slicing tomatoes.

"It's over."

"I know. I saw the phone light up."

Regina turned around and held Abby, who started to cry big, gulping sobs.

"Shush, girl." Regina patted and rubbed Abby's back.

"I can't believe it," Abby said through hiccupping tears.

"Don't you know she's passed into Heaven? There's no pain in Heaven."

Regina lowered her gently into a chair and handed her a phone.

"I'm going to go sit with my girl. Will you call Duke?"

"Yes." Both women reached for a tissue at the same time and smiled wanly. Regina insisted, to Abby's eternal consternation that tissues be in every room in the house. A lady always used a handkerchief or, if one was unavailable, a tissue. Regina insisted on ladylike behavior.

Duke immediately recognized Abby's ringtone. He answered on the first ring.

"Talk to me, Auntie Abby."

"It's all over, Duke," Abby said softly.

"I'm on my way."

"There's nothing you can do, and the weather is awful." Abby wanted to spare him coming out.

"No disrespect, but sometimes I wonder about you. We need to be together right now." He rang off.

He kissed the young woman in his bed and dressed hurriedly.

"I'll be in touch," he said to her. He meant it and she wanted to believe him.

Back at the apartment, Abby looked at the sandwich. She felt odd eating when her sister was dead. She was still staring at the sandwich when Regina came back into the kitchen.

"You eat, you hear me?" Regina said. "Funeralizing is hard work and you got to keep your strength up."

"I'm not hungry," Abby said.

"Did I ask if you were hungry?" Regina said. "No. I said 'eat' and I mean 'eat.'"

"Duke's on his way," Abby said, picking at the sandwich.

"After you finish, call Poppy," Regina ordered.

"Why bother a staffer on Sunday night?" Abby asked.

"You may have lost a sister, but the State of Texas and the U-nited States of America lost a Senator," Regina said. "This isn't just about us, in case you don't remember seeing the President of the U-nited States here an hour ago."

Duke was used to stares when he entered his keycard into the penthouse elevator slot. Thank goodness he was alone. Tears were running down his face, and he was mopping them up in a handkerchief. This one was already sopping wet. He should have brought a pocketful.

There were hugs and tears all around when he entered the penthouse.

"Would you like to see your Aunt Pris one last time?" Abby asked softly. "Totally your call."

"Let me think on it," Duke said.

Regina handed him the BLT she had made for him, a double-decker with avocado. Duke polished it off in six bites and downed a glass of milk. That man could always eat.

Regina brought out a plate of cookies and set them in front of him. They were plain sugar cookies, Priscilla's favorite. Duke polished off a handful with a second glass of milk.

"Aunt Abby, I think I'll pass. I want to remember Aunt Pris from when she was well, if it's all the same to you."

Abby patted his hand. "Sure. Fine." *I'd prefer that memory too.*

The utility room doorbell chimed. "That'll be the funeral home. You guys can stay here."

Abby opened the back door to two men in cheap dark suits, their hands fig-leafed in front of them. Their gurney was covered with a white sheet and thermal blanket that hung down eighteen inches on each side. There was a white pillow on top.

The taller one said, "We're from Nunnelly's."

"This way." She gestured down toward Pris's room.

Abby led them down the hall, the gurney between the two men. She stayed with them while they loaded Priscilla's body into a body bag. Abby kept her composure until she heard the rattling hiss of the zipper.

It hit her like hearing a rattlesnake in a sleeping baby's bed. She breathed in sharply and had the good sense to sit on the nearest chair.

The older man squatted down in front of her.

"I'm real sorry for your loss," he said. Then he put his hand on her shoulder.

Through her tears she looked into his face. She was bewildered. *Death was his business. He only came because I failed.* But as she searched his face, she saw no sign of falseness. He really was sorry for her loss.

"Thank you," she said.

She remained seated as they put the body bag in the deep stainless steel box built into the gurney. There was so little left of Pris to lift, Abby could have done it. Then they replaced the linens. The gurney looked the same before and after a body was in it, just like in the hospital. *The dead tend to frighten the living, so they go unseen.*

"Here's a release for you to sign. It says all she was wearing was a nightgown. No jewelry, is that right?"

"Yes." Abby glanced at the page and scrawled her name.

"Our files tell us no autopsy and a closed casket for the senator?"

"Yes."

"When you've chosen clothes, call. You can drop them by, or we'll pick them up."

"Okay." Abby hadn't thought of that. *Why were people buried in clothes?* She wasn't exactly sure.

"And you'll let us know about the arrangements. No hurry." The nice one put a card into her hand.

"Sure. Whatever." She wanted them out.

Poppy McElroy, the senator's Chief of Staff, arrived a few minutes after the funeral people left. Regina greeted her at the front door. Poppy was wearing a red cocktail dress and a three-quarter length mink coat. She was carrying a black binder.

As Poppy hung up her coat, she remembered Pris giving it to her at Christmas.

"You'll have to make do with black. They didn't have it in red," Pris said. Poppy was shocked and thrilled at the extravagance of the gift from her dying boss.

"Oh, Poppy, you look too pretty to be in such a sad house," Regina said, holding her tightly.

"You doing okay?" Poppy looked at Regina. "You must feel like you've lost your own child."

"Pris is in a place of peace," Regina said, tearing up. "Abby, Duke, and I are getting the bedroom back to the way it should be."

Poppy gave Duke and Abby her condolences, and said to the three of them, "If Regina's got you cleaning, I'll stay out of the way." She pointed to the thick black binder she brought with her. "I'll just be in the study."

Duke was moving all the hospital equipment into the utility area, including the detested rollaway bed. Regina and Abby were ripping sheets, egg crates, and mattress pads off the bed. They'd already filled one huge trash bag with soiled linens and sent them down the trash chute. They filled a second and third bag with pillows permeated with Pris's sweat. Thousands of dollars in exquisite linens went into oblivion.

Next they made a box for the hospice people to pick up.

Poppy had come as soon as she got the call. She'd been at a fundraiser for Senator Logan's pet charity, Bookworms. Prominent women in Washington held a book club every month for inner-city girls who loved to read. The girls not only got free books, they learned to dream big dreams. Hers was not the only fur checked that night. Fur might be déclassé in some places, but status items always talk inside the Beltway.

The binder under her arm had funeral arrangements in it. It had been in Poppy's sight for the last two weeks.

Poppy almost always wore red. She was a true redhead from the wrong side of some track, had worked her way up in Washington, largely under Senator Logan's tutelage. She was whip smart, closing in on forty, and married to her job. She looked years younger. She'd read as a child that redheads should avoid the sun and smoking, so she did. She also worked out like a fiend and dressed for power. With spiky red hair and black trendy glasses, everyone on the Hill knew Poppy. No one got to Senator Logan, except through Poppy.

She'd quietly run the office during the Senator's illness. She visited daily for signatures and quick briefings. After working with the Senator for two decades, she knew what Pris wanted. She and Lyman Woodruff, the Chief of Staff in the Houston office, were keeping the constituents happy, and that was the most important part of the job. In the last few weeks, her visits had been brief and only social. Poppy signed the letters herself. If she could have cast votes on the Senate floor, she would have. Truth be told, the office was in great shape.

Poppy knew to steer clear of Regina's cleaning tantrums, so she poured herself a glass of white wine and fired up the copier and laptop in the Senator's study. Abby would need her own copy of the funeral briefing book. Poppy had stocked the home office long ago. Soon Abby would have a briefing binder labeled "Senator Logan's Funeral Arrangements."

She pulled up the press release, and when Abby and Regina were finished, they all met in the kitchen.

"I need the time of death," Poppy said.

"It was 6:58 p.m.," Abby replied.

"As soon as you've informed the President, Vice President and congressional leadership, I'll release this," Poppy said. "I'll get them each on the phone for you."

"Abby, here's your briefing book," Poppy said gently, sliding the tome towards Abby with one hand and speed-dialing the President's Chief of Staff with the other.

The best thing Poppy could do for her beloved boss was to make sure the funeral, while not as elaborate as Princess Diana's, ran at least as efficiently, if not more so.

CHAPTER FIVE

NO ORDINARY DEATH

As Poppy was on hold for the President's chief of staff, she slid a sheet of paper across the table to Abby.

"Just read this when I give you to POTUS."

"POTUS?" Abby asked.

"'President of the United States.' There's also FLOTUS and SCOTUS."

"Got the First Lady one. Is SCOTUS the dog?" Abby asked.

"Supreme Court of the United States." Poppy was deadpan.

"Oh."

"Chaffee? Poppy. I have Senator Logan's sister for the President." She handed the phone to Abby.

"This is Dr. Adams," Abby routinely answered.

"Just a moment, please…"

"Walter Harrington."

Abby started to speak, but her throat went dry. She quickly took a sip of water.

"Mr. President," she read from the script, "this is Abigail Adams. I'm sorry to tell you my sister passed away this evening. Not long after you left, actually."

"She was a helluva gal," Harrington said with a catch in his voice.

"Yes sir, she was."

Poppy was making a cutting gesture across her throat. Abby put her head down and plowed on.

"She was genuinely thrilled you agreed to sign the Infants First Act. I think she was waiting for your visit before she let herself go."

"Well, sign it I will. I assume you'll come to the ceremony?'

"Yes, sir, if you like."

"I'll order the flags lowered to half-staff. I'd also like to give at least one of the eulogies, if I may pull rank."

"Of course." Abby was on the verge of tears at the flag remark.

"Have Poppy get with Chaffee about the funeral schedule. Thank you for notifying me." Then he was gone.

Poppy wasn't pleased that Abby had diverted from the script, but Abby hadn't nattered on.

"Now the Vice President, if we can find her. And don't expect any niceties from her. She's J. Edgar Hoover in drag. On her good days."

"Barker," the gravel-voiced woman said. *Boy was she*, Abby thought. She heard the Vice President take a long drag on a cigarette.

"Madam Vice President, I am Abigail Adams, Senator Logan's sister."

"Yeah?" Big exhale.

"I have the sad duty of informing you she passed away this evening."

"Damn," Barker said. "Cancer's a bitch." Abby heard her take a sip of something. With her voice, chances were it was hard liquor.

"I couldn't agree more. Poppy will be in touch when funeral arrangements are firm. Good-bye." Abby wanted off the phone with this woman.

"You don't hang up on the Vice President," Poppy said. "She hangs up on you. Protocol might not matter to you, but it matters in this town."

"Poppy. My sister just died. I don't really give a crap about protocol."

"Now, now," Regina chimed in firmly. Her left eyebrow however, was cocked, a sure sign her temper was locked and loaded. "Grief is no excuse for unladylike behavior. Do as Poppy says."

Abby felt like she was in a seventh-grade etiquette class when all she wanted to do was scream and cry.

The Senate's Majority Leader Chuck Schwartz was at home and offered his condolences. "I think Senator Logan's body should lie in the Capitol Rotunda. People on the Hill really loved your sister."

Abby could barely remember the last time she was in the Capitol Rotunda. Suddenly, it took on new meaning.

"That's quite an honor, sir."

"And Abigail, if there is anything I can do, please call me."

"Thank you."

And then he was gone.

"He sounded kind," Abby said to Poppy.

"He should be. He got your sister's job when she got sick." Poppy passed her the press release. "Please approve this."

"You work fast," Abby said, half-sarcastically. She scanned one page release and looked at the attached photo of Priscilla. She was sitting in a field of bluebonnets, the breeze ruffling her blonde hair.

"I've known this moment was coming, Abby. It's my job to anticipate." Poppy's voice was surprisingly gentle.

"I'm sorry," Abby said. "I know you loved her too."

"Don't start with 'nice,' or I'll go weepy. Just approve the press release."

Abby read it and nodded.

Poppy went to the computer, edited in the time of death, and hit the Send button. Then she sent Duke to turn on the television to CNN.

Within a few minutes, there was Priscilla's picture, bordered in black. Sympathetic voices on all the news channels said what the press release did about her succumbing to a long battle against breast cancer.

Poppy turned the page in the folder.

Within an hour, Poppy had everything organized. She'd cleared the funeral with the President's Chief of Staff, Logan Chaffee, for Wednesday morning at eleven at the National Cathedral. The head of the National Cathedral was instructed to rearrange another funeral into the afternoon.

"Not a problem. The President's schedule trumps old Mr. Ingraham's."

Poppy e-mailed him the service Priscilla planned, and he agreed. Then she showed Abby the obituary, and Abby nodded absently. Poppy hit more buttons, and the obit went to numerous news outlets.

Poppy called Laura Rowe, the woman at Neiman's who had dressed Pris for years. "Yes, it's all over, but the sister needs shoes for the services," Poppy said, putting a hand over the mouthpiece.

"Abby, what is your shoe size?" Poppy asked.

"Eight narrow," she replied.

"Please bring an assortment, at least one pair black, one gray or plum. See you at nine. Thanks."

Poppy's BlackBerry rang. Every one of her frequent callers had their own rings. Audrina Howell's name and number flashed on the screen.

"I just heard. My time is your time this week, Poppy. Same selection as we talked about?"

"Yes. National Cathedral. Wednesday morning, 11:00 a.m. Sound check at 7:00 p.m. Tuesday. You're at the Four Seasons. Only suite left was a junior. Do you mind?"

"Poppy, if it has indoor plumbing, I'm happy."

"Thanks."

"Senator Logan put me on the map by suggesting I sing at Walter Harrington's inauguration. She took me from a wannabe to world-class. I'm going to sing like an angel for her."

Duke had hoped for just family time with stories and memories, but this was taking on the air of a military briefing.

"I need to head back," he said politely. "Law Review deadline is 9:00 a.m." He didn't tell them his piece was already finished.

"Just one sec." Poppy held up her hand. She rapidly flipped to another portion of the binder. "Will you take the clothes to the funeral home for me, Duke?"

"At ten on a Sunday night?" Abigail asked.

"They're there," Poppy said.

Poppy went into Priscilla's dressing room and returned moments later with a very dated navy-blue suit with white piping and navy shoes. It was so old, it had humongous shoulder pads. Poppy remembered Pris picking it out for the funeral.

"Pris said to bury her in this. She wore it her first day in the Senate. She threatened to haunt me forever if I buried her in panty hose."

The women chuckled. Abby put the items in a garment bag. Duke was glad to get out of the apartment, even if it did mean a detour on a cold, snowy night.

Priscilla was a major clotheshorse. Her dressing room and closet were professionally designed. It was Pris's indulgence.

Poppy seated Regina in the room and had Abby stand on the platform in front of the three-way mirror. Each suit was covered with a fabric dust cover, as plastic is death to fine fabrics. She looked in the section in the binder on "Abby's wardrobe."

So for the next half hour, Abigail put on and took off clothes listed in the binder. A funeral suit. An outfit for the Rotunda. Another for visitation if people wanted to come by.

The sisters were roughly the same size, but some alterations would be needed. Poppy produced a plastic inset full of business cards and took one out.

"Here, call Mr. Tran's daughter. She's a whiz. Fast, not cheap. Ask her to come at nine tomorrow." She gave the card to Regina, who slipped out of the closet for a moment and made the call.

"She'll be here," Regina confirmed.

Poppy had started to pull the next outfit when Regina interrupted. "Accessories?"

"Yes, sorry. I'm tired too." Poppy referred back to her notes.

"Black Ferragamo bag, Cartier tank watch, black pearl studs, thirteen millimeter."

Regina knew where everything was. She put them in a shopping bag and hung it over the hanger. Kim would take home just the black Chanel suit. She'd change it up a bit so Abby wouldn't look like she was wearing hand-me-downs.

"Which hat?" Regina asked. "The National Cathedral will be cold as a tomb."

The black straw was too summery; the English "Fascinator" gave them all the giggles.

"Oooh, you are not wearing a bird's nest into a church, girl." Regina started to laugh, and its power was cleansing to all three women.

Finally, they found a black wool felt roll brim hat with a small black veil.

"Perfect," Poppy said. Abby wasn't so sure, and she was really starting to tire.

Abby consented to trying on one pair of panty hose to make sure the brand fit. Then she was free to add others without snaking herself into and out of them. *I hate panty hose. No, I loathe them. I work in scrubs for a reason.*

Each outfit was graced with two, not one, pairs of panty hose. Abby looked perplexed.

"In case of a run," Regina said. "You can't go around in tatty stockings for this."

"Next, we have the Capitol Rotunda. Abby, you're to wear the gray sheath, baroque opera-length pearls, and matching studs."

Thankfully, this dress needed nothing done to it. The entire ensemble was put together, complete with accessories, underwear, and two pair of stockings.

"Visitation. Pris put you in a St. John suit."

"Whatever."

Abby tried on the appointed outfit. It was fine. Poppy and Regina chose accessories, as Abigail was clearly agitated and tired.

"Can I go to bed now, please?" Abby was so tired, she wanted to suck her thumb and twirl her hair into ringlets with the other hand. "I love you Reege."

Abby hugged Regina, then trudged down the hall.

"I love you too. I'll wake you with coffee in the morning. Eight-thirty okay?"

"Yes ma'am. G'nite, Poppy."

"And don't you forget your prayers," Regina said. "We have to give thanks for her life." *And for the end of her pain.*

CHAPTER SIX

HELPERS

Abby's room had somehow neatened itself up during the day. She didn't want Regina to pick up after her, but she had only thanks for her right now.

She wanted her bed, but first she wanted death off of her. She scrubbed herself from head to toe under a furious shower, slathered on some lotion, and wrapped herself in a terry cloth robe draped over a warming bar.

"Bless you, Saint Regina," she said of the warm robe. She reminded herself Regina needed care too. She would tend to her tomorrow, somehow.

Once ready for bed, she crawled into it and hoped for sleep that did not come.

She'd been here before. Frazzled nerves fraying in the gale force winds of trying to keep death at bay. It didn't matter that she'd done everything right. She lay awake as death mocked her.

Sleep did not come, only more tears. *Priscilla is really and truly dead.*

When she smelled brewing coffee, she realized she must have slept. Then the thought returned. *Priscilla is really and truly dead.*

It would be her first and last thought of the day for many days to come. It would be a long time before she could remember the Pris in the bluebonnet photo. Now Abby saw her as the vanishing body in the luxurious bed.

She knew how grief begins: the nightmare is not a dream.

She pulled on jeans, a sweater, and loafers and shuffled into the kitchen. Regina was up and dressed in a velour tracksuit and snow boots. She even had on her makeup.

"You're up early." Regina said, looking at the clock. It was seven thirty.

"Regina. What can I do for *you* today?"

"Well, as soon as the salon opens, make me an appointment for a manicure. I'm off to take my morning walk."

"Regina. It's snowing like crazy outside."

"All the more reason to get it out of the way. Text me the time."

"Yes, ma'am."

Abby skipped the morning news. She knew the only news in her world. *My sister is dead.*

Poppy let herself in with her passkey promptly at eight. She was dressed for the office in a red suit and carried the black binder.

"Thought I'd work out of the study, in case I have questions for you."

"Coffee?" Abby held up the pot.

"No. I'm good."

Finally the salon opened, and she booked the services for Regina at ten. At the last minute, she put herself down for a manicure, pedicure, and a haircut and facial. "Yes, noon is fine." Abby hated spending time on her appearance. It showed. Winter was hell on her fair and sensitive skin.

"Don't do anything drastic to your hair," Poppy said.

"I'm thinking short, red and spiky," Abby said.

"You don't want your hair to look too 'done'," Poppy offered, not rising to the bait.

"That's *not* an option." Abby grabbed a handful of the curly mess. "Besides, I'm way overdue. My frizzies are having baby frizzies."

An astoundingly pretty young Asian woman appeared at nine. She was serene and composed.

"I am so sorry about your sister, Dr. Adams. She was always very kind, and very encouraging of my work." Kim Tran wore a gray pantsuit with a coral, navy, and gray scarf. The coral set off her long, black, silky hair.

"Thank you. Poppy tells me you are a whiz at what you do."

She dipped her head and shrugged one shoulder in modesty. The waterfall of ink black hair moved fluidly with her gestures.

"My parents support my career choice. Last month, they sent me to a modern textiles course in Paris."

"Wow, I am impressed," Abby said. This little girl was a powerhouse.

"I was looking forward to making a ball gown for your sister. Perhaps you'll let me make one for you."

"Well, fancy dress balls aren't on my agenda, but the next one I get invited to, I'll ask you to make my gown," Abby said indulgently.

"I would be honored. Now, there are some alterations? I'll wait outside while you change. And please, wear the undergarments you have planned for the outfit."

Within forty-five minutes, they were finished.

"No one will recognize your sister's suit. I will bring these back this afternoon after five, if that is all right?"

"Yes, thank you."

Abby remembered to text Regina's appointments to her. The next to arrive was the personal shopper with a trolley full of shoes.

"Dr. Adams? I'm Laura Rowe. I dressed your sister for many years. I cannot tell you…" she trailed off and burst into tears. Laura didn't mention she was a recent widow.

Abby handed her a tissue.

"I know, I know…" Abby found herself patting the older woman's back.

"May I get you some tea? Coffee?" Abby continued.

"No, thanks." She blew her nose. "I'm fine now. I'm just a big weeper."

"Tears wash away sadness," Abigail said.

"What a lovely thought," she said. "That brings me to the first thing on my list."

"It's not shoes?"

"No, handkerchiefs." She fished in her tote bag. "These are for you. They are antique. I find tissues quite useless where grief is concerned."

Laura gave her a packet of six handkerchiefs wrapped in pink satin ribbon.

"I am very touched," Abby said. "And you're right. Handkerchiefs are far better."

"So. Let's see your wardrobe."

"Oops. Kim just took it for alterations," Abigail said. "I think we can choose shoes anyway. I'm hard to fit. So I stick to the basics."

"Well, I've taken the liberty of bringing a variety of sizes, plus gel insoles. Fine shoes haven't caught up to comfort ones."

Abby chose four pair in a matter of a few minutes. As expected, only expensive Italian shoes fit her. Abby had expensive feet, and the shoes felt better with the insoles.

"As well, here's a classic black boot if the weather's too bad for street shoes."

Abby slipped it on and zipped it up.

"Oooh. Finally. A comfortable boot," Abby said.

Abby went to retrieve her credit card, but the Neiman's lady waved it away.

"This is on your sister's account."

"Um, Ms. Rowe, my sister is gone."

"Yes, but she left explicit instructions you were to be outfitted for her funeral on her nickel."

"She is one of the only people who do good deeds from the grave."

Regina appeared fresh from the ministrations of the salon. She looked a bit ridiculous holding drying fingernails in the air, but she was sure Ms. Rowe had seen worse.

"Hello, Laura," Regina said, hugging her with fingernails held out, lest they get mussed.

"Oh, Regina. I am so sorry."

"Thank you, Laura, but God has taken her home. No more suffering for her. Just loneliness for us." Regina was calm this morning. That comforted Abby.

"Reege, did you know Pris had arranged to pay for my shoes?"

"Honey, she planned this down to the kind of nuts the caterers are bringing. She outfitted all of us, down to a black suit for Poppy. Don't you go thinking you're so special."

"As usual, you put me in my place," Abby said, hugging Regina.

"And if you hadn't made your own beauty appointment, I was to drag you kicking and screaming. Pris didn't tolerate ragged cuticles."

"Hey, I'm meticulous about my hands," Abby protested.

"Well, you still need to take better care of yourself."

Laura Rowe packed up the unwanted shoes and took her leave.

"Thank you again, Ms. Rowe, for the handkerchiefs. I'll share them with Regina," Abby said, proffering the packet to Regina.

"And Poppy," Regina added. "There's plenty in here for sharing."

"We'll see you at the services, I hope," Abby said.

"I'll be there sobbing and wailing in the back."

"Thank you again."

The first of the floral arrangements began arriving about ten o'clock. By the time Abby left for the salon, there were twenty. She picked cards off arrangements and noted the type of flowers on the back of each card. It was going to be a long night for thank-you notes. Laura Rowe's was first.

"Poppy, I'm going to the repair shop. I'll be back about two. After that, I need to get some more thank-you notes. I've already got twenty to write tonight."

Poppy plunged a hand into the red lizard tote she always carried.

"Here's a box of fifty. I'll bring more tomorrow. You know the staff can write the notes."

Abigail looked at the cards. They were exactly what she would have chosen, cream flat card, thin black border, and script font.

"So you read minds too?"

"Something like that." Poppy smiled.

"If I get overwhelmed, I'll ask the staff to help."

"You will. Now go get your hair spiked."

"Thanks." She was saying that a lot today. She had lost her sister, but her sister had some wonderful people around her. Maybe she could get through this week with her sanity intact.

Breathe in. Breathe out. Repeat.

CHAPTER SEVEN

PUBLIC GRIEF

The Franklin Tower Spa catered to women who knew what they wanted. Some, usually visitors, wanted to draw out the experience, complete with cucumber water to drink and massaging sandals to wear. Busy professionals wanted to be in and out fast.

Abby disliked time spent on vanity. Two women did her manicure, while two more did her pedicure. She had a mini-facial to moisturize her winter-ravaged skin. Then she got a serious haircut by their top stylist.

"Oh, I know you," Andre Callas said. "I worked with your sister a lot. I loved her."

Abby could not forget the black guy-liner to show off his blue, blue eyes, and black Elvis pompadour. "She got my mom's Medicare straightened out, and my mom's from Iowa. Just relax, I'm a miracle worker with curly hair, and girl, you need a miracle."

He preferred to cut her hair dry, and when he finished, her hair looked fantastic.

"See? Fabulous. Other women would kill to have your hair."

Abby couldn't believe her hair was actually behaving. *Who was this guy, the hair whisperer?*

Abby was back upstairs, a better version of her old self, by two that afternoon. Another twenty flower arrangements had arrived. *The staff would definitely have to pitch in on the thank-you notes.*

Poppy asked for a few minutes of her time.

"Sure, just let me grab some food." Abby still felt vaguely guilty eating while her sister lay in a casket. Regina had put out some tea sandwiches. Abby munched on a couple while Poppy talked.

"Here's your agenda." Poppy passed her a card printed with bulleted items. "Read it and keep it in your bag."

Abby looked at it.

* 5 p.m. Clothes back from Kim Tran.

* 5:30 p.m. Hair and makeup here by Andre Callas…

"Hey, he just cut my hair," Abby said. "A real character."

"And very talented with makeup," Poppy said. "For public appearances, we'll use him."

"What if I don't like the war paint?" Abigail asked, pleasantly.

"You can wash it off afterwards."

"My sister did all this, didn't she?" Abigail asked.

"Down to the she-crab soup in the Senate Dining Room," Poppy said.

"How will I know what to do in there?" Abby asked.

"I'll be on your left, and this is like a good Irish wake. Lots of booze and lots of stories about your sister. No politics. Just take it all in."

"Okay. Would you cull these flowers, sending them to women in veteran's hospitals? Pris really tried to remember them."

"Sure, the building people can do that."

Abby went into her room, cranked out twenty thank-you notes, stamped them, and lay down on the bed. The next thing she knew, Regina was awakening her.

"Sweet Pea, it's time to get up and get dressed."

Abby looked at the clock. It was five thirty. She felt thickheaded.

"Is Kim here?"

"Been and gone."

"What if the clothes aren't right?" Abby asked in a fuzzy panic.

"They'll be right. Kim's good."

"Where's Duke?"

"Here, watching sports. Want something to eat after you shower?"

"No, thanks."

She showered quickly and put on a robe, then headed into Pris's dressing room.

"I'm trusting you to make me look like me, but better," she said to Andre when she sat at Pris's professionally lighted dressing table.

"Easy. More intense colors, as the television lights wash you out something fierce. No need for heavy makeup. Even with high-definition cameras, you have great skin. What's your secret?"

"I live in the hospital. I never see the sun."

He started by leaning her head back and covering her face with icy washcloths while he chose her products. It amped up the day's facial.

"To de-puff from crying and napping. Next time you nap, do it in the recliner with your head elevated."

He worked quickly. When he finished, he tucked the waterproof ("so you can cry") mascara and gloss in her purse for touch-ups. Poppy had already put in the five by eight card, a handkerchief, and an extra pair of panty hose. Poppy even added a tampon just in case.

For her hair, Andre pulled it up and off her face and tucked it into a loose knot.

"You have a great neck, let's show it off."

He sprayed her hair.

"This is shine spray. Wash your hair tonight or you'll feel like a grease pit."

"So I turn into a slime ball at midnight?"

"Something like that."

"I'm thirsty, may I have some water?"

"No, no." He wagged his finger. "Drink through a straw, or you'll mess up your lips."

"Okay, okay." Abby raised her hands in surrender.

For courage, Abby wore some of Priscilla's favorite fragrance, the Bulgari Green Tea. It smelled luscious on both of them. She missed her sister less when she wore it.

She had the privacy of dressing herself. She liked the way she looked in the three-way mirror. *Gray, baggy sweats and no makeup are always unflattering. Gray couture and professional grooming are a big step up.*

Abigail appeared at precisely six. Poppy gave her a thumbs up. Regina bustled down the hall, patting herself with a handkerchief. She looked wonderful in an eggplant-colored suit, with matching shoes, bag, and hat. Regina believed in one-color outfits. Duke stood up and turned off ESPN. He looked handsome in a navy cashmere blazer, a white shirt, and an Hermés tie from Pris. His gray flannel pants broke exactly twice. His Italian tassel loafers were shined to a mirror finish.

"My sister would be proud of her family," Abigail said.

"Auntie Abby, don't you make me cry," Duke said. "If I start, you know Reege is next."

"And I'm the worst," said Poppy. "It takes a lot to make me cry, but when I start, get out the mop."

He helped each woman into her coat, put on his own overcoat, and they all stepped out to wait for the elevator.

"You know Pris preferred to wear her furs, but since it isn't politically correct at a public function, she bought the most expensive 'cloth' coat she could find," Poppy said of Abigail's cashmere coat. "You can get a fur for less."

"Sounds like Pris," Abigail said.

"Remember," Poppy said, "levity is fine in the Dining Room, but somber in front of the cameras.'

"So if Aunt Abby cuts one, I can't laugh?" Duke asked.

"Stop it," Regina said, half smiling and reaching across Poppy to slap him on his arm. "I can't believe I raised a boy as bad as you."

Their car was waiting under the *porte cochere* when they exited the building.

The four fit easily into the back. Poppy and Duke sat facing backward.

"Members' entrance to the Senate, please, Robert," Poppy said.

"Dr. Adams, Miss Regina, Duke, I'm real sorry the Senator passed. She was always real good to me. Once she called the VA herself to get my benefits straightened out. And I'm not even from Texas."

Abby was beginning to understand public service and the graceful generosity of her sister.

Once they were outside the Rotunda, Poppy stopped them.

"Okay. Don't let the lights freak you out. And watch out for cables on the floor."

Abby was grateful. The Rotunda was as bright as an operating room, and cables snaked the across the floor.

There was an honor guard at her sister's flag-draped casket. None looked more than twenty. Each was ramrod straight, eyes front.

Abby stood and looked at the casket, aware Pris was resting on the catafalque that held Abraham Lincoln. The flag over her casket flew over the Capitol on the day of her death. Abigail's breath caught in her throat.

Get Pris out of there. She can't breathe. Abby fought down panic, a foreign emotion to her.

Duke and Regina followed her, and Abby could hear the stoic Regina softly crying. She went to comfort her. Duke was on Regina's other side. Cameras clicked by the dozens. Poppy hung back, for once dressed in black.

Suddenly it hit Abby. She would never hear her sister's laugh again. She would have to give in to the grief, but now was not the time, and this was not the place.

Members of Congress followed them. The public would file through until the casket was removed to the National Cathedral on Wednesday morning.

In the Senate Dining Room, Poppy arranged them in a short receiving line.

The first person through was the Vice President, who is the President of the Senate.

"Damn shame about your sister," the Vice President said in her whiskey and cigarettes voice. The woman's handshake was like a vice. The phrase "Junkyard Dog" came to Abby's mind.

"Thank you, Vice President Barker," Abigail said.

She robotically greeted everyone, shaking some hands, accepting many hugs, and enduring air kisses and cheek kisses by the dozens. She was glad she had been able to keep all these people, and their germs, away from Pris for the last months.

She passed off each person to Regina, with the "Queen of our Family" line. Regina passed them to Duke, who pointed them toward the bar. The noise level rose and soon the toasts began.

"To Pris Logan," one Senator said. "Pretty as a picture and tough as nails."

"Hear, hear," said Majority Leader Schwartz. "To the woman who not only made the President sign her Infants First Act, but made him fund it, to boot!"

"To my kind friend, who brought me Regina's chicken soup, even if I only pretended to be sick," Peggy Mellon said.

"To the woman who should have been the first female President," the junior Senator from Texas said, and he was of the opposing party.

Abby saw many Senators with tears in their eyes.

By nine thirty, the four were back in their limo. They dropped off Poppy and then Duke. Regina and Abigail went home to pecan balls, Priscilla's favorite dessert. Vanilla ice cream shaped into a ball, then rolled in Texas pecans and topped with hot fudge sauce.

"A lot more comforting and a whole lot less dangerous than alcohol," commented Regina, who didn't like to see her flock drink.

"My hips would disagree," Abby said drily, dropping a kiss on Regina's forehead and wolfing down the dessert.

CHAPTER EIGHT

THE FUNERAL

Wednesday morning broke frigid, overcast and threatening sleet. A thick mattress of clouds all but obliterated the sun.

My sister is dead. I am now no one's sister.

Abby cried softly into her pillow, feeling terribly alone. Sure, she had Regina and Duke, whom she loved with greater ferocity than ever, but her solitariness seeped deep into the marrow of her bones.

I don't know how to live without my sister.

Rationally, she knew other people did this. She just didn't know if she could do it. *How come we don't have a term for people who have lost a sibling or, worse, a child?*

She dreaded the funeral. All she wanted was to pull the covers over her and wait in place for oblivion. If it didn't come in a month or so, she would get up and wander back to a life somewhere.

Her grief was punctuated by moments of remembrance: the stethoscope on the silent chest, the moment she saw the flag-draped casket in the Rotunda. *Get her out of there, she can't breathe.*

She couldn't tamp down the terror of a world without her sister. Death would triumph again today. She'd have to look at the box with her sister in it.

Regina's faith sustained her. She really believed that Pris was free, out of pain and in Heaven. Abby believed only that Pris was out of pain. Maybe that was Heaven. As long as Pris was alive, there had been hope. Hope was all Abigail lived on. Now it too was gone.

Today there would be people she didn't know, mouthing platitudes she didn't want to hear about a side of her sister she didn't know. They knew nothing about the bond between the two sisters, of the sorrows they had shared, or the silliness they could generate just being together.

Stop this.

Abby had eaten virtually nothing, drunk only the occasional glass of water. She wanted to magically fast forward to the end of her own life. The only thing she had to show for her grief was dull, saggy skin and dead eyes in dark sockets.

Regina knocked on her door and walked in.

"You've got to get up," Regina gently commanded. "And you are going to eat a proper breakfast. You are not going to faint in front of the President of the U-nited States, do you hear me?"

"Yes, ma'am," Abigail answered as if she were thirteen, not thirty-six.

Her private time was over. Abby kicked off the covers and stumbled into her bathroom. The shower helped put her into the camp of the seemingly alive. Abby had a quick, small breakfast and brushed her teeth. Poppy had forbidden her to go to the funeral with coffee breath. *Jeez, did everyone in Washington do breath checks every few hours?*

Regina was percolating as usual, even if she was doing it out of rote. Duke would be there in plenty of time for the ride to the National Cathedral. Poppy was in the living room supervising the caterers.

Abby was grateful to have a printed schedule, a planned and clean outfit to wear. She would have omitted something important, like her skirt. Of course, this support came from her dead sister. She knew Abigail would not go quietly into the funeral all in one piece.

After tomorrow, when she would plant her sister in the ground at Glenwood Cemetery in Houston, life would have a gaping hole in it. She knew she was Pris's executor, and that would take another year out of her life. She'd say daily, "My sister died." Maybe by then, her anger would be spent. Perhaps in a year, her first thought on awakening would not be "My sister is dead."

Abby read the outfit off today's card and pulled out the Chanel suit she was going to wear. There was a note taped on its cover.

"I changed the neck and sleeves, as your arms are longer than your sister's. Kim."

The suit, minus the iconic Chanel buttons, was transformed. Kim put gray silk frogs in their place. She'd added a grey lace modesty panel to the deep V of the neck, and matching ruffles peeking out from the sleeves. With the gray baroque pearl earrings, she would look elegant and dignified.

External grooming countered her internal chaos.

Andre appeared with a smock to go over her suit.

"I don't mind getting makeup or hair spray on a ratty old bathrobe, but I draw the line at a Chanel suit. Besides, you gotta get these shoes ready, girlfriend. No slipping and sliding allowed today. And today will be long."

He handed her some sort of file and told her to rough up the soles of her new shoes.

Pris's dressing room lighting was brutal, but perfect for a woman often on high-definition television.

"You are not looking good," Andre said gently. "Any worse and you'd scare small children. Believe me, in my crowd, I've gone to way too many funerals. You gotta eat, and you've gotta drink lots of water."

They started with the iced salt water on her face for a few luxurious minutes. Then things went quickly. Her makeup was similar to the other night, but he chose to put her hair in a French twist.

"How retro," Abby said.

"There is nothing 'retro' about a classic. Nothing retro about Catherine Deneuve." He wagged an index finger back and forth like a metronome. *Was this his favorite gesture?*

Abby liked her hair. When she was finally ready, even she felt she looked as good as possible. This time, instead of shine spray, he sprayed a holding hair spray.

"Your hair won't move in a hurricane. Your head may come off, but your hair will still be perfect."

She managed a half chuckle.

When she was in her suit and shoes, Andre pinned her hat in place. Abby realized veils let women weep in private. This one was grossly inadequate.

She picked up her bag. Everything was there. Especially handkerchiefs.

Abby walked into the living room. Poppy was directing placement of the flowers. She had kept arrangements that complemented the décor, relegating the others to female veterans in the area.

"We leave in five. Go to the restroom."

Poppy left nothing to chance. Telling another adult to go potty was just part of her job.

The "Lacrimosa" movement of Mozart's *Requiem Mass* oozed from the National Cathedral's organ. Duke, Abby, and Regina entered the first pew from the family area. The Cathedral was cold, gray, and gloomy. It smelled faintly of damp stone. Everyone was already seated, including the President and Mrs. Harrington across the aisle.

They exchanged nods. She was prepared to see the flag-draped casket, but the unexpected scent of Casablanca lilies threatened to undo her. She must think of something else, or she would panic again at the thought of her sister in the box.

Instead, she looked around the Cathedral. It would have been lovely on a sunny day. Today, the stained glass was dull. The Great Organ had what was it, ten thousand pipes? She silently counted windows until the service began.

Mechanically, she went through the motions of the service. She hated every moment so far.

Then Walter Harrington took the pulpit and gave his eulogy.

"Priscilla Adams Logan was a giant in the Senate. Everyone knows that. She was also a true Texas woman. She was a lady when it suited her, and a brawler when necessary. She had a first-rate mind, and if logic didn't work, she pulled out her secret weapons of charm and beauty. I've personally seen one senator ignore her intellectual argument, only to change his mind when she turned on the charm and crossed those long legs. The man never knew what hit him.

"Most importantly, she was tenacious. She never gave up. Literally on her deathbed, she made me promise to sign and fund the Infants First Bill. Would I have signed the bill otherwise? I don't know. All I know is that when I die, Pris will likely be sitting on St. Peter's right. If there is one person I do not want mad at me, it is Priscilla Logan."

Everyone nodded sagely as the President sat down.

Abby could have spoken, but preferred Duke speak for the family. His massive body seemed to dwarf the space where the President had just stood; his voice, resonant and strong, commanded everyone's attention. With his first word, he upstaged the President. Unlike the President, he spoke without notes.

"Ours, as you may have noticed, is an unusual family. Regina Temple and I are aunt and nephew. Abby and Pris were sisters. Through untimely deaths, we were forged into a family.

"We all lived together in the Adams home, in a comfortable neighborhood in Houston, though not a particularly integrated one.

"I was a babe in arms when I came to them. I remember three beautiful women rearing me: Auntie Regina, Auntie Pris, and Auntie Abby. To say I was doted on is to say the sun rises in the east. And, as is true in parental love, it came with limits.

"There was no unauthorized brownie cutting. There was no taking the last of the ice cream. There was no television on school nights. Not even for the World Series or the Super Bowl. There was 'yes, ma'am' and 'no, ma'am.'

"I could have gone to public schools, but Pris invested—heavily—in my education. When she figured out I could perform well in a competitive academic environment, she let me know that my best was her minimum expectation. Every day.

"Once I slammed the door of my room in an adolescent huff. Pris was home, and she slammed that door right back open.

"Young man," she said, "Regina and I own this house, so *we* own this door. If you ever disrespect it again by slamming it, it comes off its hinges. Forever. Got it?'

"I knew to say, 'Yes, ma'am.' I never slammed a door again. I also could extrapolate similar punishments for more rebellious behavior, so I toed the line. I might be six five, but I was low man on that totem pole. Being raised by three alpha females will keep any young man in line.

"Pris married the wrong man, and her divorce was full of dark days. She came out of it a different person, a person devoted to public service. She drummed into me, 'Those who need not work must yet serve.' She served tirelessly for a quarter century to make this idea we call America a better place.

"Priscilla Logan believed passionately in the rule of law. She believed passionately we need the best from every citizen to make our future fit its promise. She also believed a mark of a civilized society is how the strong help the weak, how the whole help the broken, how the civilians support the warriors.

"I have been blessed far more than any man could hope to be. Auntie Pris set high standards and made sure I met them. Then she gave all the credit to me.

"In looking for the right words to say about my Aunt Pris, I will borrow from Shakespeare, as Robert Kennedy did for his brother John. On this day, at this time, I shall say of Priscilla Adams Logan:

"'And when she shall die, take her and cut her out in little stars
And she will make the face of heaven so fine
That all the world will be in love with night
And pay no worship to the garish sun."

"Goodbye, Auntie Pris. I will see you in the stars."

Abby realized while she was weeping silently, the crowd was crying with her, some in audible sobs. Regina's face too was washed in tears as Duke finished and left the pulpit; the President stood and shook his hand.

The singer Audrina Howell closed the service.

She would sing *a capella*. She simply opened her mouth and out came magic. Not the operatic oration of the trained voice, but the sheer talent God grants once in a generation.

"Amazing grace, how sweet the sound…" She sang several verses in her clear, pure voice of incredible range. She changed to a higher key with each verse.

The church was gray and chill as she began, but as she sang, sunlight came flooding into the church in full radiance. Beaming through the stained glass, sunlight turned into the colors of rubies and sapphires and emeralds.

The gloom of the occasion lifted. The elegiac music of Mozart gave way to the voice of an angel singing comforting words.

Everyone was enraptured by the various verses of the well-worn hymn. The light show made it all the more sacred. Howell chose not to close with a coda of the first verse, but to end with her favorite one:

"Yea, when this flesh and heart shall fail,
And mortal life shall cease,
I shall possess within the veil,
A life of joy and peace."

People sat numb in the brilliance of the Cathedral. Powerful people who had seen it all, done it all, and were justifiably jaded sat slack-jawed at the transformation of a gray and gloomy church to the inside of God's jewelry box, complete with an angel's song.

It took everyone a few moments to collect himself.

The President was the first to pay his condolences, and then a seemingly endless line of the nation's government leaders filed past. A parade of members of Congress, dignitaries, and prominent figures left Abby numb. She was somewhere deep within herself. Condolences by the rich and powerful did nothing for her.

But the voice of Audrina Howell and the illumination of the Cathedral portended better times to come.

CHAPTER NINE

THE GREEN, GREEN GRASS OF HOME

Few of the dignitaries came to the house. Most of Priscilla's staffers came, and since she served on several committees, those people came as well. As well, people from the building, social friends, friends from Bookworms came, as did some of the girls themselves. Abby headed back to her room to rest. No sooner had she kicked off her shoes than Regina appeared.

"What's the matter?" Regina asked gently.

"I don't know those people. I want to curl up in a ball."

"Of course you do, but you don't get to do it today," Regina said. "Now get out there and let people give you their condolences. You might even learn something."

Abby touched up her makeup and went into the crowd.

"Bob McKenna, Armed Services Committee legislative aide," said a beefy young man. "Your sister saved my life."

"How did she do that?" Abby was genuinely interested. *Lifesaving is my bailiwick.*

"She visited me at Walter Reed when I was a wreck with PTSD. She told me I was a hero just by staying alive. That put me on the path to recovery. Now I work in the field."

"I'm glad my sister came into your life. I'm sorry you've lost her," Abby said. Bob was just the first of a stream of people whom she found herself consoling. Everyone knows the family hurts, but the dying person is like a pebble in a pond, the waves of sadness radiate outward to hundreds.

A few of the people were lobbyists, though it took Abby a while to figure them out. Their introductions were simpler.

"Frank Olsen. Baker and Fox. We're going to miss our friend in the Senate."

"Who, or what, is Baker and Fox?"

"We consult on pharmaceutical matters."

"Ah." Abby would nod and look at the owner's shoes. Funny, men and women like Frank Olsen never wore cheap shoes.

This was the underbelly of Pris's life she didn't want to know about. Sure, it was the way things got done, but Abby viewed lobbyists like drug reps. If their view was valid, there would be no need to push it. Every time anyone leaned on her to do something, she knew there was something in it for him. Whose wallet was picked in the process? In medicine, it was the patient's. In Washington, it was the taxpayer's.

She gave short shrift to anyone who appeared to be a lobbyist, listened closely to everyone who had an interesting story to tell. By two, the crowd was gone. It was just the four of them: Regina, Poppy, Duke, and Abby.

All except Duke kicked off their shoes and fell into the sofas, finding soft spots for sore feet.

"I'd take off my shoes, but you ladies wouldn't like the smell," Duke said.

"Well, you may this once put your feet on the coffee table," Regina said. Duke was glad to get them up.

"You know you were the star," Poppy said to Duke. "People thought your eulogy was phenomenal."

"Being a star at a funeral is no honor. I just spoke from the heart."

"Well, don't be surprised if party people start courting you," Poppy continued.

"I haven't even finished law school," Duke laughed.

"So what happens now?" Abigail asked Poppy. She had a rough idea, but needed Poppy to fill in the details.

"Tomorrow the four of us fly the Senator's body to Houston, wheels up at 7:00 a.m. from Reagan National. There will be a graveside service attended by some of the Houston staff, the local dignitaries, and Houston friends. A reception will follow at the house in Tanglewood. Pretty much like today, except lower key.

"Abigail, I'm sure you'll have estate matters to deal with there. Reege, you can stay or come home. Ditto for you, Duke."

"If Aunt Abby can spare me, I'd like to come back," Duke said.

"Sure, you've got school. Uh, Poppy, what airline are we flying?"

"John Lafferty has loaned us a Gulfstream 650."

"Why?"

"He owns Lafferty Weapons Systems and is head of the Strategic Defense Political Action Committee. Your sister sat on the Senate Armed Services Committee."

Abby didn't like taking favors, but it was too late now.

Houston

From the air, Abby knew Houston would be green, and it was. The live oaks did not lose their leaves in the fall; the new leaves simply pushed out the old ones, usually in March. As a result, the city was a green sea of trees, festooned with highways and hung with clusters of gilt skyscrapers.

February in Houston can be anything from summer to winter. She couldn't tell from the air. Stepping off the plane, she realized spring was in its glory. Driving to the cemetery, she saw the azaleas, the southern cousins of rhododendrons, were in full bloom in many yards.

Abby was glad they had no fragrance, or the city would gag on it. Everywhere there were pink, purple, coral, white, and red azaleas blooming. The Bartlett pear trees were also in bloom, as were the redbud trees. It was still too early for dogwood, but clearly winter was on the run.

From the airport, it only took about twenty minutes to get to Glenwood Cemetery along the banks of Buffalo Bayou. There had never been buffalo, but this overblown drainage ditch was the primary navigable waterway in Houston's early days. It still was a drainage ditch, but slowly, Houston put things along its path that would tolerate being inundated in muddy water every few years. Jogging paths, sculpture, even gardens. Farther upstream, people put high-dollar homes on the higher banks, tolerating such things as water moccasins and mosquitoes the size of ultra-light airplanes.

The graveside service at Glenwood Cemetery was small, the mourners already there in the shade of a tent. Staffers from the Houston office were there, as were a few neighbors. Abby saw no one from her hospital. A few military men were there, as was an honor guard like the one in the Senate.

It took Abby a moment to recognize Governor Lawson Gray. A big man, he looked deflated and low. He had come alone. The Mayor was there, though Abby did not know her.

Even Miss Penny from next door was there, ninety if she was a day, and perfectly groomed and coiffed, wearing a chic black suit that, at her age, probably got lots of use.

The Governor was silent and sad. All he could manage was to take her hand in both of his and weep silently.

There was also a tall man in a gray Stetson, a freshly laundered white shirt, blazer, jeans and boots. Abby didn't recognize him, but he carried himself well.

Then it was time for the service.

Priscilla would lie next to their parents. Her dad had bought four plots in one of the times he'd been rich. Abby realized with a lurching stomach that the fourth was for her. She had never before thought about where her body would go when life left her. She imagined her body like a cicada shell, fully formed, but empty at the end of it all. Her parents were just pictures and stories to her. The thought of their bodies beneath her gave her pause.

There was a carpet of artificial turf on the ground next to the open grave. Abby was in the middle of the first row of chairs, Regina and Duke on either side of her. Abby hoped this would be short. The marathon of death was wearing her out. She longed to sleep for days. *Just get through today and it will all be over.*

An Army Chaplain named O'Toole cleared his throat, and the group quieted. Regina took Abby's hand and held it.

"Senator Logan was a great friend of the military. She realized what many people overlook. The absence of warriors always makes for war. Only the presence of men and women who will sacrifice their lives for their country keeps warmongers away from us.

"She was a student of military history and asked me to read MacArthur's words as she is laid to rest beside her parents. Her father was a veteran, a member of the 101st Airborne. She thought of herself as a part of the military in her service on the Armed Services Committee.

"'The Long Gray Line has never failed us. Were you to do so, a million ghosts in olive drab, in brown khaki, in blue and gray would rise from their white crosses thundering those magic words: Duty. Honor. Country.

"'Those three hallowed words reverently dictate what you ought to be, what you can be, what you will be. They are your rallying points: to build courage when courage seems to fail; to regain faith when there seems to be little cause for faith, to create hope, when hope becomes forlorn.'"

The casket was lowered, the flag folded and handed to Abby. She was weeping openly but smiled up into the face of the man who handed it to her.

She was unhinged by the playing of "Taps."

She buried her face into the flag and wept. She did not remember Duke holding her up and walking her to the car. All she remembered were the words.

Duty. Honor. Country.

CHAPTER TEN

A TIME OF GRIEF AND SHOCK

The reception at the house was small, and people knew Regina, Abby and Duke must be tired. Everyone brought food, but no one stayed long. The man in the Stetson left it on the hall table.

"I'm Mason Ingram, from Logan Ranch. I just wanted to come by and pay my respects," he said, offering Abby his big callused hand. "I can't think of an easier person to work with than your sister."

Abby introduced him to Duke and Regina.

"She was the heart of Logan Ranch," he said to them. "And I can tell you, she loved you three very, very much. She talked about y'all a lot."

He shared a few stories and then said he'd best be getting back.

"Don't y'all be strangers," he said as he put his Stetson back on and left.

Before Poppy and Duke left, Poppy produced another five hundred black-bordered notes.

"You know the staff can write these," Poppy repeated.

"I have a system," Abigail said. "Besides, chores are a passable balm for grief."

"You'll be okay?" Poppy asked.

"I can't find the bathroom without you, but I'll learn." Abigail hugged Poppy.

"Just doin' my job," Poppy replied with tears in her eyes.

Poppy and Duke flew back to Washington on the Lafferty jet. If Duke was impressed, he had the class not to show it.

Abby tried to go through the mail at the house. She'd filled one entire trash bag before she realized she was throwing away the real mail and keeping the circulars. So she dumped everything onto the dining room table and headed for bed.

Regina was already in her nightclothes and reading her Bible when Abby went to kiss her good night.

"Well, Reege, we got through the hardest part."

"I wish you were right. But now the hard part starts. There's no ritual to carry us along. We just grieve."

"I want to curl up and sleep for a week."

"Then you go right ahead. Me? I do best sticking to my routine. Don't forget Miss Penny made you her chocolate pecan pie. You don't want to waste that."

Miss Penny looked the same at ninety as she had at seventy. She lived next door and Abby had known her, to use Miss Penny's phrase, since Before the Flood. She made her own chocolate pecan pie. The other neighbors had just brought takeout from one of the neighborhood's fancy places. All the women claimed they'd forgotten how to cook.

Abby cut herself a serious piece of pie and topped it with vanilla ice cream. That was her supper.

She shut off the house phone and her Blackberry and went to bed. She did not remember her head hitting the pillow.

My sister is dead.

She must have slept because Texas sunshine was tap dancing on her eyelids and the damn mockingbird was singing his fool head off. She pulled her drapes and went back to bed.

My sister is dead. I wonder what time it is. I want some of Miss Penny's pie.

Her watch said eleven, but her clock said ten. She'd forgotten to change her watch. She got up, drank a glass of milk with another piece of Miss Penny's pie, and went back to bed. The next thing she knew, it was either four or five o'clock.

Her big chore of the day was changing her watch.

Somehow, over the weekend, she managed to sort the mail, write a pile of thank-you notes, and avoid getting dressed. She found it odd, writing to the President. Those cards that lacked addresses, she put aside to talk to Poppy about on Monday. Lafferty had to be thanked for his jet, even though it was too cozy for Abby's tastes.

She tried to go for a jog along the leafy Tanglewood Boulevard, but her feet felt like stones, and she gave up after a block.

Back at the house, Regina was dividing up the food in the two refrigerators.

"Run to the grocery store and get me some disposable containers, would you?" Regina said. "Most of this is going to a shelter."

Abby complied.

For the next hour, they packed up food, washed dishes, and loaded coolers, wedging cold packs between layers.

Regina kept enough for them for the weekend, but waste offended her. She'd give the food away rather than have it go bad.

Abby put the coolers in the back of Regina's car. When she saw Regina head out, Abby was suddenly panicky.

What if Regina doesn't come back?

At least Regina didn't see Abigail burst into tears. Abby knew her fears were grief for Pris, but they stung anyway. Exhausted, she went to bed as soon as Regina was home safely. Sleep overtook her like a drug, putting her down into hours of blackness. When she awoke, her first thought was the same.

My sister is dead.

Awakening earlier seemed like a good sign, so she showered, dressed in jeans and a shirt, put her hair in a ponytail before she ate more pie, this time with a cup of strong coffee. Going from ice cream to milk to coffee with her pie struck her as progress.

She paid her bills online. Long ago, Pris had made sure the finances would be seamless. Abby had been paying all the bills for over a year and the balance in the account was still staggering.

She had no idea when she'd feel like returning to work, so she e-mailed her boss and said she needed a few more weeks. He didn't reply. She had no idea if she still had a job. She didn't really much care.

No, everything could wait until after her Monday meeting with Pris's lawyer and CPA.

Abby continued her electronic silence over the weekend. Regina, of course, went to church. Abby didn't feel like any more sermons, so she slept in. Her weekend goal was to finish Miss Penny's pie and rest. She did both. She did deign to shower and put on clean pajamas daily. Monday was soon enough to consider mundane things like contact lenses and underwear.

Abby, again well dressed and well groomed, appeared at Marston Mills's office at nine. He had been Priscilla's lawyer for decades. Despite his lawyerly name, Abby thought he was rather affected. His office was full of British hunting prints, there was a stand of antique canes in the corner, and he actually had a tea table.

"May I offer you a cup of tea, Abigail?" he asked, gesturing to an antique caddy filled with an assortment of tea bags. To a true tea lover, bags were perfidy.

"Yes, please, English Breakfast. Two lumps." Abby had read so many English novels, she could tell you which teas took milk and which took lemon.

Just then, a perspiring Eliza Pierce appeared in a black pantsuit, rolling a document carrier behind her. Her shiny black bob and Franck Muller watch spoke of the firm's stratospheric rates.

"Traffic," she said, the generic Houston apology for tardiness. Abby had to smile. Even on a March morning, a harried Texan works up a sweat.

"May I have coffee? I need a heart-starter," Eliza said.

Abby calculated the pleasantries had cost her in the neighborhood of at least a thousand dollars, but said nothing.

Two hours later, she staggered out of the office with her own set of documents, their accompanying CDs, and two new shocks to absorb.

The will was drawn as Pris had said. Abby was the executor. There was a bequest to endow a chair devoted to children's law at the University of Texas Law School, a bequest to Bookworms, her favorite charity, a very generous nest egg for Poppy, and another the same size for Mason Ingram, the guy in the Stetson.

The greatest assets, Logan Ranch and Logan Oil, were in a corporate structure of some sort. Upon Pris's death, Abby owned fifty-one percent, while Regina and Duke divided the rest. This guaranteed that Abby had the final say.

Duke's was in trust until he was thirty-five, with Abigail as sole trustee. In the meantime, he'd get the income quarterly.

The rest of the estate was also extremely substantial, far greater than Abby could imagine.

The letter Marston handed her was the second shock. Written ten years ago, it was to be delivered upon her death. She wanted to read it in private.

She was shaking so hard when she left the office, she decided not to drive. She crossed the street to a Starbucks, got a decaf latte, and found an upholstered chair in which to read the letter. She was grateful for her anonymity. She closed her eyes and inhaled the aroma of the coffee. Then she read the letter, slowly. The sight of Pris's handwriting momentarily jolted her. She felt as if Pris was talking to her.

"Dearest Abby,

Few people know the story of my divorce. You should know. You're old enough, and the consequences of that marriage are coming at you.

Lawson Gray and I were seriously in love in law school. One day, I caught him making out with one of my sorority sisters, and I broke it off.

On the rebound, I found Lance Logan, whip smart, movie star handsome, and a perfect gentleman. It didn't hurt that his dad owned a huge chunk of North Texas dotted with wellheads and pump jacks.

In short, he was the catch of my class, and he was after *me* big time. I thought it was nice not having a man trying to get into my panties every five minutes like Lawson did. We dated for several months before we slept together.

Once we'd married and settled at the ranch, I noticed he only wanted sex between my periods. He was polite, but he'd married me as a "breeder." I didn't know what to do, and before I could talk to Regina about it, fate slapped me upside the head.

One day, there was a problem, and I went looking for Lance. I walked past the bunkhouse and heard moaning. Since everyone should be out working, I thought someone was ill. I opened the door. There was Lance, naked and "in the saddle" with an older guy named Mike.

I ran back to the house. Somewhere on the High Plains of Texas, I lost my breakfast. I was more dangerous than a nest of water moccasins. It was the early days of AIDS, and if he'd infected me, I was a dead woman.

I locked myself in the house. Dad Logan came banging on the door. I racked two shells of buckshot into my shotgun.

"Goddammit, Pris, put down that gun. Lance's at my house. We've got to talk."

I bawled my eyes out, and Dad was great. He'd worried about Lance's sexuality and was relieved when I showed up. A widower with one child, he wanted grandchildren the way a man in the desert wants water.

Long story short, Dad had all three of us tested for everything under the sun. The week of waiting nearly did me in. We were all fine medically, and sixty days later I was divorced.

Dad Logan and I negotiated the settlement. Twenty million outright, with a bunch of royalties thrown in. Plus, if I kept Lance's sexuality quiet and kept the Logan name, he'd back me in any political race.

Six months later, my tests were still negative, and I ran for State Senate, then U.S. Senate. Dad Logan was a kingmaker, and I was the son he never had. Lance went on to die of "cancer," which of course, was AIDS.

Dad Logan died not long ago, leaving me everything. Now this blessed burden falls on you once you're thirty-five.

You've got three first-rate helpers. Mason Ingram runs the ranch. He's an Aggie with a degree in Ranch Management as well as an MBA, is as honest as the day is long, and will do you a good job. He's underpaid, so that's why I left him a nest egg.

Marston and Eliza are honest, hardworking, and expensive for a reason: they're good.

So if you ever wondered how I afforded the penthouse at Franklin Tower, now you know. If you wondered why I wanted to pay for med school, now you know. (Pigheaded cuss that you are, you took out loans and lived on a shoestring. If they aren't paid off yet, do it with a check, today.)

I think this legacy will make you, not break you. I wouldn't hurt you for the world. And remember, those who need not work must yet serve.

I love you three more than you can ever know. I hope that this legacy will bring you joy, as you, Regina, and Duke have brought me incredible joy. You've been a wonderful sister, a good "daughter" to Regina, and a great "aunt" to Duke.

I just wish I could see the look on your face.

All my love, Sissy Prissy.

Hmmm. I'm going to have more money than I know what to do with. I never have to work another day. What will I do? Work is all I know.

Why can't I just have Pris?

This is my responsibility. I must be a good steward of this. If I learned organic chemistry, I can learn estate management.

Abigail breathed in and out for a while. Then she went to the bookstore and stocked up on titles like *Accounting for Dummies* and *Estate Management*. At twenty bucks a pop, they were a lot cheaper than Eliza explaining things at a thousand dollars an hour.

"What in the Sam Hill is all that?" Regina looked up from her crossword puzzle and asked about the load of books in Abby's arms. As usual, her glasses were threatening to fall off the end of her nose.

"Reege, we're rich. Pris left us rich."

"I hate to be the one to break it to you, but I've been rich for decades. The only problem money cures is poverty. We have enough. What's a five letter word for *silly?*"

"Goose. You silly goose. I love you."

CHAPTER ELEVEN

AN APPOINTMENT

The day held another shock for Abby.

That afternoon, Lawson Gray called her, apparently for the tenth time. This time her phone was on.

"Abby, this is Lawson Gray. Don't you ever return your damn phone calls?" He was not a happy governor.

"I'm so sorry, Governor Gray, I turned everything off for the weekend, sir," Abby said as politely as possible. "Just to grieve silently. How are you?"

"I'm walking and talking, but I'll never be the same, not after losing Pris," he said candidly. "One way or another, she's been a part of my life for over thirty years."

"Well, I am sorry you lost her back then, and I'm real sorry we've both lost her now."

"Listen, you and I need to talk about your appointment."

"Oh, my goodness, did I forget something? Did we have an appointment?" Abigail asked, horrified she might have stood up the Governor of Texas.

"No. Your appointment to your sister's Senate seat."

"I don't understand." Abby's mind was blank.

"I made your sister a deathbed promise to appoint you to her seat. You will serve until a new Senator is elected in the fall. I will be running for that seat with her blessing."

"This is the first I've heard of this, Governor."

"Aw, sheee-ut. I thought you were up to speed on this."

He then explained the whole process, and Abby listened with growing panic. *I'm not a Senator, I'm a doctor. What the hell was Pris thinking?*

"May I sleep on this?" Abigail asked.

"Sure. I could strangle Pris for not telling you."

"How about me? She wants to hijack my life from the grave. Talk about controlling."

Abby hung up, confused, angry, complimented, and suspicious. She would think about it and call Gray in the morning.

She and Regina had a simple supper, and then Regina watched television. Abby retreated to her room. *When in doubt, make a list.*

Finally, she made her choice. She decided she could do more good for children in the Senate than she could at her old job. Besides, it might be fun to slip into Pris's life for a while. To be with grown-ups, to wear better clothes, maybe even to meet a new man. It would be a sabbatical. She was burned out, who wouldn't be? Besides, at the end of the year, she'd still be a doctor. She'd never have a chance to be a U.S. Senator again.

Abby was pleased she'd pushed Priscilla to sponsor the Infants First Act. It had, after all, been Abby's idea.

Most people thought babies were blobs, but they learn more in the first year of life than in any other. The hardwiring of their brain changed with the kind and amount of stimulation they receive every single day. Many parents were clueless about what babies need. So parents would have parenting classes, the babies would join them for infant stimulation classes. Kids would be screened for developmental problems, and if any were present, intervention would start immediately.

The school would be a social hub for young parents, just as it was for parents of school-age kids. Perhaps with a support system, postpartum depression could be decreased.

Each school would get a social worker and cop to make sure families knew how to get help.

She called Lawson Gray on his cell at nine o'clock.

"Governor, I would be honored to serve out my sister's unexpired term," Abby said in a clear strong voice.

"And you promise not to run."

"Cross my heart."

"Okay, you're in. What do you need?" he asked. She could hear him tapping a pen on a piece of paper.

"I think I need some training in how to be a Senator." Abby laughed.

"Well, Poppy can teach you that. She's practically been one for the last year."

"That'd be great," Abby said. "But I'm really afraid of someone sticking a microphone in my face."

"Ah, media training. I'll get you fixed up with Wicker Washington. Three days is all you need. I'd like to make the announcement tomorrow, here in Austin. Say two o'clock."

"That's fine."

"Bring me fifty packets with your head shot and a bio. I'll need them for the press."

"What's a head shot?" Abby knew what one was in her business, but doubted Gray was referring to a gunshot wound to the head.

"A publicity portrait. Put on some makeup and the top to a suit. Head to any office supply store, and they can do one for you. Bring fifty color copies with you."

"Gotcha."

"Then we'll see you and Regina both about two?"

"We'll be there with bells on."

"If you don't put on something with them, you'll definitely make page one, above the fold." He chuckled and hung up.

Next she called Poppy, who was already at the office, trying to keep things running until someone showed up to fill the seat.

"So that was her plan all along," Poppy said thoughtfully. "I didn't want to ask her. I thought it was rude."

"Will you stay as my Chief of Staff? Please?" Abby asked.

"Abby, you can't find the bathroom. Of course I'll stay."

"And I won't be running."

"Duh. Lawson Gray thinks this is his seat now."

"So, tell me what I have to do for tomorrow."

"Show up. Stand up straight. And don't say 'fuck.'"

Abby laughed.

"I'll e-mail you some remarks," Poppy said. "Oh, and keep your phone on."

Abby laughed again and hung up.

Regina was in the kitchen when Abby came in.

"I have something to tell you," Abby said.

"Yes, I know," Regina said.

"You know?"

"Abby, I raised you. I can tell when you are about to bust a gut with news."

"Do you know what my news is?"

"Yes indeed-y, I do," Regina said with a smug smile.

"Who told you?"

"Priscilla. Well, actually, she asked me what I thought. I told her you'd make a fine Senator, assuming of course, you got yourself some better clothes. Especially bras. You wear the rattiest undergarments. God gave you a nice bosom, and if you don't start supporting it, it'll be at your knees before you know it."

Abby laughed. Just once in her life she'd like to outwit Regina. It hadn't happened yet.

"Thanks. Will you go with me tomorrow to Austin to be sworn in? Will you hold your Bible for me?"

"Yes, of course, but you aren't sworn tomorrow. The Vice President or the President Pro Tem of the Senate does the swearing. Tomorrow, the governor just appoints you."

"Thank you, Miss Constitutional Law."

"You're welcome, but we need to go to Austin tonight, dear."

"Why's that?" Abby asked.

"In case we have a flat, or the car breaks down. Why don't you call and book us a room at the Driskill Hotel? That's a real slice of Texas history."

"As usual, you're right. I'd best go pack. Right after I get a head shot done."

"Oh, 'fore you go, I've got something for you," Regina said.

She went to her capacious purse and excavated around in it. Out came her Bible, a fat wallet with an industrial strength rubber band around it, a large disco ball keychain, a roll of duct tape, an enormous six foot metal measuring tape, a plastic bag of knitting, a flashlight the size of a billy club, and a tin of breath mints. Regina finally unearthed a small leather-bound book.

"You'll need this. It was your sister's copy of the Constitution. She always kept it in her purse, even though she'd memorized it. I suggest you do both."

Abby looked at the small book. It was no bigger than her hand and it had run a nation for over two hundred years. Her heart did a little flip-flop.

Each headed off to her room to pack. First Abby called the Driskill and got a two-bedroom suite. Regina deserved a treat.

Abby pulled up her *curriculum vitae*, the medical equivalent of a resume, on her computer, and edited out the more arcane medical jargon. That would work as a "bio."

Abby swiftly did her makeup, adding more color to her lips and cheeks as Andre had taught her. Luckily her hair was clean and it was easily arranged into a casual updo. She grabbed her Chanel suit jacket and headed to the copy place.

She got her picture taken four or five times, picked the proof she liked, paid extra for rush service, and extra again for a little digital editing, what the pimply faced girl called "electronic concealer."

Abby had them make fifty copies of her bio, then found a plastic chair. There she sat, reading the Constitution and waiting for her photos. She remembered how proud her civics teacher was to introduce this document to them. As teens obsessed with hairdos and boy bands, they'd been underwhelmed.

Now the Constitution was immediate to her. She had to really learn this document. As short as it was, she could master its content before swearing-in. She had this intense urge to apologize to her teacher for not joining in his enthusiasm.

She picked up the photos and copies, bought a few office supplies, and went home. They were on the road in less than two hours. Abby had packed two outfits and four pair of panty hose. She was learning.

It was too early for the bluebonnets. Lady Bird Johnson's view of Texas became more evident every year. Just like New England had its "leaf peepers," Texas had its "wildflower wanderers." The state was awash in bluebonnets, buttercups, primrose, Indian blanket, and Indian paintbrush starting the first week in April.

Still, even in March, the grass was greening up, and trees were leafing out. Their new leaves were fat with precious moisture and looked a fresher, neon green. By the end of summer, they'd be thin, dusty, washed out, and frankly tired of making all that oxygen.

When they were on the other side of Brenham, Abby brought up her visit to Marston Mills.

"Reege, I talked with the lawyer about the will yesterday."

"Ummm," Regina said, not looking up from the cap she was knitting. She and her Mission Ladies made hats for premature babies at the county hospital. If half were as productive as Regina, the hospital would need offsite storage.

"Do you know how Pris left things?"

"I imagine she left everything to you," Regina said, plastic needles tapping away.

"No, she didn't. She left fifty-one percent to me, and the rest divided equally between you and Duke."

"I can understand leaving something to Duke, but who passes money up?" Regina asked, somewhat puzzled. "You're s'posed to pass it down. And Duke is too young to get any money."

"Well, it's in trust until he's thirty-five. I'm his trustee. He gets the income off it as soon as the estate settles, but at age thirty-five, he gets the whole amount."

"Whooo-eee, are you in for a ride. Do you have any idea how stubborn that man-boy can be?"

"I wonder where he got it." Abby shot Regina a glance. Regina ignored her, flipping the knitting to the next row.

"Reege, you're going to get a lot of money."

"I already have a lot of money."

"Yes, well, this is probably more than you have." Abby was scared to tell her the full amount lest she have a heart attack.

"Well, that was certainly generous of her."

"Once I know the full amount, I'll let you know. Of course, Uncle Sam gets his cut."

"Oh, he always gets the biggest piece of the pie," Regina said emphatically.

Regina put her knitting down and looked at Abby.

"Like I've said before, the only problem money solves is poverty. I'll enjoy some of it, but I'll try to do some good with my money. But I'll do it very, very quietly."

"Whatever you like," Abby said.

"Screaming 'money' is worse than screaming 'fire' in a crowded theatre," Regina pronounced it *thee-ATE-er*. "Pretty soon, someone's going to get trampled, usually the person with the money."

Austin's traffic was worse than usual, if such a thing was possible, but they made it to the front of the of the Victorian era hotel, where valets and bellmen took care of the car and luggage.

Once inside the door, Regina said in a stage whisper, "Sixty years ago, I wouldn't have been welcome here. Now you tell me I can buy the place. Is this country great or what?"

Poppy's e-mailed remarks were boring. After dinner, Abby wrote her own remarks and got ready for bed.

Maybe it was sleeping in a different bed. Maybe it was no mockingbird. But sleep flowed over her like fresh water. For the first time since her sister died, she awoke refreshed. *Yes, my sister is dead, but something new is starting because of her.*

Abby slept late, and she and Regina had brunch in the hotel.

The Texas Governor's Mansion is a white Greek revival mansion of impressive proportions nestled in a grove of trees near the Capitol.

Abby was a bit nervous, but Governor and Mrs. Gray put her at ease. Of course, both the governor and his wife knew Regina, so there were no handshakes, but warm hugs and kisses in a small parlor off his study. Refreshments were iced tea for the ladies and bourbon for the governor.

"Is my husband still trying to get you to marry him?" Lorena Gray asked Regina.

"I think he took it back when I told him I'd quit cooking," Regina said, shooting the Governor a dirty look.

"Why that's a cryin' shame," Lorena said. "Regina, may I give you the nickel tour while Lawson and Abby talk what Texans call 'bidness'?"

"Certainly. I haven't been here in years."

Lawson and Abby went into his study with its antique maps of Texas and dark-paneled walls.

"Great maps," Abby said.

"My favorite's the one that goes all the way to Colorado," Gray said.

"So what happens now?" Abby asked.

"Well, first you have to sign this. It is consent for an FBI background check. They'll fast track it as you'll have a need to know. Besides, I've checked you out pretty thoroughly in the State databases, and you're clean."

"I should be. I've never even gotten a parking ticket."

Abby read it and signed it.

"My press guy has the press assembled, has given them the packets," Lawson said. "We'll do remarks, photos, no questions, out in twenty."

"Gotcha," Abby replied. *Did everyone in politics speak as if they were texting each other?* "Ladies' room?"

Gray showed her the way.

Abby freshened up, deepening the blush and lip color for the photos.

"Pretty day," Gray said when she reappeared. "We're outside, by the way."

"That's fine." They went only as far as the verandah, where the air was soft and warm, with a southerly breeze ruffling the trees.

The podium was arranged so trees would be the background.

The microphone bouquet was large, and beyond it were a dozen or so reporters and photographers. Television cameras and still cameras on tripods flanked the reporters' chairs and were already aimed at where they would be standing.

Governor Gray, his press guy, Bob Philips, and Abby walked to the podium.

As the Governor and Abby approached, the reporters stood.

Bob Philips opened the briefing.

"Have a seat, guys. Everyone have a bio and head shot?" The crowd nodded. "Let's go."

Lawson Gray took the podium. Regina and Lorena slipped into the back row of chairs, unnoticed.

He then paused for what seemed like a long time. Abby would later learn to do this herself. It gave the video people a little extra time for editing.

"Today I am appointing Dr. Abigail Adams to fill the unexpired Senate seat held by her late sister, Senator Priscilla Logan..."

Abby fixed her eyes on him and listened. He seemed more animated in front of the cameras. He didn't drone on, he got to the point, and then shut up. It was her turn.

"Hello. My name is Abigail Adams and I am deeply honored to be here." Abby looked at the reporters and smiled.

"Even though my sister and I wore the same size shoes, I can never fill her boots. I am honored and humbled to be asked to serve my beloved Texas. Only an appointment by Sam Houston himself would be a greater honor.

"I was born in the shadow of the Alamo at the Nix Hospital in San Antonio. If you cut me, I don't bleed, Guadalupe River water runs out. I believe in the Lone Star and the Big Bend, the live oak and the giant cypress, and the wildflowers that come every spring. I believe in Texas rivers and beaches, football on Friday nights and on Thanksgiving Day. I also believe in chili with beans, corn (not flour) tortillas, tamales at Christmas, barbecue, and doing things like going into space. I think it's neighborly to say 'Hi' to people you pass on the street.

"I think it's important we find a way to run this planet so that Mother Nature doesn't get even madder at us and flick us all off of it.

"I'm a doctor, so I believe that health is good and disease is bad. I believe that bad people can't beat good ones, if the good ones keep a 'coming. In short, I believe in Texas and all that she stands for.

"I am deeply honored to be asked to represent *all* of you in Washington. It is a duty I take quite seriously. I am well aware I've never been elected to anything. While in the Senate, I will devote myself to the service of all Texans, present and future. Whether you were born here or got here as fast as you could, I'll be there for you.

"Thank you."

Various people started shouting questions, but Gray motioned for Abby to move away from the microphones.

"That's it, guys. No questions. Oath of office in Washington within a week. Details to follow from the Senator's office."

He stood off to one side of the podium, put his arm around Abby, and raised his right hand in a static wave. Abby did the same with her left.

"Smile like you mean it," he said into her ear. "And lower your arm, or you'll show skin above your skirt."

Abby did as she was told. Then they turned another direction and did the same thing. A third turn and all was over.

"Great remarks," Gray said. "Tell Poppy I want her writing for me when I'm in the Senate. Of course that last bit about illegal immigrants was a bit much, but…"

"Thank you." Abby didn't tell him her words were her own. It never crossed her mind that the last remark could be interpreted as a remark on illegal immigration.

I've got a lot to learn.

CHAPTER TWELVE

OPENING DOORS

Abby e-mailed a quick letter of resignation to the Chief of Staff at the hospital before they began the drive home. She should have gone by in person before the announcement, but frankly, she forgot. In the e-mail, she said public hospitals would have a friend on the Hill, which was true.

He'd still be ticked at her for not coming back. He needed all the warm bodies he could get. The economy was shoving people off insurance by the hundreds of thousands. The Health Care Reform Act hadn't fully kicked in yet, and until it did, public hospitals were stretched even further. Her hospital regularly ran at 110 percent of capacity. That meant no reserves, ever, even for a disaster or an epidemic. Unless of course, the trauma crowd got sober, put away their knives and guns, and stayed home to watch *Ice Road Truckers*. *Fat chance.*

On the way home from Austin, Abby was still up from the ceremony, but Regina was busy doing her knitting.

"Abby, I've been thinking," Reege finally said about twenty minutes out of Austin.

"'Bout what?" Abby asked.

"After you're sworn in, I think I want to come home," Regina said. "I'm plain tired. Bone tired."

"If you want to be here, be here. Spend time with your friends; rest up a little, Lord knows you've earned it."

"Besides, the building is full service—from room service on down. They'd probably floss your teeth if you asked them. If you get in a pickle, Duke will bail you out."

Abby didn't want to remind Regina she could take care of herself, though not half was well as Regina did.

Driving east into the gathering evening put a little gloom into both of them. It was full dark by the time they pulled into the garage.

"I think I want some tea. How about you?" Regina asked.

"Me too. I'll bring in our luggage."

Abby put their bags in their respective rooms.

As usual, she couldn't wait to get out of her clothes. She took a quick shower, exchanged contacts for glasses, brushed out her hair and put on loose, soft clothing. She felt instantly relaxed. She called the process "unzipping the day." She usually did it as soon as she walked in, no matter what the time. It helped her put the gore of the hospital behind her. Unzipping, reading for pleasure and exercise kept her sane in her world of mayhem and tragedy.

Regina had a natural charm in all things domestic. She made a pot of tea and nuked some lemon cookies from the freezer. She put everything on a tray, and even though nothing matched, everything went together in shades of pink and white and green. It smelled divine too.

This was one of the gifts she would miss from Regina. Left to her own devices, Abby would have a soggy teabag sitting in her mug and broken cookies out of the bag.

Regina could be a bossy boots, even a curmudgeon, but the things she did in a home were elegant, welcoming, and reassuring. Regina made all things right for Abby, and anyone else fortunate to be under a roof with her.

"Have you thought about what this money will do to Duke?" Regina asked, as she poured them both a cup. The fragrance of the tea was calming. No wonder the Brits felt a "cuppa" was the appropriate response to anything from a bad day to a bombed-out house.

"Not really. I just know that I have the responsibility for managing it and giving the proceeds to him. I don't have any choice."

"I knew this day would come." Regina sighed "I knew Old Man Logan left it all to her."

"How'd you know that?"

"I met him once. Really a fine man. I saw through Lance pretty quick. But Pris didn't ask my opinion, so I didn't give it. I probably should have. No, I knew she'd gotten it all when she bought the penthouse about a year after Dad Logan died. Who else would he leave it to?" Regina stirred her cup three times. As always.

"Having Duke become wealthy is not a catastrophe, Regina. You raised him right."

"I know, I know, but I'm so afraid some woman's going to break his heart to get at his money."

"Regina, he's a good man. You can stay here, be with your friends. You don't even have to go to Washington if you're tired."

"Oh yes, I do. You will put your hand on my Bible, just like your sister did." Regina popped a small cookie into her mouth and chomped down on it for punctuation.

"Yes, ma'am," Abby said. She was glad to see Regina's spunk return.

"No, you go on up, and I'll follow in time for the swearing in. Then I'll come home."

Poppy was adamant that Abby do no interviews until after her media training, so Abby consented to get to Washington within a couple of days. Her media training with Wicker Washington was scheduled for Monday, and the swearing-in on Thursday.

Abby had very little she needed to take to Washington. Her life was pretty much in her electronics: a Kindle, a Dell minicomputer, her BlackBerry. She had a wallet and a little bag of old makeup, all of which went into a shabby ten-year-old backpack that looked decidedly non-Senatorial. The bag itself probably harbored enough hospital germs to start a small plague.

The next morning, Abby was at the luggage store in the Galleria when it opened at ten. She found a black calfskin tote with compartments and a zippered top. Of course, the price cut into her sense of frugality, but perfection was worth it.

She decided to humor Regina. She went and got fitted for all new lingerie. She bought enough (all beige) to last her until her Senate gig was over. The woman insisted that spandex slips and such were essential to good grooming, so she bought those too.

Too cheap to pay a lot for panty hose, she stopped at the drugstore and loaded up on it in nude, black, and navy.

"I swear I will never again wear panty hose after I'm out of the Senate," Abby told Regina, holding up three bags of them.

"If you buy anything else, you'll have to buy a new suitcase. No sense in doing that, as Pris had just bought all new luggage before she got sick."

After a quick bite of lunch, she booked her flight to D.C. Then she called Pris's Houston Office. She spoke to the Houston Chief of Staff, Lyman Woodruff.

"I'll be by later this afternoon just to say hi. Would you have Fuzzy's send in pizza and soft drinks for about four o'clock? I'd like to meet everyone."

She put on her St. John suit, carefully packed her new tote bag, and drove over to the office. It was right in the neighborhood, actually. A mid-rise just off Memorial Drive held not only her office, but those of a Congresswoman her sister called Porkette Blowhard. She'd have to pay a call on her too. She hoped Porkette wasn't there, for fear she'd say, "Hi, Porky. How are the little piglets?"

She got to the office about three thirty. Lyman Woodruff was rangy and rumpled, about five years her junior. He was friendly and open and a nice counterpoint to Poppy.

"Sorry I couldn't pay my respects at the service. My grandmother passed away," Lyman said. "Let me show you around."

They wandered among the office. Most everyone was involved in helping constituents solve their problems with the federal government. One group handled veterans, another dealt with immigrations matters, one focused on retirees. Even people hassled by the IRS had a friend in the office.

One section dealt only with luring businesses into Texas, a relatively easy job for a state with no state income tax. Each of these people had a counterpart in the Washington office. As a rainmaker for Texas jobs, Pris was a champion. When the rest of the U.S. economy was in the toilet, Texas was growing new, and good, jobs.

Abby went into Pris's office while the staff waited on the pizza delivery. The office was foreign to her. She'd been here maybe once. Pris collected political memorabilia. An old U.S. flag was framed on one wall. Faded but intact, it had forty-eight stars. The plaque beneath it said, "This flag flew above the U.S. Capitol on V-E Day 1945." There were other things framed: an "I Like Ike" button, a Kennedy pennant. Pris was a nonpartisan collector.

She sat at her sister's desk. Of course, the chair fit her. There was a gavel, a nameplate, a U.S. Senate mug of pens.

There was only one picture. It was Abby, hanging upside down from the monkey bars when she was about eight or nine. Her long strawberry-blonde curls almost touched the ground. She was at the age where her teeth were still too big for her face, like beaver teeth.

She remembered Pris taking the picture on a cool fall day nearly thirty years ago. Tears threatened to swamp her, but she fought them back and strode into the conference room, redolent with the garlic and tomato smells of hot pizza.

The room went silent for her.

"You guys have done a wonderful job the last year while my sister was so sick," Abby said. "I know that her death was a loss for many of you personally. I'm going to need you more than she ever could. Why? She knew what she was doing, and I haven't a clue. But I'll study hard and take your advice very seriously, so please don't hesitate to give it to me. Now let's have some pizza, and you guys can take a well-deserved break."

Lyman offered her a piece of pizza, but she declined.

"I need to go down to pay a call on the Congresswoman. I don't need garlic breath and a tomato stain on my clothes."

"Oh, I called. She left early. You're off the hook."

"Then I want that pizza, and a very large napkin."

CHAPTER THIRTEEN

TOOLS OF THE TRADE

Abby was excited when the wheels screeched down at Reagan National. For the last decade, she'd known roughly what her day would be like. Now, she had no idea what her days would hold. That was exhilarating.

"Hey, thanks for meeting me," Abby said as she air-kissed Poppy, who was waiting for her at baggage claim.

"No prob," Poppy said. *Poppy looks a bit grim.*

The suitcase took its time appearing. Poppy was mostly quiet. When it finally appeared, Abby grabbed it, and they were out the door in seconds. If Houston was in full spring, Washington was in full slush. *I'm glad I wore my boots.*

They were at Poppy's mud-splattered Toyota in a few minutes, long enough for Abby to remember she didn't own a true winter coat of her own.

"I hope you've got on dancing shoes, because you are going to be very busy. Tonight you have off. Tomorrow, Laura Rowe and Kim are at your place at nine sharp. After they leave, you do your three days with Wicker Washington. The following day you are sworn in." Poppy's affect was flat.

"So why so glum?"

"We're getting blowback on your illegal immigrant remark."

"Oh, for crying out loud, I wasn't even talking about illegal immigrants. I was referring to the bumper sticker that said, 'I'm not a native Texan, but I got here as fast as I could.'"

Poppy kept her eyes on the road and they crawled through traffic.

"Abby, I sent remarks. Why didn't you use them?" Poppy's tone was terse.

"Because they didn't represent what I wanted to say?" Abby offered.

"Next time you have an idea about what you want to say, send it to me and let me take out the word bombs," Poppy said. It wasn't a request.

"Whatever." Abby hated that word. But she was ticked off.

"Will you be with me at Wicker Washington?" Abby tried to sound cheerier.

"Actually, no. I'm taking a couple of days. Going to a spa. I need some time away."

Abby noticed she was not asking.

"I imagine you are whipped."

As they pulled up to the Franklin, Abby turned to Poppy.

"Would you like to come up for a drink?"

"Nope. I'm on my way right back to Reagan. My flight is in two hours."

"Poppy, I could have taken a cab."

"No, I wanted to tell you in person that I am worn out. I'll get you through to the end of the year, but then I'm getting out of politics. It's not you. Well, not exactly. It would be easier if you didn't think, if you just did as I told you to do." Poppy was serious.

"Well, thanks for your candor. And I hope you have a wonderful rest. You do deserve it," Abby said. *If she thinks I'll 'mind,' she's got another think coming.*

Poppy popped the trunk open, and that was Abby's cue to get her stuff and get out.

Abby was glad she hadn't yet told Poppy the size of her bequest. In her mood, she might quit on the spot. Besides, Poppy would have to wait for the estate to settle before she got it.

The apartment was immaculate. Undoubtedly, Regina had called ahead and given lots of instructions. The refrigerator had been emptied and restocked with basics. Even her bed was turned down with a mint on the pillow.

She read through the schedule cards Poppy had given her. Tonight she had nothing on her list. Laura Rowe and Kim Tran both came in the morning at nine.

Abby had a sudden urge for a root beer float. She was celebrating. She was going to be a Senator. She went to the fridge. No root beer. She opened the freezer. No ice cream.

She'd already undone her hair and taken out her contacts. She left her hair hanging down, grabbed the parka, and headed to Tran's. Dusk was gathering in the shadows, and the color was leaking out of the sky. Trees looked inky, but there was still some blue in the western sky.

The bell jangled as she pushed in the door of Tran's Store. As usual, it smelled of freshly cut ginger. Abby suspected he cut a piece every day just for the fragrance.

"Hello, Mr. Tran," Abby said.

"Hello, Missy." He smiled back at her. Abby had never figured out if he called every female that, or just her.

"I want some root beer and ice cream, please," she said, heading for the cooler and freezer.

"Want straws to go with that?" *He was always up-selling.*

"Sure, why not?" Abby didn't tell him she'd just thrown out boxes of straws from Pris's illness.

"Got a date tonight?" Tran asked.

"Me? I'm an old maid. You know that."

"Men must be crazy. You nice. Not like a lot," he said, handing her the purchases and change for the twenty she handed him.

She thought about asking after Kim, but decided the ice cream felt a little mushy, so she'd best hurry home.

"Bye," she called from the door, as another woman entered. Abby waited a beat, but didn't hear Mr. Tran call her "Missy."

Abby put a book on the U.S. Senate on her Kindle—for ninety-nine cents. It was a glossary of Senate terms she'd best learn, things like "cloture." *Handy reference.* She had her root beer float while she skimmed it.

Tomorrow she was going to get all new clothes. She was feeling a little like Cinderella getting outfitted for the ball. Much better than the last time she was with Laura and Kim. She wished she had Pris to share this with. Pris had not only been her sister, she'd been her best friend. When you're orphaned, you tend to be real tight with your siblings.

Her hospital friends were just colleagues. Besides, none had even bothered to come to the graveside service in Houston. No one even wrote a note. Sure, they were nice when they wanted her to cover a shift for her, but they dropped her like a hot potato when she left to care for her dying sister.

"Gotta look out for your sister," was as close as anyone came to sympathy.

She wanted her sister to share the joy of a new wardrobe and a new life with. Of course, in a perverse way, Pris was there to share it. She had made it all happen.

Before tears could engulf her, she concentrated on Cinderella and all the characters. What were the ugly stepsister's names? Was Griselda one? Drusilla?

By noon she, Laura, and Kim were ready for a break. Abby had chosen two weeks' worth of new work clothes and accessories. Kim had picked through Pris's closet and chosen some special occasion outfits that she could change up enough to make them unrecognizable.

Abby had ordered lunch sent up, and the three women ate at the table rolled in by room service, complete with a bouquet of tulips and Gerbera daisies.

"The women in this town will roast you alive if they catch you in your sister's clothes," Laura Rowe said, sipping her mineral water.

"There is only a small chance of that," Kim said pleasantly. "A long full gown becomes a cocktail dress with self-fabric roses along the neckline. That sort of thing."

"So do I have everything I need?" Abby asked, after eating chicken, grape, and walnut salad.

"You have everything you need except a ball gown," Laura said.

"I told Kim that if I ever needed a ball gown, I'd let her make it," Abby said.

Kim was blushing.

"What's up?" Abby asked.

"I brought you a few sketches and swatches," Kim said. "For your ball gown. But only if you feel you need one."

The three women passed them around. Laura Rowe was slack-jawed.

"Do you have anything already made up? I'd like Neiman's to see these."

"No," Kim said. "The gowns I have made are all bridal. But I have a portfolio of them at my studio." Her "studio" was her bedroom, so she usually slept on the sofa to keep the studio pristinely clean.

"Kim, I love this fabric and that second design," Abby said. This girl was going places, no reason not to help things along.

The dress was a long and covered up, but very sexy.

"First, I shall have to get more detailed measurements and make you a dressmaker's dummy. I would then make it in muslin for fit. Once I cut the fabric, there's no going back. So I could do it in about two weeks minimum."

They discussed price and Abby was glad to give Kim the work. Kim would be thrilled to have the exposure when Abby wore the dress. Besides, with her custom dressmaker's dummy, Kim could then make Abby virtually anything.

March 11

Wicker Washington was on K Street in the midst of all the lobbying firms. *There's some serious money floating around here.*

Abby couldn't imagine three days of training to speak into a microphone. She wore one of her new outfits and felt quite chic. *I like chic.*

A well-coiffed older woman greeted Abby at Wicker Washington.

"You must be Dr. Adams," she said, standing to shake hands. "I'm Barbara McCord. If you'll come with me, please?"

"Certainly."

The two crossed an elegant lobby to a door. Barbara pushed it open, motioning Abby to move through ahead of her into a dim hallway.

"Motion sensor lights. Mr. Wicker is waiting for you. He's at the end of the hall. Can't miss him."

Abby walked a couple of steps, and a barrage of blinding flashes of light from every angle hit her. People started calling her name, and microphones shot toward her. The cacophony of voices became quite loud.

"Dr. Adams, over here," a man's voice yelled at her.

"Senator, what were you thinking?" A woman sounded angry.

She put her hands in front of her face to protect herself, and finally a door opened.

"Hello, Dr. Adams. Welcome to the big leagues." Bob Wicker held out his hand to shake hers. "Let's see how you did on your first ambush."

"First? Is there going to be another?" Abby said, laughing.

"You never know." He motioned her into a seat and offered her a glass of water. She was grateful for it.

He sat down and pushed a button. The whole horrible scene replayed on a large monitor on the wall.

"First of all, your behavior is entirely normal. Pretend you are a viewer. Let's call you Doris. And Doris is from Dubuque. Pretend that Abigail Adams has been accused, wrongly, of something, and the media catch her as she exits an office building. What comes to mind?"

Abby sipped her water and watched the videotape in horror.

"She looks guilty as hell, hiding behind her hands, not responding."

"Correct."

Media training was definitely a good idea.

"After you finish our course, you will be able to use the media effectively: to put across your message effectively, and to do damage control when necessary. Would you like to try the ambush again?"

"Yes. I would, as a matter of fact."

Bob opened the door into the darkened hallway. She thought it would start when she got to the other end of the hall and turned to come back. However, the barrage started when she was halfway down.

She held herself more erect, put a small smile on her face, and walked until she nearly bumped into the door at the far end. She turned and walked back. She said nothing and faced straight ahead.

"You play dirty pool, Mr. Wicker," Abby said at the replay.

"So does the press, Dr. Adams. Let's let 'Doris' watch you again."

"She looks kind of prissy, maybe smirking," Abby said of herself. "She's not hiding, though, that's good."

"Excellent. Excellent. Let's go into the studio."

He raised the lights in the dreaded hallway. It was empty. The Wicker staffers and their equipment retreated behind the closed doors. Once in Studio One, there was a small area to sit and watch a large monitor.

"Harry, cue our walk through the hall, please."

There was Abigail walking down the hall with Bob.

"What do you notice about us?"

"Well, that you still play dirty pool," she said, laughing.

"No, I'm trying to teach you something. There is always a camera on you. Always. Always. Always. When you are sworn in, you cease being a private person. Period. And while complimentary pictures are nice, ugly ones are valuable—especially if you should happen to do something ugly, like have sex with an intern. A picture of you, say, picking your nose or pushing your glasses up with your middle finger matched with a negative story is major cash to some people."

"So don't pick my nose or sleep with interns. Got it."

"Actually, just touching your nose is a bad idea," Wicker said. "Harry, cue the nose shot."

There was Abby picking her nose not five minutes earlier in Bob's office.

"But I didn't do that!" she yelped.

"Oh? You put your right index finger on the right side of your nose. The picture was shot from the left. Therefore, you're 'picking your nose.'"

"Okay. I'm putty in your hands."

"First, we are going to talk about neutral face."

"Harry, give me a head shot of Dr. Adams walking down the hall with me."

"Now, 'Doris,' what do you see?"

"I see someone who looks unhappy, even angry."

"Were you in fact unhappy?" Wicker asked.

"No, I wasn't."

"The expression we have when we are thinking nothing in particular is called our 'neutral' face. Very few people have one that is positive. Most of us have our mouths turn downward."

"Okay," Abby said, slowly, nodding thoughtfully.

"Harry, give us a head shot of me walking down the hall."

"'Doris,' what do you see?"

"I see a very pleasant-looking man."

"I had to learn that face. That face is my stock in trade, and your assignment tonight is to look into the mirror and come up with a neutral face. It is basically a half-smile that conveys empathy.

"After a short break, I'm going to turn you over to Hillary, our voice coach. She'll get you into shape in that department. Then you and I will meet again in the morning." Wicker handed her *The Wicker Media Manual*, a three ring binder. *Tonight's reading*.

Hillary appeared presently. She was heavyset and horsey looking, but her voice was lovely.

"How do you do? I'm Hillary Warden, and I'm your keeper this afternoon."

"Your voice is lovely and rather familiar," Abby said, chuckling at the pun.

"Ah, well, thank you. I make most of my living doing voice-overs. I have, as they say, a face for radio." She laughed a melodic laugh. "I occasionally consult for Wicker."

They went into an audio booth. The walls and ceiling were covered in gray foam and the door sealed tightly. There was just enough room for two chairs, microphones, a webcam, a video monitor, and two headphones.

"We are going to start by critiquing your remarks at the Governor's Mansion. Before we start on diction, however, I want to congratulate your writer. He did an excellent job."

"That'd be me."

"Then keep on writing your own stuff. You've got what it takes."

"Thanks." *Tell that to Poppy*.

"Put on these headphones."

They listened to the audio only of the remarks.

"Tell me what you noticed about your voice."

"I don't sound like me."

"Correct. No one does. Speech resonates in our heads as we hear it. That resonance is absent in any recording."

"Okay. Got that."

"So I'm going to teach you some professional techniques." And indeed she did, for an hour or more. Abby learned exercises to relax her facial muscles before speaking, some tricks to make her voice fuller, even to make her voice project more. All their work was on a DVD for her.

Before Abby left, Hillary fitted her with an earpiece.

"Which ear do you prefer?" Hillary said.

"No preference."

"Then we'll put it into your right ear. Put your left ear onto the desk. Are you comfortable?"

"I feel silly but fine."

Hillary mixed a powder and a liquid together that smelled strongly like superglue.

"Now don't freak, I'm going to put it in your ear. You can't move or talk for three minutes."

Abby stayed still while Hillary filled her right ear with goo. Then she set a timer.

"Don't lose this, or we'll have to do this again. This is called an IFB for independent feedback. This earpiece will be drilled and have a clear, curly tube come out of it. At the other end will be a jack. When it is plugged in, someone in the control room of a television studio can talk into your ear."

The timer went off. Hillary tugged Abby's ear backwards, and the mold slid out.

"Your IFB will be ready tomorrow. We'll have another afternoon session."

"Thank you, Hillary."

"Last year I nursed my sister after a bone marrow transplant. She made it. I'm so sorry Senator Logan didn't. She was a helluva Senator."

"Thank you. As I said, I've got big boots to fill."

"You'll do just fine. Most people who come in here are so full of themselves. You aren't. You're a real person. The Senate needs a few dozen more like you."

"Why, what a lovely thing to say. You've made my whole day."

Hillary sent her home with a tape recorder and some speeches to read into it.

"Remember, the best speeches are really poetry. Churchill wrote his, not in paragraphs, but in lines, even noting when to pause or take off his glasses. So when you think about writing and giving a speech, think poetically. Your remarks at the Governor's Mansion were really very poetic. So rewrite them as poetry and speak it that way."

"Great tip," Abigail said. "I doubt I'll be giving many speeches, though."

"You never know. And the power to persuade is the most important power of all."

CHAPTER FOURTEEN

CINDERELLA

That night she ordered her "unzipped" wardrobe: a bunch of new yoga pants and loose tops and hoodies. No, she wasn't going to do yoga; she was just tired of living in her bathrobe after work. She even ordered a new bathrobe as well as some cozy pajamas. She could give up sleeping in her worn-out shirts.

She e-mailed Marston Mills to set up a blind trust for her while she was in the Senate. That way, she could never be accused of voting on a bill that would help her financially. She specified the management fee would not exceed one percent per year. *About the time the estate is settled, I'll no longer need the blind trust.*

Abby checked in with Mason Ingram, Pris's ranch manager, assured him that nothing would change and that she was only a phone call away.

"Have you got everything you need?" Abigail asked.

"Yes, ma'am. I'm set up. You know how to get into the website and check up on things?"

"Yes."

"Then you can follow along any time you like and see how things are going. Don't be a stranger."

"I'd love to come, I just don't know when," Abigail said.

Abby couldn't imagine owning a chunk of Texas that size. The biggest thing she'd ever owned was a used Prius. Now she, along with Duke and Regina, owned something almost as big as Rhode Island, but with oil wells, not people. At least it was in good hands right now.

She texted the car service for nine in the morning. She laid out another chic outfit. *So far, this is fun.*

A row of black Lincoln Town Cars waited downstairs in the morning. Hers said "Adams" in a large font on a piece of paper on the dashboard. *Carpooling with a twist. Ford should definitely be making money in this market.* Her driver, Robert, kept tabloids in the backseat, and she was transfixed all the way to Wicker.

"So, Barbara, good morning. What chamber of horrors do you have for me today?" Abby asked the receptionist.

"Today is a fun day. You first get to do makeup and hair."

"Well, that's a relief. A girl could get used to this."

"That's the problem. Too many people get addicted to themselves. Then no one wants to watch them anymore."

"I'll try to remember that."

"Yes, once you start to believe your own PR, it's all downhill from there. Andre is ready for you, if you'll follow me."

"Andre Callas? I know him. He's very nice. How did you know to use him?"

"Poppy recommended him."

"Of course."

"Poppy's the best Chief of Staff on the Hill."

Couldn't prove it by me, at least not right now.

Andre and Abby greeted one another, and Barbara left. As usual, Andre had on his guy-liner and wore his Elvis pompadour. He had his two tackle boxes as well as an assistant with him.

Abby introduced herself to Bette, Andre's assistant. A multiply-pierced Goth, Bette looked maybe fifteen. With her black hair, nails, and lips, Abby wondered what Bette offered the beauty business, but kept her mouth firmly shut.

Andre draped her with a smock.

"When you do your own makeup before an interview, baby girl, always use something to protect your clothes. Even paper towels tucked into the top of your suit will shield you from a disaster."

"Won't there be people to do it?" Abby asked.

"No, budget cuts everywhere. You have to do your own most times. From a small bag that fits in your tote."

"Okay. I'd best pay attention."

"First we start with threading," Andre said.

"Huh?"

"Abby, darling, 'Huh?' is only one step up from 'Do what?'" Andre said, wagging his head from side to side and rolling his eyes. "Ladies in your position say, 'Pardon me?' or 'Excuse me?'"

"Noted. 'Pardon me,' but what is threading?"

"A way to tame your brows. Left to your own devices, you'll have eyebrows like the late Andy Rooney in a few years."

"You get the Candor of the Year Award."

He took a length of thread, made it into a loop, and then wrapped it the way kids do when they want to spin a button on it. Within moments, each of her brows was perfectly groomed.

"See, that didn't hurt a bit, did it? And look, your eyes appear more open."

"You're right."

"Now for the lip. Put your tongue up under your upper lip."

Another minute or two, and her lip was completely fuzz free.

"That hurt," Abby said. "But then again, it was my lip."

"There's no whining in beauty. Now. I am going to apply products to one side of your face, and then you will do the other. Like in the cheesy stores, but with better results. Bette will write everything down and get it for you. It will all be here in the morning. A regular-sized set for home, and travel sizes of everything for your tote bag. Don't leave home without it."

"Face prep is everything. Exfoliate daily and moisturize twice daily. Wear a sunscreen on your face, décolletage, and backs of your hands."

"Why?"

"The neck and hands are age giveaways. And use a primer on your eye makeup, or it slides off in the District's heat.

"Don't forget concealer." He used something that clicked a dab onto a brush.

"Do I need primer with it?" Abby asked.

"Only if you want your under-eye area to look like sheetrock."

"No thanks."

"For you? Cream blush on moisturized cheeks, brow bones, and into your hairline."

"My hairline?"

"You are supposed to glow, not look like a puppet. Lips stain, blotted, then topped with a gloss. If the gloss comes off, you have color, which is youthful."

"But what about foundation?"

"Not for you. Everyday? Show off that perfect skin. If you get oily or sweaty, use a blotting tissue. For camera work, a dusting of powder and powder blush. They deepen color and reduce shine," Andre said. Bette kept notes of shades he chose.

"And don't forget artificial tears just before you go on camera. Makes you look bright-eyed; the pros all do it."

With practice, Abby could do this in five minutes at home. Abby liked her look in the lights. She looked like herself, just better.

"Now we go to hair. Bette, get the hair sheet for curly hair, would you?"

Bette flipped through a file box she toted. "Got it."

Andre was fluffing her hair.

"Great hair. Really, really great. Never colored, great body. Your hair makes a statement."

"Yeah, it says 'I frizz for fun,'" Abby retorted.

"In part because you aren't brushing it correctly. Mason Pearson paddle brush, every night. Now that you've got the cut down, I'll teach you two styles. One down, one up."

"This I've got to see," Abby said.

Andre misted her hair with water, and then parted it asymmetrically, from the point of her crown to just above her left eyebrow.

"Look, there's almost the same amount of hair on both sides."

"Yes?" Abby said. Then Andre tucked her hair behind each ear, and it looked great.

"Top it with a shine spray, and you won't frizz."

Next came the updo.

"In general, women in positions of power should not have hair confusion. Remember President Wells's wife and her awful parade of hair styles?"

"Yes, she was dreadful."

"It completely undercut her credibility. So find a style you like—that I approve of—and wear that every day. And it should not cover your face or your collar. Show me how you wear it in the hospital."

"Well, I usually keep it up in a banana clip."

Abby took the brush, and in ten seconds demonstrated.

"No. Look." He pointed into the mirror. "You're wearing a hair pom-pom on top."

Abby had to laugh. Even "Black Bette" cracked a smile.

"This photographs poorly, but you're close."

He gave her a loose figure-of-eight chignon just above the nape of her neck. "Lots of fullness, even the charming escapees," he said of the hairs that sprang out of the style.

"Better?" he asked. "You know you're a grown-up when you stop fighting your hair."

"Fantastic," she replied.

"Okay, now you do it."

Abby did it without difficulty.

"Last thing. You have complicated hair, so wear simple earrings. Pinkish baroque pearls are lovely with your coloring. Get a variety of sizes and colors online. No diamonds or CZs. Too flashy."

"Bette will have your kits ready for you today. Tonight I want you to practice this makeup and hair. You should be able to do this in your sleep. We'll stop now and send you to Bob for lighting and studio work."

"Thanks so much. I hope you'll come to help for special occasions?" Abby said.

"Of course. Poppy has already booked me for the swearing-in. Show me your nails."

Abby proffered her hands. Her nails were short, neatly filed and bare.

"You, my dear, need solar nails."

"I can't have them in the hospital."

Andre looked at her as if she were daft.

"You are a S-E-N-A-T-O-R. Bette, get her set up for them, day before swearing-in."

"Yes, Andre."

"Baby, your grooming is a *huge* part of who you 'are' in the public eye. As soon as you take your oath, *you are public property*. You'll have a standing appointment with me every month for a cut, condition, and threading. Nails every two weeks. A pedi at least once a month, as you will be on your feet a lot. Remember, you are never to go out of the house unless you are CR."

"CR?"

"Camera Ready. You may *not* go out of the elevator without the fab five: concealer, eye-liner, waterproof mascara, lip and check color. Anything less and you'll look like a hag."

"Why waterproof?"

"In case of rain or tears."

"Got it. Lucky for me you're at Franklin."

"No, lucky for me. You, at least, take advice. You should see some of the livestock that comes into the salon. They want hair like a yak. I swear one woman looks like a wildebeest. Won't let me thread her chin hair that is all but a goatee."

"What do you do about them?" Abby asked, laughing.

"Charge them double and make them swear not to tell a soul who does their hair. Goatee Lady? I charge her triple."

CHAPTER FIFTEEN

MEDIA MAVEN

Bob Wicker took her to Studio Two. Just outside it, a full-length mirror allowed for one last image check.

"We call it the spinach check." He looked at his teeth in the mirror. Abby did the same and discovered lip gloss on her teeth. She quickly wiped it off.

The studio itself was a cold, cavernous room, with a political interview set, three robotic cameras, and a huge monitor off to the side of the set. A large man in the shadows was fiddling with something. One wall was painted lime green. The floor was full of snaking cables, only a fraction of which were taped down.

"Watch your step. Every studio is a minefield. Literally and figuratively." He pointed to the cables.

"Time to check out how you look. Andre will come in for a camera check, then it'll just be us. You sit in the seat on the left. Rusty, come here. I want you to meet someone."

"Hi, I'm your floor director." He extended a meaty hand.

"I'm Abby," she said. "What does a floor director do?"

"Well, the trolls in the control room control camera position, audio levels, cut to commercials, and the like. I'm human backup. Also today, I'm here to make sure you learn how to sell it."

"Sell it?"

"In television, your image and voice go through a thousand digital manipulations before they get to the viewer. So you have to be 'up.' Have you ever done cocaine?"

"No." She was shocked at the question.

"Good, but bad. People on coke are more animated, more intense. That's what you're here to learn today."

"I gotta mike you. One reason to wear suits. Dresses are tricky. Normally you'll do this yourself, so pay attention. Take off your jacket, please."

He clipped a small mike onto her jacket, ran its slim wire under the jacket's shoulder. She put the jacket on, and the microphone cord hung down from the back at the waist.

"You plug in to the hole in the desk."

"Yes, got it."

"Now, put your IFB into your right ear and loop the tubing over your ear."

Abby did as she was told.

"See the other jack hole in the desk?"

"Yes."

"Plug into that."

Someone spoke into her right ear. "Hey, Senator, you're looking great."

"Wow," Abby said. "Are you sure I'm not going to catch fire, being plugged in on both sides?"

"Nah," Rusty said. "It only gets tricky when you're standing outside in a puddle."

Bob set up at the other seat.

"Now, Abby, as soon as that mike is plugged in, you need to remember the entire world can hear everything you say," Bob added.

"Weird."

"No, wired." Bob and Rusty laughed.

"What do I do if I have to sneeze?"

"Excellent question. See that little button on the right, the white one?" Rusty said in his slight Southern drawl.

"Yes."

"That's a 'cough button.' It cuts off the feed from your mike while you hold it down. If you take your finger off, the mike is open again. Now I'm going to light you."

Overhead, there was a forest of incredibly bright lights on high tracks. "Those light the set, not you."

"Your lighting is here." He fiddled with lighted silver umbrellas on stands with the inside of the umbrella facing Abby.

"This is 'bounce' lighting, the most flattering. If you're ever not in a studio, get them to bounce some light off a wall and then onto your face. Without good lighting, everyone looks horrible. You gotta know this yourself, in case your press person is sick."

Do I have a press person? Another question for Poppy.

"Good tip."

Then he pointed a light meter at her and nodded. He spoke into his headset.

"I'm happy, you happy?" he said to the people in the control room.

Andre came in and stood in a corner.

"Bit shiny," he said, pulling out a compact he'd brought.

He dabbed her nose and forehead and turned to the monitor.

"Great. This will be in your makeup kit. See you tomorrow." He blew her a kiss and was gone.

"Now, Abby, take a good look at yourself in the monitor," Wicker said. "Tell me what you see."

The monitor was huge, at least three feet square.

"I see someone with hideous posture."

"Good girl. Sit up ramrod straight. And sit on the front half of the chair. Now lean into the camera without losing your straight back."

"Better, but my jacket is bunching up," Abby said.

"So stand up, pull it down, and sit on it."

She did. *Sit on my jacket, perch on the front of the chair, lean forward, sit up straight, and act like I'm on cocaine. All this to look normal.*

"Now tell me what you see?"

"I see a better me." *To heck with better, I look damned good.*

"Good." Rusty gave her the thumbs up sign. Then he went and stood sequentially in front of each of the three cameras.

"Your camera is camera two. When the red light is on, it's focused on you."

"The tally light?" Abby asked proudly.

"Good girl, you read the book last night. You won't know how tight a shot it is unless you can learn to catch the monitor in your peripheral vision. That's the shot going out to the world. It's just under the clear part of your desk."

Abby found she could follow it without looking at it. Very useful trick.

For the next hour, Bob and Abby did rehearsals of various interview scenarios, from chatty to confrontational.

In between each segment, Rusty told her to "ramp it up a bit." Or "Sell it to me."

They had her do an exercise: close your eyes, think of the sexiest man in the world, and envision him in the camera, even blow him kisses. He is your lover. The love of your life. They were quiet while she did this. She didn't need to think about this one: Michael Aston, the movie star.

He was the epitome of tall, dark, and handsome, greying at the temples, and his brown eyes melted hearts. She thought of him, standing behind her, kissing her neck as he slowly undid her dress. His touch was gentle but electrifying.

She could get into this.

Then they did another fake interview, and even Abby could see the difference in her performance. She lit up the screen. *The camera as lover is an intense performance enhancer.*

Lastly, Bob taught her about split focus.

"The viewer is the third person in our conversation. So, you want to include him or her. To do that, you simply look at the camera with the red light on."

And to think, Abby thought television was for simpletons.

"What about my hands? I talk with my hands."

"Then use them. Just keep them away from your face and hair."

The next day was a half-day, and it went much faster.

Abby came in, Andre taught her a sleek updo "for when you want to kick ass." Then he and Hillary disappeared into the control room.

They shot her doing her Texas speech again, and in a confrontational interview in which she defended the Infants First Act. Everyone was amazed at how far she had come. She owned the screen when she chose to.

She was that rarest of things, a natural who wanted to learn.

Abby was just glad it was over. A lot of work, just in case she might have a camera in her face.

Maybe Poppy was right after all. *Smile. Shake hands. Shut up.*

Tomorrow was the swearing-in. She had no idea when and where she was supposed to be. She didn't even know what the oath was. *Where the hell was Poppy?*

CHAPTER SIXTEEN

GETTING READY

Regina arrived at the apartment about seven. Abby hugged her as if they'd been apart years, not days.

"I'm so glad you're here," Abby said. "Poppy took this time to disappear. To a spa."

"That doesn't sound like her," Regina said, slipping off her mink coat. Abby hung it in the coat closet. Then she put Reege's suitcase on the luggage rack in her room.

"I still haven't heard from her," Abby said. "Can I make you some cocoa and cinnamon toast?"

"That'd be great. But she'll show up. Besides, I know where to go and who to talk to." Regina laughed. "I've been down this road once before."

Abby was in the kitchen heating the cocoa when the phone rang. *Finally.*

It was Duke calling for his "marching orders," but Abby had none to give him until she spoke to Poppy. *Where was that woman?*

Abby and Regina both got into their bathrobes and slippers and enjoyed a "meal" of cocoa and cinnamon toast.

Poppy's ID appeared on her phone about eight. *Finally.*

"How was the spa?" Abby asked, deliberately smiling so her voice would sound pleasant. *Who in the hell do you think you are, just disappearing at a crucial time?* "I hope you got some rest."

"Actually, I did. Sorry I was such a bitch."

"We all are sometimes." *Don't try it again, babe.*

"You've figured out the car service, I take it?"

"Yep, plus wardrobe, hair, makeup, and media. And I have my appointment all signed and sealed. I have my passport for identification." *I've even memorized the Constitution.*

"You're a fast study. That's good. You and Regina can pick me up at nine. We'll take it from there. I'll give you your dance card in the morning."

"Okay. Can you please e-mail me photos and bios of the Senate leadership?"

"Now?" Poppy asked. "It's kind of late."

"I only have one chance to make a first impression. I need it within the hour. We'll pick you up at nine. Bye." Abby hung up. *Poppy needed to up her game.*

Abby called Duke, who answered on the fourth ring.

"Talk to me, Auntie Abby." Abby heard a party in the background. *Ah, the joys of grad school.*

"You still on for tomorrow?" she asked.

"Sure. It's not every day my Aunt Abby gets sworn into the U.S. Senate."

"Great, we'll pick you up at eight thirty."

"I can't wait, Aunt Abby. And don't you worry, I'll wear my best sweats."

"Here," Abby said, handing the phone to Regina so the two could catch up.

Abby padded back to her room and ordered the car online. There was indeed a link to the Senate leadership in her e-mail.

Abby tried to match names and faces, but it was hard. Most were the pale, male Medicare crowd that ran the country. Fifteen women. Six African-Americans. Virtually no Hispanics, or Vietnamese. The Senate looked very unlike the nation.

She double-checked her bag: passport, appointment, oath printed from the Senate website, makeup bag with sanitizing wipes, tampon and spot removal pen, wallet, extra panty hose, handkerchief. Oh, and most importantly, Pris's copy of the Constitution. Abby had already memorized the meat of it. After memorizing a zillion medical things, it was a snap.

She put a pen in the pen slot. She connected her BlackBerry to its charger and left it to dangle over the open bag, ditto for her mini-computer and Kindle. *Since when had it become normal to plug in your purse?*

She realized she'd be carrying a black bag with a navy suit, so went online and ordered the same bag in navy and another in red.

She laid out her clothes for in the morning, from underwear to accessories.

She would also wear her sister's custom-made gold Seal of the United States. Pris had always worn it to ceremonial occasions. She kissed it before she pinned it onto the left shoulder of the suit. According to Bob Wicker, a pin there made it into a head shot. Lower, it would be a distraction.

Of course, she would wear her watch, an eighteen-karat gold Ebel Wave that Pris had given her when she had started medical school. She took it off only when the battery needed changing. She remembered when her sister gave it to her.

"Here, Sissy, a waterproof watch with a sweep second hand. I had my choice between this and a Mickey Mouse watch," Pris said with her husky laugh.

For her thirtieth birthday, Pris had given her a monogrammed pinky ring. That too she always wore on her right hand.

Oh, God, I miss you so much, Pris. Look at me. You have given me everything.

She was almost as nervous as the first day of residency. Back then she was scared of making a mistake on some defenseless baby. She hadn't. But now she had to laugh out loud.

She was the defenseless baby.

CHAPTER SEVENTEEN
SWEARING-IN

Today's the day.

The rain last night washed away the dirty dregs of snow. The city looked clean for a change. Winter was on its way out.

Abby was dressed and ready to go, her hair sprayed into submission, her nails Frenched to perfection.

Regina was in a burgundy suit with a hat of the same fabric. For a Regina hat, it was restrained. Some looked like headdresses on Star Trek. One summer hat had alternating white and pink ostrich feathers around it. Any bigger, it could be a beach umbrella.

Abby and Regina picked up Duke, who looked quite dapper in a dark suit, pale blue shirt, and Harvard tie.

"You want me to do a little hip hop, maybe bust a rhyme at this swearing-in? Liven the place up?" Duke said to Abby. Then he put his fist to his mouth and began to rap. "I'm going in the Senate. Yeah, yeah, I'm in it, in it, the Senate, the Senate."

"I'm sure the Vice President's Secret Service detail would be amused," Abby replied.

"You're going to behave yourself," Regina swatted his arm. "Unlike you did at Pris's swearing-in. You threw up and ruined my brand new dress."

"What did you expect, taking a baby?" Duke protested. "Did you think I'd remember it?"

"I just wanted you to see history being made," Regina retorted. "No fault in that." Bickering was their specialty, and Regina always got the last word. She claimed this was good training for marriage.

Poppy was ready when they pulled up. She was in red, as always, though she looked a bit pale. *Who goes to a spa and comes home pale?*

"Hey, Poppy, you're looking mighty red today," Duke said. "Is this some red letter day?"

"Let's just all get through it," Poppy said. "Then we can get down to the real work on Monday."

They inched along through D.C. traffic up to the Russell Office Building.

"I'd like to spend some time in the office this weekend," Abby said to Poppy.

"That won't work for me," Poppy said. "Sorry."

"Oh, well, I can go alone," Abby said.

"I'd prefer you didn't."

Abby let the matter drop. *Poppy did not have their roles straight.*

Poppy brightened when she got them all into the Russell Office Building. Suddenly, she was the lead scout, and they followed her blindly through security and up to Abby's office.

"As a senior senator in the majority party, Pris had prime real estate," Poppy said. "You ought to see people scramble for office space after elections. Like a cutthroat game of musical chairs."

"Are there any floor votes this afternoon?"

"No. Friday afternoons people try to get out of town."

The Beaux Arts building was spacious and the Rotunda in it impressive, though it was dwarfed by the one in the Capitol itself. Their steps rang out as they crossed the floor. Thank goodness Laura Rowe knew to put insoles in all her shoes. These floors would destroy feet. *I'll miss working in athletic shoes.*

Abby was "camera ready," had a "positive neutral" face, and stood up straight. She knew the Constitution by article and section, would not say the f-word and would emulate her sister's charm. As a skill set, it wasn't much, but it was all she had.

The office was crowded, and the addition of the four of them made things even tighter. The high ceilings and impressive woodwork helped, but not a lot. Just inside the door, an intern sat at a reception desk.

The blonde-maned young woman with a blinding white smile stood and offered her hand.

"Hello, Poppy, Senator, I'm Sally Ann Porter, from Dallas. Welcome. Hello, Miss Regina, Duke." Sally Ann obviously knew the pecking order.

"Thank you, Sally Ann," Abby replied. *There must be men after her like flies on honey.*

Sally Ann sat back down, and Poppy gestured to the bullpen of desks and chairs, crammed into the spacious room.

"It would be a cube farm, but it would cost money and not look 'senatorial.' We've tried to cluster people in similar areas. In the far corner, constituent relations, other side, press/public relations. Left corner, legislative aides, right front, committee aides."

Abby noticed everyone wore his photo ID for the building.

"Hi, guys, I'm Abby Adams," she paused so the room could quiet. "I'm going to be working here for a few months."

That got a chuckle.

"I really appreciate all you do for Texas, and all you meant to my sister. By the time I get up to speed, it'll be time to leave, but I'm still going to work hard. Your help will be essential, and I thank you for it in advance."

Poppy had a pickle face during Abby's talk, but frankly, Abby was past caring. Poppy took them through a set of double wood doors with ornate carvings, and into another room that had obviously been chopped in two.

"This is my office," Poppy said of an area with a U-shaped desk and three chairs in front of it. "By custom, most people enter your office through mine. Before we go into yours, let's go into Mikey's office."

"Michael Molloy is still here?" Duke asked. "He was older than God when I first met him."

'Yes, and, like God, he doesn't seem to age at all," Poppy said.

Michael occupied the other half of the chopped-up office. He too had a door into Abby's office.

Michael Molloy stood. He was about Abby's height, but stooped. His Irish coloring hadn't aged well, and he had lots of age spots where red hair used to grow. What he had left was snowy. He probably had bushy white eyebrows, but kept them trimmed. His eyes were still a sparkling blue.

"How do you do?" he asked, rather formally as he offered his hand and bowed slightly. "Mikey Molloy at your service, ma'am."

"I'm Abigail Adams, and I am delighted to meet you. If you merit your own office, why haven't I met you before now?"

"Unfortunately, I was incarcerated in a hospital at the time of your sister's funeral. I escaped, however, though not unscathed. I fear I shall never wear a Speedo again."

Everyone laughed.

"What do you do?" Abby asked, feeling a little stupid.

"I do what you need for me to do. I am, as you can see, past retirement age. As such, you could think of me as your very own greeter, like at Wal-Mart."

That, too, produced titters.

"I am an 'old Washington hand.' I prefer to think of myself as your liege. I am at your service. Some of the youngsters call me Obi Wan for some reason."

"I am truly delighted to have you on my side. I am going to need a lot of teaching. Between you and Poppy, I'm sure you'll keep me on the straight and narrow."

"A very boring path, Dr. Adams, but these days, one must walk it, or the press will eat you alive. If you are available either day this weekend, I would be delighted to come in and begin your Senatorial tutelage. Monday's busy. There is a floor vote."

"Shall we say one o'clock both days?"

"Yes. I like a hard worker."

Poppy was studying a fingernail.

"Miss Regina, how are you faring these days?" Molloy asked as he took Regina's hand in his two bony ones.

"I'm tired, Mikey. Just bone tired."

"I was too, until I went back to work. I thought I'd putter. But there's nothing with which to putter. We never repair things, we just replace them."

"And Duke? Where are you in your schooling?" He turned and smiled up into Duke's face.

"Second year, Georgetown Law School, sir."

"Ah, yes, I remember law school. I think I attended during the Lincoln Administration."

"Last time you told me it was Teddy Roosevelt," Duke said.

"Oh, dear, the mind wanders."

"If I don't see you later today, I'll see you here at one tomorrow," Abigail said.

Poppy escorted Abby, Regina, and Duke into Pris's office.

Regina promptly declared that her feet hurt, kicked off her shoes, and sat in the most comfortable sofa in the room. Duke prowled around the room and read everything on the walls. Plaques, certificates, signed pictures with all sorts of luminaries.

Abby took in the décor first. Wood-paneled walls. Dark blue carpet, yellow and blue chairs, matching Chippendale sofas in front of a faux fireplace. The office had traditional furnishings. The styles would have been quite at home in the drawing room of John Hancock, who at the time of the Revolution was the richest man in Boston. It was obvious that these were mere copies; otherwise they'd be in a museum. Even the color scheme was period appropriate.

The most modern decorative items above the sofa were Audubon prints from the early 1800's: a roseate spoonbill and a brown pelican. Alas, they too were fakes.

The natural light from the windows was abundant, for which Abby was grateful. She glanced out her window, and was thrilled to see a view toward the west. The afternoon light would be bright.

She walked behind the desk and sat down. The chair fit her, as she thought it would. The desk was a massive thing, far too big, but she was stuck with it. It was a far cry from her locker and cubby at the hospital. The computer seemed up to date, with a large flat monitor and a pull-out keyboard. The phone looked simple. Phones made her think of germs, and she flashed back to the crowded office.

"Poppy, can you get disinfectant wipes, hand sanitizer, and a box of tissues for every desk?" Abby asked.

"Sure. Why?"

"Infection control. We have too many bodies in too small a space. I'll bet the last time the flu went around, you were half staffed for weeks."

"You're right, we were."

"Now we won't be." Abby smiled. "And tell people who have a fever of 100 or greater to stay home. Period."

There was a credenza behind the desk that held a number of reference books as well as a few family pictures. Duke in first grade, smiling hugely without his two front teeth. There was one of Regina at the beach in a hot pink muumuu and lime green sun hat. Abby's graduation picture from medical school gave a little tug at her heart.

Still, for some reason, Abby could not see her sister in this room. Perhaps because it had been nearly a year since Pris had been in here. Oh, she'd been wheeled into the Senate chamber for a few squeaker votes, but those stopped months ago. Pris had once been vital and active, a woman for this office. Over the last year, she was reduced to a shriveling body fighting to hold onto the dwindling molecules one called life.

"Let's go get me sworn in," she said to Poppy.

Abby took out her makeup bag and checked herself in the lighted magnifying mirror. She added a little lip color and gloss, a quick dust of blush. Then the four of them were off to the swearing-in.

"Would Mikey like to come?"

"It is really family only," Poppy said. "The only reason I am going is to show you where to go. Besides, Mikey would deliberately do something to annoy the Vice President. He despises her."

"Does anyone like her?" Abby asked.

"It's unclear whether her mother does or not. Her lifelong partner, Jane, seems to tolerate her at best."

"How did she get to be Vice President?"

"Fifty-five electoral votes," Poppy explained. "She might be a junkyard dog, but she's California's junkyard dog."

The President of the Senate's Office was grandiose and largely ceremonial. The Vice President hung out there if she had business on the Hill. Of course, there was the occasional swearing-in, like today.

There was a still photographer and what appeared to be a permanent video camera set up on a tripod. The videographer miked both the Vice President and Abby.

"You're late," Vice President Barker said to Abby. "I have to be out of here in ten minutes." Her breath was a combination of coffee, cigarettes, and last night's booze. *Dragon breath from a dragon lady.*

Abby looked at her watch and smiled pleasantly.

"Oh? Are we? I'm so sorry. By my watch, we are five minutes early, and my watch is set to the time on the office computer." Abby faked pleasant confusion.

Abby was not going to start her term taking crap from anyone.

"You bring your credentials?"

"Yes, ma'am." Abby presented the folder with the appointment by Governor Gray.

The Vice President perused it briefly and handed it to the Secretary of the Senate.

"Have you attained the age of thirty years?"

"Yes, ma'am." Abby took out her passport and offered it to the Vice President.

"Are you a citizen of the United States?"

"You can tell that by the passport."

"Would the person carrying the Bible approach."

"This is Regina Temple," Abby said. "She was my legal guardian when I was growing up."

"Yes, I know Regina. Makes cheese grits that I would kill for. Good morning."

"Good morning," Regina said stiffly. She'd be damned before she'd make that witch any cheese grits. Not unless she had some arsenic to put in them. Vice President Barker never came to see Pris even once when she was sick.

Not that Barker's job was anything special. It wasn't worth a bucket of warm piss, according to John Nance Garner. Of course, the press had cleaned it up to a "bucket of warm spit." Either way, Vice President Barker had the manners of a Rottweiler, with apologies to Rottweilers everywhere.

Duke and Poppy remained on the side of the room. The Secretary of the Senate was there with a leather-bound book in which she entered Abigail's name, date of appointment, and state.

The Vice President asked Abby to raise her right hand and put her left hand on Regina's Bible. The videographer turned on his light, and the Vice President paused for a moment or two. Abby could hear the clicking of the shutter on the still camera. She remembered her posture, her diction, and her pleasantly neutral face.

"Okay, ma'am, any time," the video man said.

"Please repeat after me. I do solemnly swear…"

"I do solemnly swear…"

And in a few moments, Abigail Adams, MD had become Senator Abigail Adams.

"Congratulations, Senator Adams. Welcome to the Senate." Barker shook her hand long enough for the video and still guys to get the shots they needed.

Then she dropped Abby's hand and reverted to her sourpuss expression.

"Sign the register, and Poppy will take you to Barbara Lansky. She'll get you logged into the computer, put you on the payroll, and so forth."

"Thank you, ma'am."

"Oh, and Poppy, don't forget to show her where the bathrooms are. For nearly two hundred years, it was all males in the building. We women have fought some serious battles for potty parity, I can tell you that."

Then the woman was gone. She had the gait of a person always in a huff about something. Maybe if she didn't smoke so much, she wouldn't huff and puff all the time.

CHAPTER EIGHTEEN

FIRST DAY OF SCHOOL

Abby said good-bye to Regina and Duke after the swearing-in.

"I'm going home to watch my stories," Regina said.

"I love you," Abby said, hugging Regina tightly. *She'd be asleep in a muumuu before the opening music and wake up in time for Naomi, the woman who took over for Oprah.*

"I love you too, Senator Sweet Pea."

"Duke, thank you too for coming."

"Wouldn't have missed it. I'm the only brother with two white Aunties who have been U.S. Senators." He beamed down at her. The man had charm.

Abigail followed Poppy through the bowels of the Capitol to the Senate administrative offices. The Secretary of the Senate was the official administrator of the Senate, but Barbara Lansky, her clerk, did much of the work in a generic-looking basement office.

Barbara peered at her over green sequined half-glasses.

"Credentials, please?" She had a thick New Jersey accent. The sign on her desk read, "Failure to plan on your part does not constitute an emergency on my part."

The woman examined the papers.

"Photo ID, please?"

Abby handed her the passport.

The woman turned to a computer and punched in some information. When she had finished, she returned Abby's documents. Barbara heaved herself up and walked to an area for pictures. She chose one of several colored screens and pulled it down.

"Please step to the line on the floor for your photo."

Abby stood, smiled slightly, and in a click, it was over.

"Now, I need to fingerprint you."

"My prints are on file for my DEA license, as well as my medical license."

"Rules are rules," she said.

Abby submitted again. At least the ink came off with special wipes.

"While you wait for your ID, please fill this out for payroll and such." Barbara pointed Abby toward a chair.

Abby filled out everything. By the time she returned it, her official ID was still warm but ready, complete with a bar code at the bottom, a decent picture, and her right thumbprint.

"Wear this at all times in the building. Inside your clothing is fine. The bottom of the card is a key card. It will open the doors you may enter. If you attempt to enter a restricted area, security will be alerted."

"Got it."

"If you loan this ID to anyone for any reason, it is a federal crime, do you understand? If you lose it, report it immediately to the number on the back of the card. Put that number in your phone."

Then Barbara smiled and offered her hand.

"Welcome, Senator Adams. I really miss your sister, and I am quite sure you are cut from the same cloth."

"Why, thank you. Do I need to do anything on her behalf for the Senate?"

"No, but thank you. I took care of it myself. I'm Barbara Lansky," she said with an even thicker Jersey accent. She pointed at herself with a thumb. "Between you and me, I run this joint. You need anything? You call me."

They both laughed and Abby thanked her. Then she and Poppy left.

"Before Nine-Eleven, it was all very casual. No longer. People wear their IDs. They need to be able to identify the bodies."

"How reassuring. I'm surprised we're not micro chipped, like dogs."

"Don't say that or someone will run with it," Poppy said, smiling for the first time that day.

On the trek to the Senate Dining Room, Poppy briefed her on lunch.

"I'll fetch you at one thirty. Lawmakers, their guests, and staff can eat at the Senate Dining Room, but many prefer to *schlep* across to the House Cafeteria."

"Why?" Abby asked.

"Well, House food is better, cheaper, and you get some exercise," Poppy said. "Whatever you do, don't eat the bean soup. It's famous, all right. You'll have gas for days."

Abby laughed.

"I'm serious," Poppy said. "I won't work for Senator Gasbag."

Poppy delivered Abby to the Private Dining Room, across from the main Senate Dining Room.

"If you'll give me your electronics, I'll have them brought online."

Abby produced them.

"The Senate Majority Leader is your host," Poppy said. "I'll pick you up at one thirty." Abby was totally lost and was grateful Poppy would reappear to lead her to her office. There were so many corridors, not to mention the Capitol subway system, she'd probably figure out the lay of the land just in time to leave the Senate.

Abby was glad she'd studied the materials Poppy sent. As Abby entered the room, she put on a smile. *Showtime. Pretend you are your sister.*

The room had red carpeting and crystal chandeliers. Everyone was standing, glasses in hand, when she entered the room. Obviously, no one minded having a drink at lunch.

"Senator Adams. Welcome," the Majority Leader said.

"Why, thank you, Senator Schwartz," Abby said, shaking his hand. He deliberately kept his drink in his left hand to keep the right one warm. *Good tip.*

"At the risk of saying something sexist, you look lovely." He smiled kindly. Abby snagged a glass of iced tea from a passing waiter. With her left hand.

"Thank you, Senator. I feel a bit better than the last time we met." Abby referred to the funeral.

"That boy of yours, what's his name? Dick?"

"Duke," Abby ignored the use of "boy" about a grown black man.

"Gave an amazing eulogy. He's going places."

"He is an amazing young man. Phi Beta Kappa at Harvard. Second year at Georgetown. Law Review."

"I don't think I could get into law school these days," Senator Schwartz said. "I majored in beer."

Abby laughed. "I thought that was the only degree plan at the University of Texas."

"Let me introduce you. And please, call me Chuck. This is a bipartisan event. Much of the politicking you'll see on the news is just for show. We try to get along as often as possible."

She was introduced to men she'd only seen on television. The two most senior female senators were there as well. The first one reminded her of an antique teapot: short, stout, but still quite lovely in her own pastel way.

"Hello, Abby, I'm Peggy," Margaret Alden Mellon said. "Your sister and I were big movie buffs. Sometimes we'd sneak away to a matinee."

"Oh, yes, I remember you," Abby said. "Don't you have a dog named Friend?"

"Yes. There's an old saying. If you want a friend in Washington, get a dog. So I named mine Friend."

If memory served, she also had a huge stud farm in Kentucky where the Queen visited from time to time. She was one of "those" Mellons, a family present at the creation of the country and many of its industries.

Abby tried not to be impressed, but she was. This woman had no reason to engage in public service. It was money out of her exceedingly deep pockets. But she was the Senate's guru on women's issues. She and Pris had been a formidable duo.

"Yes, we figured out a long time ago that when Pris and Peggy wanted something, it was easier to just give it to them than to try to talk them out of it." Chuck Schwartz laughed. "'Yes, dear' works as well in the Senate as it does in marriages."

"And he should know," Peggy said, patting his arm. "He's been married to the same woman for forty years."

"I'd love it if we could have dinner one evening. Just the two of us?" Peggy said.

"I'd like that."

"Shall we say Sunday? My house? Six thirty?"

"I'd be delighted. I assume Poppy has your address?"

"She does. See you then." Peggy said, turning with a little wave.

"I wondered how long it would take you two to become co-conspirators," Chuck said, rolling his eyes theatrically.

Chuck steered her toward the other woman in the group, Cordelia Laurus. She was the exact opposite of Peggy Mellon. Tall, thin, and ageless, this light-skinned Afro-Asian woman was known for her love of publicity. She wore her snowy hair in a thick braid wound around her head. Pris had called it her "crown." She had come from "the projects" and had risen to be a Senator from Louisiana. Her love of publicity was famous.

"The most dangerous place in the universe is between her and a camera," Pris once quipped.

"Hello, there. I'm Senator Cordelia Laurus. Welcome." Her voice was deeply resonant, and her strong Louisiana patois came through. Her affect was condescending in the extreme. Abby suspected she and Pris had not seen eye to eye on many things.

"So very nice to meet you, Cordelia." Abby offered her hand. The woman stiffened and took it. *Apparently, she thought her first name was "Senator."*

"I do hope you will be a friend to New Orleans," she said, breaking the taboo about not talking business until after lunch. "We still have a long, long way to go."

"New Orleans is one of our unique cities. And everyone in Houston was happy to help after Katrina." Abby sidestepped the pitch. Even before Katrina, Abby wished New Orleans had a more intimate relationship with bleach. The last time she'd visited, the French Quarter smelled of equal parts drunken throw up and mildew.

"Yes, well, that was nice, but there is so much more that we need."

Abby kept her anger in check. Houston took in a quarter million refugees with one day's notice. Abby was one of the doctors working nearly full time at the Astrodome in addition to her regular job. That couple of weeks were the longest of her life. Not only did she see almost every conceivable illness, she gave enough tetanus shots to give herself tennis elbow. *I'll bet I did more work to help Katrina victims that you did, sister.*

Abby sat on the Majority Leader's right. "You must try the bean soup," the Majority Leader said. "It's quite famous."

"Oh, I've had it. I was here with my sister once." Abby found lying pricked her conscience very little. Abby ordered the tomato aspic and a chicken breast and was saving room for chocolate pie.

The aspic was dull and dense and the chicken dried out. The chocolate pie was a puddle of cheap pudding in a shell that required a steak knife. Abby would be bringing yogurt to the office.

Abby chatted with the Majority Leader during the first course and with the Minority Leader, Ted Clarke of Rhode Island, during the second course.

"Tell me, Ted, how does a Senator from the smallest state rise to such a lofty position?" Abby asked.

"Everyone else had enemies except me. Now, no one dares confront me. They're afraid I'll have another heart attack." He tapped the left side of his chest and chuckled.

"Do you know Mike Molloy?" Abby asked.

"Of course. Once he learned that you were to be appointed, he came out of retirement."

"And when was that?"

"Your sister told him well before she stopped coming to the office." Abby sipped her tea to conceal her surprise. *Just like Pris to change my life without even warning me.*

Over dessert, the Majority Leader told her he'd like to see her in her office about three.

"My time is your time," Abby said with a smile. "I'm honored."

"No honor involved. I've got to walk off the damn bean soup."

CHAPTER NINETEEN

REALITY BITES

By three, she had found the bathroom, not said the f-word once, had her electronics bugged, and eaten dreadful food. She'd found no reason anyone would want her job. Abby was trying to figure out how her sister organized her desk, when Poppy knocked and brought in the Senate Majority Leader.

"Thanks again for lunch. May I get you something to drink? Iced tea? Coffee?" Abby inquired, leading him towards a sofa and chair for their chat.

"Do you have bourbon and branch?" Schwartz inquired.

"The bar's not stocked, I'm afraid." Abby was not going to serve alcohol in her office.

"Diet cola. No glass." He popped the can and took a big swig. He tried to muffle the large belch, for which Abby gave him scant points. "I need to talk to you about two things. One is money."

"I hope the other isn't religion or sex," Abby said cheerfully.

"Money first. Your sister died with a significant war chest."

"I don't know anything about that," Abby had learned to keep a straight face in medicine, so she used the trick of cupping her hand in front of her mouth, thumb under her chin.

"That money would help other candidates' races."

"I see," Abby said.

"I'm pretty sure she would have insisted on using that money in other, tight races." *The guy buys me a crap lunch and thinks he owns me.*

"Funny, I'm her executrix. I know nothing about this." Abby played dumb to keep from strangling the man.

"I do hope you'll do the right thing with it. We have some critical seats this year that might put us out of power."

"I will definitely look into it." Abby rose and made herself a note on her desk. "I'll start on it on Monday morning."

"Thanks. Oh, and there is a floor vote on Monday. We're for it."

"What is it?" Abby asked pleasantly.

"It's a bill banning stem cell research from cord blood."

"I'm afraid I don't understand," Abby said. "Cord blood is either banked for the baby's later needs or thrown away."

"Well, we feel that the stem cells will be used for cloning."

"Chuck, have you ever known someone who died waiting for a transplant?"

"No, but…" he crunched his empty can, setting Abby's nerves on edge.

"Well, I have. You forget, sir, that I am a doctor. The first time you attend the funeral of a little girl who died waiting for a transplant, I think you'll be for using cord blood to make her a new liver, or kidney, or bone marrow."

"But it's a 'sanctity of life' issue."

"Amanda Louise Morgan's life was very, very precious to me. She was a brown-eyed blonde toddler. She would sit up in the bed and ask for her purse and sunglasses. She could barely say 'purse.' And the things she put on her eyes were her 'sun gasses.' She was three when she died. Not only did she die wearing her beloved 'gasses,' but the purse and glasses went with her into her grave. Would you deny Amanda a shot at life from cells in throwaway blood?" Abby tried to sound thoughtful. *I am irate.*

"Well, I guess…"

"I'll make you a deal, Senator."

She had his attention.

"You bring Amanda Louise Morgan back to life, I'll vote for your bill," Abby said.

"Now, Abigail. We need your vote. It's a squeaker."

"I will read the bill. Unless there is something unexpected in it, my vote is no."

The Majority Leader snorted. "The bill is six hundred pages."

"Have you read it?" Abby asked.

"Well, not word-for-word, no. But my staff people have vetted it."

"Who is the sponsor?"

Abby wrote down the names of the Senator and Representative behind it.

"Texans are very pro-life," Schwartz said.

"And cord blood is as pro-life as it gets." Abby stood up and extended her hand. "I think we are through here, Senator. Please come back any time. My door is always open."

He walked through the door slightly bewildered.

Abby wanted to slam the door. Instead she turned to Poppy, who was sitting at her desk, watching as Abby gave the bum's rush to the Majority Leader.

"I want a copy of the Ford-Wilson bill, please. Please print it out for me. Then I want five law school grad staffers in here with the printed bill."

"Okay, why?"

"We are going to read the bill."

"The party wants this bill," Poppy said.

"I want to read it. Do I or do I not have that right, Poppy?"

"Yes, ma'am, you do." Poppy sounded irritated.

"Those first two words make me very happy."

"May I ask why you want only law school staffers?"

"Someone has to know how to read the damn thing. I certainly don't."

This was not at all how she planned on spending her weekend.

Her next visitors were two FBI agents. She stood to greet them. Both were tall, angular, and had crew cuts.

"I'm Abigail Adams," she said, offering each her hand to shake. Each did his best to break it.

Abigail hoped her hand would stop hurting in the current decade. She grabbed a glass of ice water to soothe it.

Their names were irrelevant, as everyone entering her office was logged in and out electronically. Ditto for phone calls. Abby gestured for them to sit.

Crew Cut One and Crew Cut Two congratulated her on passing her background check.

"Tell me what I need to know."

"You have an Interim Top Secret Clearance so you may attend closed sessions of the committees on which you sit. 'Interim' means it expires when you leave the Senate. Please sign this form."

It said basically she could spend her life in federal prison if she divulged Top Secret information. Abby read and signed the form. They handed her the combination to her Top Secret closet. Then she stood, handed them the forms, and wiggled her fingers "bye-bye." Another handshake would likely cripple her.

Next in was Bob, the IT guy for the Senators. He was bearing her electronics, so she was glad to see him.

"You're good to go with these," he said. "Just sign this form that says you know we've added keystroke software."

"What's that?" Abby asked, turning her electronics over to make sure they were okay. *As if I could tell.*

"That means you have no expectation of privacy on these items. We can always know what you are doing, electronically. So if you want to visit weird sites, do it on your home computer."

"Not a problem,"

"It also says you may not put Top Secret materials on any of your other personal electronics."

Abby signed that as well.

"Report lost or missing electronics immediately. One guy couldn't find his laptop for a couple of hours, and then it reappeared. Someone had hacked into a CIA site."

Bob walked her through the creation of her various e-mails, and showed her the "members only" section of the Senate website. Ditto for other governmental websites she could enter.

"For your private e-mail, we use your door number. If you forget it, just look out the door."

He was in and out in ten minutes. Her hand was still hurting from Crew Cut One and Two.

"Poppy, please get me Marston Mills on the phone. Ditto for whoever was treasurer of Pris's campaign. I also want a printout of every donation to her last Senate race."

"Okay. May I ask why?"

"I need to look into a few things." Abby hung up the phone. *No, you may not ask why.*

So much for a peaceful first day. Abby was waist deep in alligators and had to have the swamp drained by Monday.

She stuck her head into Mike Molloy's office. His head was gently bobbing as he tried to stay awake. The squeak of the door roused him.

"Yes, fair lady. How may I help you?"

She ran her ideas past him and saw his eyes light up.

"Oh, that will be delicious. Naughty but delicious."

"Do you think I am being unrealistic?"

"Not at all. First, it was damned cheeky, and possibly illegal, for the Majority Leader to presume to make a grab for the money. Second, he hit a nerve with trying to tell you how to vote. You stand your ground now, and you won't regret it. Your oath did not include doing as the party elders wish."

"Thanks, Mikey. See you tomorrow at one?"

"Yes. I'm going to head home now, if you don't mind."

"Not at all." Abby had an urge to kiss him on the top of his forehead, but restrained herself. "Thank you."

Abby and her five law school grads met in her office about four o'clock.

"We have work that might impinge on your weekend plans," Abby said. "Groaning is allowed."

They groaned.

"Excellent groan. Does anyone have a wedding, birth, or funeral to attend this evening?"

No one did.

"Then text your date and bail. Here is the Ford-Wilson bill banning the use of cord blood for stem cell research. I understand the party is for it. I propose that we read it."

Abby dealt out sections to all the readers.

"With all due respect, Senator, if we read every piece of legislation that is up for a vote, nothing would get voted on," said a young man in a bow tie and horn-rims.

"And, Mr. Bow Tie, what is your name and what law school did you attend?"

"Fred Pierce, Yale."

"Mr. Pierce, has it ever occurred to you that *not* reading a bill is a dereliction of duty?"

"You have a point."

"I am not a lawyer, but I can read, so let's get started." They all sat around the conference table and read page after page of boring legalese.

"Jeez," said one young girl.

"Yes?"

"Felicity Wyeth. Stanford. Here's an earmark for an ice-making plant in Alaska. Eighty million dollars. To help keep salmon-spawning water cool."

"Very interesting. Please mark it and print me a hard copy."

The pizzas and sodas came about five when the largest part of the Friday afternoon exodus was over. *The Senate kept bankers' hours.*

The young people fell onto the food with big appetites.

One of the readers excused himself and came back with his laptop.

"Senator? Frank Koenig, NYU. The meat of the bill matches, just a sec, roughly ten thousand words from the Voices for Life platform."

"So what you are telling me is the Voices for Life drafted the bill?"

"Basically."

"So Ford and Wilson didn't even draft it?"

"Not the meat of it, no."

"Thanks, guys. I think we've found what I needed. Frank, would you highlight both the bill and the Voices for Life information and print them out for me? You can all go back to your weekends. Thanks a lot."

As she was packing up to leave, Marston Mills was put through.

"She made no provision for the campaign funds. None at all."

"Thanks. That's all I needed to know."

The only puzzle piece left was Harrison Hatcher, Pris's campaign treasurer, whose call came in just as Abby was starting to leave. After the briefest of pleasantries, Abby said, "I need an accounting, please, of all the monies in my late sister's campaign fund. As well, I need the donor list and amounts."

"That was nearly six years ago," Hatcher snorted.

"I'm sure your records go back that far," Abby said pleasantly.

"It'll take me quite a while to find them, and I'm quite busy." *And I am not?*

"You and I both know it's a very few minutes on the computer. You have a fiduciary responsibility. It is time to account to me for those dollars. Here's my e-mail. I'll expect the information no later than close of business on Monday."

Abby rattled off her e-mail, confirmed that he got it, and hung up on him.

Why wasn't there something between doormat and bitch?
Abby called Poppy in.

"Pops, please have a seat. I need some leadership here."

Poppy looked a little more interested.

"The Ford-Wilson bill was copied verbatim from Voices for Life literature. Some ten thousand words. I am not going to vote for the bill, but I wonder what I can do with that information?"

"You could put out a press release saying why you are not voting for the bill."

"What would happen?"

"The shit would hit the fan and splatter all over you. Also, Ford and Wilson would look like morons and be on your case until you left office. And the Majority Leader would have a stroke."

"Okay, now something else. Did Pris ever tell you what she wanted done with any leftover campaign funds?"

"Not in so many words, no."

"Did she intimate she wanted them to go to the party for tight races?"

"No, she was planning on running again, until of course she found out that she was terminal."

"Was she a fan of the Majority Leader?"

Poppy laughed out loud.

"She loathed him. He always tried to tell her what to do."

"Ah, well, I must say I can see her point."

"Abby, you have to be careful. If you don't want Ford-Wilson to pass, just vote no. Don't play games. This town runs on 'face.' If you embarrass your 'esteemed colleagues,' even if they are morons, you will regret it."

"But I'll be out of office when the new Senators are sworn in."

"A lot can happen between now and then. You want to make as few enemies as possible. Trust me on this. You know maybe one percent of what you need to know to be a Senator."

"That's humbling. But I have you and Mikey."

"Mikey's great on principles and history. I do the nuts and bolts. I need you not to wander off into uncharted territory. There be dragons there."

CHAPTER TWENTY

MIKEY

Abby smelled chicken cooking when she opened the door. *Yum.*

"How was your first day?"

"Long." Abby dropped a kiss on Regina's cheek and headed down the hall to "unzip." She reappeared a few minutes later. Her face was bare of makeup, her hair down, and her contacts out. She was wearing yoga pants, a loose top, and slippers.

"It'll get easier. I'm making us chicken and dumplings. That okay with you?"

"Is the Pope Catholic?" Abby said as she went to set the table. That, and doing dishes, had been her chores as long as she could remember.

Regina ladled the fragrant concoction into bowls. She'd made a pear, arugula, and walnut salad on a separate plate.

"Politics isn't my thing. I assess a situation, fix it, and move on."

"I know what you mean. Kind of like me and microwave bacon. If I want food, I want real food."

Abby smiled at Regina's lopsided logic.

"Abby, speaking of 'moving on,' when do you want to tackle Pris's stuff?" Regina asked.

"Not now."

"Okay, baby, but when you're ready, you call me and I'll come help."

"I appreciate that." The dumplings were the best part of her day.

"And how do you feel about living here alone?"

"I don't feel alone. The office is like a beehive. I'll enjoy the solitude."

"Good. I've got reservations to go home in the morning. I've ordered a car to take me to the airport. I want you to sleep in."

"Reege, I don't mind taking you. Pris's car needs driving."

"I said you are going to sleep in." Regina cocked an eyebrow.

"Yes, ma'am. I seem to still crave sleep. I'm meeting Mike Molloy at the office tomorrow at one. He's going to tutor me. Apparently he knew Pris was going to arrange my appointment. Did you?"

"We talked around it, but nothing was carved in stone," Regina said, pouring herself a cup of coffee. She knew better than to offer any to Abby, who cut off caffeine at noon.

"Why did she want this for me?" Abby made patterns in the tablecloth with her fork tines.

"I'm sure she thought you'd be good for the Senate and vice versa." Regina reached over and patted Abby's hand.

"Oh, please," Abigail protested.

"You listen to me. You took the oath, so this is your row to hoe. So do it right and don't whine." Regina had spoken. The conversation was over.

Abby was glad Laura outfitted her for everything, even a weekend foray into the office. And, to appease Andre, she had on makeup and had restrained her hair. The weather was still chilly, but she could at least go without a top coat. Her brown cashmere blazer was adequate.

Abby drove Pris's white Lexus sedan to the Russell Office Building and figured out the weekend parking with time to spare. She was in the office by twelve thirty. She started by dumping out Pris's junk drawer upside down on the top of the desk and quickly sorting through it. Most things went in the trash. Abby could not work in a messy office.

Mikey Molloy came in just before one. His face lit up at the sight of Abby.

"My dear, you make an old man's heart leap for joy," he said expansively.

"Mikey, you have the gift of gab."

"At my age, that's the only gift I have. That and my memory, thank God." He sat in the chair in front of her desk.

"Thanks for giving me your weekend afternoons."

"It's not yet baseball season. So it's no skin off my nose."

"Who's your team?"

"The Red Sox and whoever is playing against the Yankees. There is nothing like a game at Fenway Park. They've been sold out for something over seven hundred games at home. It's a cross between an appearance by the Pope and the Fourth of July for every game."

"So you're from Boston?"

"Born and bred in Brookline, just down the street from the Kennedys. Of course by the time I came along, Jack was off to college, even baby Teddy was older than me by a few years."

"What did you do in Kennedy's administration?"

"I was an advance man. Went ahead to places to make arrangements. Perfect job for a very young man, and I was."

"What was he like?"

"Restless, charming when he wanted to be, cussed like the sailor he'd been. More charismatic than smart, if that makes any sense. But he had good people around him. Terrible womanizer. She deserved better."

"Where were you when he was killed?"

"I was sick in bed when he left for Texas, so I was here in Washington. The day he went to Dallas, I came in to do a couple of hours work. Next thing I know, the televisions were on. The teletype machines were going wild with rumors of a Russian coup, a Castro hit. And all the phone lines collapsed under the volume of calls all over Washington. It was horrible. Finally, even people in the White House heard the news from Walter Cronkite, just like everyone else. The country simply stopped for four days. A dead stop."

"Gives me chills just thinking about it."

"He was just the first. Then there was Martin Luther King, then Bobby Kennedy. People thought the country was coming undone, but of course, it didn't."

"What do you mean?" Abby asked.

"Government perpetuates itself. So Senators do the things that keep them getting elected. The Senate's a real gravy train. If you resigned tomorrow, you'd get your Senate pension for life."

"That's outrageous."

"No, that's Congress."

"Constituents want two things. They want you to solve their problems with the government, like a late Social Security check. And they want jobs in their state. That's where the pork comes in. When the Senator brings home the bacon…brings jobs to an area…he or she gets re-elected. And the more senior the person, the more pork he can bring home."

"And why is that?"

"Because committee appointments are based on seniority."

"Ah, I see. And my sister was a very senior Senator. I think of myself as an independent."

"Whoa, there Abby. You ARE your sister until the end of her term, and that includes her party affiliation.

"But what if I don't like it?"

"Tough noogies. You'd lose all your seniority, all your committee appointments. You'd even lose this office. You'd be a zero, a placeholder."

"Thanks for the lesson. I am dedicated to the party, just like my sister was."

"Much, much better."

"Yes, very senior. After Nine-Eleven, the senior leadership got concerned. The President Pro Tem was the longest serving Senator in the majority party. Everyone realized we couldn't have a nursing home patient with a palsied fist running the country. And that's what the two most senior senators were.

"But when both of them died, that left a younger tier of senators on the Rules Committee. They voted to change the rules on the Pro Tem. The Rules Committee decided that if there was some sort of terror attack, and the President, Vice President, and Speaker of the House all died, the last thing we needed was an Alzheimer's patient with orange hair running the country. So now, the President Pro Tem of the Senate rotates through the six most senior senators, under eighty, in the majority party."

"That's pretty sensible."

"Oh, I've brought you a book to read. P.J. O'Rourke's *Parliament of Whores.*"

"Catchy title," Abby said, accepting the old paperback.

"It's laugh out loud funny, but spot on about the citizens and their government."

"And that is?"

"Everyone is a hog at the trough of the federal government. Whether it is a farmer being paid not to plant crops, or a homeowner counting on that interest deduction, we are all welfare queens."

"Sobering."

"Abigail, self-interest trumps all. Any time you frame an argument so it is in the opponent's self-interest, nine times out of ten, he'll buy it. You just gotta figure out what it is he wants."

"Well, I can see I've got my weekend reading cut out for me. Can I give you a ride home?"

"Why, thank you. It will save my man a trip. Just let me call him."

Abby crammed the books into her tote while Mike called home.

"Harold is making us tea. I do hope you can come in for a few minutes."

"Sure thing," Abby said, as they headed for her car. Mike gave her directions into the heart of Georgetown. He and his late wife restored the home on N Street when they moved into it in the late fifties.

"Kathleen and I were married over fifty years. She's been gone ten. I tell people we married young so we could go to bed together. Best decision I ever made." He had a real twinkle in his eye. "Her father gave us the house as a wedding gift. I protested, but he said this way, I could work at what I loved, politics, and he would know his daughter always had a roof over her head. We re-did the house, and since children didn't come along, she collected pictures with her money. I ended up living across the street from my boss for a while, until Jack went into the White House. Of course, now everyone wants a mansion, but I don't need more than this."

Abby pulled up in front of the skinny house of deep red brick. It had steep steps up to the front door. A fanlight topped the door, and given the waviness of the glass, it was probably original to the late 1790s. Mikey climbed the stairs without effort and Harold opened the door.

"Abigail, this is Harold, who does for me. Harold, this is Senator Adams."

Harold nodded his head, and then stepped aside.

"Welcome, Senator. Won't you please come in?" he said in a plummy accent. "I've taken the liberty of serving tea in the sunroom, sir."

Abby followed Mikey down a flight of stairs into a room with a brick on three sides, and a fourth wall of French doors that opened onto a formal garden. As nothing was in bloom yet, there were masses of hothouse red cyclamen in urns. The back wall was covered in ivy, now just a mass of grey webs on the wintry day.

"I'll bet this is great in spring," Abby said.

"Thank you. Please take any seat you please."

Abby chose a chintz armchair, while Mike took a seat on a green sofa. It was obvious he'd done nothing after his wife's death. Harold offered Abby her choice of teas.

"I'll have whatever Mikey's having," she said.

"Then you'll have Scotch, Senator. I don't recommend it with scones," Harold intoned.

"I adore scones, so I'll have Darjeeling, please, Harold." Abby had to laugh.

The sterling tea set was shined to perfection. Harold offered her a napkin monogrammed with Mrs. Molloy's maiden initials. Even the tiered tray of scones was silver.

"Delicious scones, Harold."

"Thank you, ma'am. It's Her Majesty's recipe, though I did add the dried cranberries."

"Harold used to work at Windsor. But when his only niece moved to Washington, he came to work for me."

"The weather is better here," Harold said, then he retreated to the corner and pretended to silently buff something.

"This, of course, is just a casual room, but the light is lovely. See the three pictures on the wall behind the sofa?" Mikey asked.

"Yes, I do," Abby answered. There were three companion pieces; two were signed Picassos.

"Do you know who did the middle one?"

"No. I know who did the other two," Abby said. The one in the middle was smudges of the Picasso blue.

"But you are quite sure you do not recognize the piece in the middle?" Mikey took an interrogatory tone.

"No, I don't," Abby said. "Did you do it?"

"No, but you are very close. A chimpanzee did it. I couldn't resist it. You have no idea how many people have gone on and on about our three Picassos."

"You are truly a naughty man," Abby said with a laugh.

The living room and a small kitchen were on the first floor, the bedrooms on the second floor. Art was everywhere. There was an Ingres pencil drawing of his wife on their wedding day, a Corot landscape, a tiny Canaletto in the bedroom, and a sweet Renoir little girl on the stairway.

"No wonder you don't want to move. The house is perfect, Mikey. I feel I would have loved your wife. I love the art she has chosen."

"They were just 'her pictures.' Then after she died, I took an art appreciation course and realized there was a whole side of her I never knew."

His eyes misted up and Abby knew it was time to leave.

"Mikey, thanks for the book. I'll return it. Do you want the day off tomorrow?"

"No. I've taken your tutelage very seriously. You will start with the amusing books, but you will get through some real sloggers. How fast do you read?"

"I'm not telling. You'll weigh me down. Shall I come and fetch you tomorrow?" She felt so British around Harold.

"No, I can get to the office just fine."

"On second thought, why don't you come to my place?"

"Harold, you heard her. She invited me to her place. And me a recent widower."

"Yes, sir. I heard her. Do you think I should accompany you as a chaperone?"

"No, I think I can do this on my own," Mikey said with some gravity.

"Franklin Towers," Abby said. "Top floor. It was my sister's, and I'm crashing there until I finish in the Senate."

"My dear, no one 'crashes' at the penthouse of the Franklin Towers."

CHAPTER TWENTY-ONE

CO-CONSPIRATOR

By Sunday evening, Abby's head was swimming.

She'd had two sessions with Mikey, digested the best of P.J. O'Rourke and his hilariously jaundiced view of politics.

It took her fifteen minutes to program the television to record *The Sunday Hour*, so she had to hustle to be on time to Peggy's. Thank heaven, again, for Laura Rowe, who had outfitted her with everything. She could not see herself showing up at Mellon's home, or at Mikey's, in jeans and a baggy sweater.

She tried to tell herself that she simply was having dinner with a friend of Pris's. But that was an understatement in the extreme. The florist in the building was closed, so Abby called the concierge about a bouquet to take.

"Not a problem, Senator," Rafael said.

Abby grabbed it on the way out.

"Just between us, Senator," Rafael said. He looked to the oversized bouquet on his desk and shrugged. He'd snipped out a few flowers and tied them with a bit of shopping bag handle. He handed them to her.

"It will be our secret." Abby tipped him well and wondered if he was legal. If he wasn't, he should be. He had a talent for flowers.

Peggy Mellon's home was legendary in Washington circles. It was almost as big as the White House, and probably better furnished. According to Pris, Peggy Mellon might as well have been her own small nation. She had a permanent staff of forty based out of an office building a block away. She had a chief of staff, Rudolfo, who had a corner office with a view.

According to Pris, Rudolfo was "lapsed royalty." Born to royals that lost everything in some war, he was steeped in the ways of manners. He had resigned an enormous salary as chief of staff for the sultan of somewhere because of the "lax morals" in the household.

He saw that Mrs. Mellon's three homes, horse breeding farm, oceangoing yacht, seventy-foot teak sailboat, airplane, fleet of cars, and nine thousand Christmas cards ran with the precision of a Swiss watch.

Housekeepers, gardeners, security, technology people, and horse trainers all reported to him. As well, he hired all the outside people Mrs. Mellon required, whether it was a vet for a horse or a caterer for a party aboard her yacht off the Cote d'Azur. As a result, Peggy only had to talk to one person. Rudolfo kept everyone else on speed dial.

So Abby was nervous as she approached the gates of the Mellon estate. She pushed the button on the call box, and Peggy answered.

"Great! Just pull up to the front."

"The front" was several hundred yards away and around a bend. Large oaks laced airily across the gravel drive in an *allee*. Peggy must spend a small fortune on arborists to keep those trees so lovely. Off to one side were masses of azaleas and spirea, and in front of them the crocuses were coming up. Spring was not far away.

Peggy was outside waiting for her, her red brick house behind her. Lights in the windows were welcoming.

"Abby, you look so lovely. Do come in."

In flats, Peggy was even shorter and rounder than she was in her office clothes. Her black turtleneck did a good job of covering her wattle-y chin, but nothing could cover the fine web of lines in her face. Years of smiling summers on horseback or heeled over in a racing yacht had done their damage. If it bothered Peggy, she gave no notice. Her face radiated happiness.

"Here's a little nosegay for you," Abby said, noticing that it had perfumed her car.

"Ah, stock, such a lovely fragrance. How thoughtful." Peggy ushered her inside. *So stock is the fragrant white flower.*

"I thought we'd eat in front of the television. There's a segment on *The Sunday Hour* I want to see. Do you think me terribly rude?"

"Not at all. I set the TV to record it."

"Ooh. I'm impressed," Peggy said.

"I set it. That doesn't mean it will work. And even that took me fifteen minutes." Abby laughed.

"I forgot to ask. Do you have any allergies?"

"No."

"Good. People are too picky these days. Used to be, you served people food, and they either ate it or waltzed it around their plates. Now, they give you a dissertation on their preferences."

"I'll remember that next time I entertain." The thought of having people over gave Abby pause. She couldn't remember the last party she threw. *Was it really three years ago? Did she really serve pizza and beer?*

The television room was cozy and comfortable, rather small, but full of books. A chocolate Lab snoozed in his mistress's chair. Abby loved the room; you could put your feet up. Nothing looked priceless or pretentious. She could relax around Peggy. She understood the bond between Peggy and her sister.

Peggy put the flowers in a water glass and sat them on the coffee table on top of the stack of Sunday papers.

"Perfect," she pronounced. The little bouquet did liven up the room.

"Friend, get your lazy bones out of my chair," Peggy said in mock seriousness to the Lab.

Friend complied, jumping into Abby's chair. The two women laughed.

"What's that saying? You're never fully dressed without a little dog hair?" Abby said.

Peggy gently shooed Friend out of the chair.

"I'll slip you a little something." Abby enjoyed petting behind his silky ears. He looked adoringly at her.

"He seems quite taken with you."

"He's a Lab. Love them a little, they'll follow you anywhere."

In a few minutes, two people in uniform appeared with their dinners on trays.

'Thank you, Imelda. Thank you, Felipe."

Abby echoed her thanks.

The trays were simple, and set with a single charger of Italian pottery ringed with an exuberant wreath of hand-painted fruits and a cobalt border.

"Self-garnishing," Peggy said of the plates. Abby chuckled.

Their dinner was simple, a filet of sole topped with halved green grapes, and skinny French green beans, oven-roasted new potatoes with rosemary and sea salt. A fresh salad with blueberries, bleu cheese, and walnuts finished the dish.

"Would you like wine?" Peggy asked.

"Only if you would," Abby replied.

"I'd just as soon save the calories for dessert."

"I couldn't agree more," Abby concurred.

They ate and chatted, muting the first piece on an aging rocker. Abby was able to eat with her right hand and keep Friend occupied with the other. *This is fun multi-tasking.*

They watched the next piece with interest. Ford-Wilson would ban the use of cord blood for stem cell research. Senator Ford and Congressman Wilson came across as two men who needed to go on a diet, as well as born-again Christians just "doing the Lord's work."

Steve Johann gave them enough rope to hang themselves. By giving their side extra air time, he let them reveal the inanity of their positions. All their backers would be happy, but undecided voters would mostly want to retch.

"Ick," Peggy said, clicking it off before Armand Rowley could kvetch for his living. "People like them make me sick. Harold Ford is sanctimonious and on his fourth wife. George Wilson is sincere, as in sincerely stupid."

"Don't spare me, Peggy, tell me what you really feel." Abby laughed.

"I forget you aren't Pris sometimes. I do miss her so. I shouldn't have been so opinionated."

"Opinions are good. I'm voting against the bill," Abby said reassuringly.

"I told Schwartz I'd vote for it when hell froze over," Peggy replied.

For dessert, the staff brought in tall multi-colored Murano glass cones filled with three scoops of sorbet: lemon, blueberry, and peach. A single chocolate mint stick stood up in the glasses.

"So do you think the bill will pass?" Abby asked as she ate her sorbet.

"It's a squeaker. Yours may be the straw that breaks this camel's back." Peggy eyed her. "Are you ready for that, first vote out of the chute?"

"Yes. It stinks. It's full of earmarks and at least ten thousand words came verbatim from the pro-life group."

"You know that for a fact?" Peggy put her spoon down and lasered in on Abby.

"Yes. We read the bill on Friday. I told Poppy I wanted to comment on that, and she told me to keep my mouth shut."

"She's smart," Peggy said. "But I don't have to keep *my* mouth shut."

"Wait a sec." Abby got up and fished out the papers from her tote. "Here are the matching areas from the website, and the bill, and here is the list of earmarks."

"May I keep these?"

"Sure." Abby shrugged.

"Great. We'll get these bastards yet."

When Abby got home, she wrote Peggy a thank-you note. She had long since turned over the funeral notes to the staff.

She laid out her clothes for the next day, and got ready for bed. She set up the coffeepot on its timer. She was content to read the first part of Mikey's latest recommendation, *No Ordinary Time*, by Doris Kearns Goodwin. A bed buddy would be nice, but a human one wasn't on the horizon. She didn't feel she had time for a canine one, so she simply read.

In the morning, the smell of coffee awakened her about the same time as her alarm. Pris had been a news junkie; with televisions all over, all state of the art, all alike, varying only in screen size. You could walk from room to room without missing a word.

Abby flipped on the kitchen set as she poured her coffee.

There was Matt Sands interviewing Peggy Mellon via remote.

"Can you believe the bill has ten thousand words in it, direct from the pro-life website?" Peggy asked, holding up two sheaves of paper. "Ford and Wilson didn't even write their own bill."

"And you said something about earmarks?" Matt asked evenly.

"This bill authorizes eighty million dollars to make ice for Alaska. Really. Have you ever heard of anything that stupid? What's next? Sending sand to the Sahara and calling it foreign aid?"

Abby had to laugh. Peggy was a fast worker. And a very effective one. Abby dressed and went to the office. She scanned all the major papers in the back of the car service. The leads were all different. *Ergo*, according to Wicker, nothing had happened. If a story was important, it was always the lead in every news outlet.

The office was in chaos when she walked in.

"Poppy, what's up?" Abby said as she hung up her coat.

"Peggy Mellon went on *AM America* and told everyone to e-mail their Senator to vote no on Ford-Wilson. Our server has crashed, and the phone lines are about to melt with call volume."

"In which direction?" As if Abby didn't know.

'Twenty to one against."

"I'll be glad to vote the opinions of my fellow Texans," Abby said, heading into her office. *Yes.*

"Did you have anything to do with this?" Poppy asked suspiciously. "After all, our people did find the connection to the website."

"Ask me no questions, I'll tell you no lies," Abby said. "Do you have my schedule for me?"

Poppy reluctantly handed her the printed cards for the day. One was the Senate calendar as it pertained to Abby, with her appointments filled in. The other cards were information on the scheduled appointments.

"I see I cast my first floor vote at two?" Abby asked. "Is there anything going on there now?"

"No. Probably someone is talking to an empty chamber for the *Congressional Record.*"

"Can you show me my desk, please?"

"Sure." The two women walked briskly toward the Senate Chamber. Abby loved the movement; its rhythm was familiar to her from the hospital. The long indoor hikes were her exercise, and Poppy had a stride to match hers.

Most people greeted Poppy by name, and some nodded at Abby.

The Senate chamber was impressive; its dark-blue patterned carpeting was set off by the lovely ceiling. She'd been in the visitor's gallery once to see Pris give a speech, but other than that, the room was foreign to her.

"Here's your desk, number thirty-four. It's one of the originals," Poppy said, referring to the original set of desks ordered after the War of 1812 when the Capitol was burned. They were little more than school desks of the era.

Abby gently opened the drawer and gasped. Former Senators had carved their names into the old wood. *Naughty boys.* She ran her fingers along the names, and a chill ran down her spine. Tears welled up when she saw "S. Houston."

To think that she would share a desk with Sam Houston was beyond anything Abby could imagine. Sam Houston is to Texas what George Washington is to the United States.

Now she was sharing his desk. *I am standing on the shoulders of giants.*

"Let's go," Abby said. "I'm feeling a little overwhelmed."

She was on remote control the rest of the morning, Poppy escorting her places, Abby pasting on a smile and shaking hands.

"Oh, that group of fifteen school kids at eleven thirty?" Abby asked.

"What about them?"

"Do we have presents for them?"

"No. They get a group photo."

"Not good enough. Here." Abby fished into her tote and came out with her AmEx. "Go get some kid books about the Senate at the gift shop."

"Abby. We have over five hundred school children coming to your office this month alone."

"So get five hundred."

"Why?"

"I want to get them dreaming big. If I can sit at Sam Houston's desk, so can they."

Abby found her way back to the office, had a quick cup of coffee with Mikey, and then chewed a couple of pieces of gum. Kids, she remembered, not only hated coffee breath, they called you on it.

The fifteen kids from the Rio Grande valley had somehow raised enough money for a class trip. That area was traditionally poor and

Hispanic. Abby wanted them to sit in her desk, to feel like a Senator. For the pictures, she would stand slightly behind them, offering them an autographed copy of *The Kid's Book of the Senate* for the photo.

"After all, guys, you taxpayers are the boss. I'm just here to serve you."

They seemed to come alive, and Abby let them open drawers and pick up the phone. It put her twenty minutes behind schedule, and she got her foot rolled over a couple of times, but she fantasized that the kids walked out a little taller than when they came in.

She gave each of them her business card as they left.

"Write me anytime. Tell me you visited, and I'll try to write you back. No promises, but I'll try. You're Texans, so dream big dreams. That's what Texas is all about."

"Bye, Senator Abby," they said on the way out. Some said, "Señora Abby," but that too was fine. The last person out of the room was a chaperone.

"Thanks for lighting up for these kids. Most people just tolerate them."

"It was my pleasure."

After they left, Poppy plopped into a chair.

"Let's hope you can work a room of adults like you did them," Poppy said.

"Nah. Grownups are mostly morons."

For lunch, Abby had vending machine yogurt at her desk while she did her morning e-mail. Then, she signed all her morning correspondence and spent time browsing the Senate's internal website. Just before the roll call vote, she re-groomed for the afternoon. She begrudged the time, but was getting it down to a minimum. In the full-length mirror, she noticed the little darling who ran over her shoe had also put a run in her stocking.

She locked her door, slipped on new panty hose, and cursed the inventor. Perhaps she could ban them in the United States. *To heck with burning bras, burn the panty hose.*

She flipped through the Senate's directory and made a check mark by each Senator she could name. She chose five more at random to introduce herself to this afternoon.

She was early into the chamber, where a number of Senators were milling around. Abby found the first person on her mental list and walked up to him.

"You must be Senator Whitman," Abby said pleasantly. "I'm Abigail Adams. I think I'll be on the Judiciary Committee with you."

"Why, yes I am, young lady." He smiled broadly at being recognized. "Are you finding your way around?"

"I left a trail of breadcrumbs this morning so I could find my way back."

He laughed heartily. Abby was vaguely repulsed by the thirty grand worth of cosmetic dentistry the man flashed at every chance, as well as his obvious face lifts.

"Well, if you need a scout, you can count on me."

"I'll remember that," Abby said pleasantly. "If you'll excuse me, I see someone I need to speak to."

She'd done three of the five on her list when it was time to sit.

At the banging of the gavel, people took their seats.

In a roll call vote, the names are called alphabetically, so for Abby's first vote, she was the first person called. She had no luxury of seeing how the wind was blowing. She noticed the Vice President was present in case of a tie. She looked bored and angry, but then again, she probably was.

"In the matter of the Senate Bill 3434, Senator Adams, how do you vote?" the Secretary of the Senate asked.

Abby rose, fingertips on Sam Houston's desk, and said in a clear, strong voice, "I vote no."

She sat down and made ticks in each column. About midway through she made eye contact with Peggy Mellon, who winked at her. Abby winked back.

The bill went down to defeat by twenty votes.

The first person at her desk was the Majority Leader.

"I am very unhappy with your vote." Schwartz glared at her.

"And with all due respect, sir, I'm at peace with it. My bosses told me loud and clear their opinion this morning."

"Your bosses?" He had his brows knitted tightly together.

"Yes. I believe they are called constituents?" Abby gave him a broad smile and walked away.

Outside the chamber there was a posse of photographers and reporters. Abby was grateful for her media training, but glad they were after the Senate leadership, not her. She strode purposefully past the throng, posture perfect, a pleasant look on her face, and not a hair out of place.

Everyone stood and cheered as she entered her office.

"What?" Abby asked. "Why are you cheering?"

"You cast your first vote, my dear," said Mikey. "You are no longer a virgin Senator."

Abby blushed.

Abby had thirty minutes blocked out with Mikey each afternoon. It varied with his nap, but was always instructive.

"So, how do you feel about your vote?" Mikey asked.

"I feel I did the right thing," Abby replied.

"You'll shortly find out that doing the right thing 'sucks,' as the young would say. Be prepared for someone to stab you in the back."

"Why?"

"The public sees Mellon's fingerprints. The Senate leadership sees yours. They know you found the link."

"Oh. And who was my leaker?"

"It doesn't matter. The only way any two people can keep a secret is for one of them to be dead. Probably one of your eager young beavers spoke to a roommate Friday night, and then the information was out."

"So how do I control the flow of information?"

"You might as well ask me how to make lead into gold."

"Thanks."

"There are a few rules."

Abby took out her notepad.

"Never say anything in an e-mail. It lasts forever. Never say anything in a letter that you can say on the phone. Never say anything on the phone that can be said in person. Never say anything in person that should remain unsaid."

Mikey rose to go.

"You did the right thing, my dear. But you will have to pay for it. Just be prepared."

"Oh, and here are your clippings." He offered her a folder with the date on it.

"My clippings?"

"Yes. I've decided to be your reader. I pass along items of note—the old-fashioned way. Things you need to know."

"Thank you, Mikey, this is incredibly wonderful of you."

"Keeps me off the streets. How are Eleanor and Franklin?"

"Not well. Eleanor has found out, after ten years and five children, that Franklin's having an affair with her beautiful social secretary. Eleanor was fine with a divorce, but her mother-in-law would have none of it." Abby was incensed.

"Rather Gothic, I think," Mikey replied. "No wonder Eleanor turned into the most modern of women."

CHAPTER TWENTY-TWO

BLOWBACK

The blowback was fast. Ford and Wilson were so intent that Abby was behind their humiliation, it took less than a day for Abby to be the target of a smear on one of the right wing cable stations.

"Just who is this woman behind the defeat of the pro-life's mission critical bill? More on Abigail Adams tonight at seven," conservative cable channels blared.

"Is Abigail Adams really a member of the party in power? Senate Majority Leader threatens to oust her if she doesn't toe the line. Tonight on *Right is Right*."

Abby watched the video clips the next morning with Poppy, Mikey, and Bob Wicker from Wicker Washington.

"All I did was *A*, cast a vote and *B*, cast it as the people of Texas wanted," Abby pointed out.

"Abby, face is everything in this town," Poppy said.

"And, my dear, I did tell you that no good deed goes unpunished," Mikey added. "You should still do them, just be ready for paybacks."

"I'm going to set you up with a mock interview and then you, Abby, are going out there tonight to show the American people what you're made of," Bob Wicker said.

"She's a newbie," Poppy protested. "Fresh meat. They'll maul her."

"I hate to see her get roughed up, first vote out," Mikey said.

Wicker knew what they did not: Abigail was a media natural.

"Oh, good grief," Abigail said. "I did nothing wrong. To *not* answer them would be weak. What time am I on?" Abby asked.

"Tonight, at eight."

"Fine. Worst-case scenario, I go back to my day job." *And enough money to never have to work again.*

Abby spent part of the day in mock interviews at Wicker Washington. The questions were ridiculous, obnoxious, and even insane. Abby was to answer slowly, thoughtfully, and with good manners. Then she was to shut up and smile a small smile.

"I don't know if I want to do this," Abby said at the end of the mock interview.

"Well, it's either that or get hammered."

"Okay, but I'm not pulling any punches. Most pro-lifers are good people, but the radical fringe has shot doctors, for crying out loud."

"Okay," Bob Wicker said. "They just got you. You cannot get angry or they win."

"So what can I get?"

"You can get condescending. You can use the line, 'I've heard worse.' Or you can just shrug your shoulders, do a Dr. Phil, and say no matter how thin the pancake, there are always two sides."

"Hey, I like those."

The rest of her day dragged. She had an Armed Services Committee meeting at which she was introduced and otherwise kept her mouth shut. Testifying was The Extreme Bloviator, otherwise known as the Secretary of Defense, Patrick J. O'Neal. He was, as they say, a legend in his own mind. *Maybe he is our secret agent in case of a war. He could bore the enemy to death.*

Abby was even less impressed at the long-winded diatribes produced by committee members for the *Congressional Record. These guys must get paid by the word.* She took out her BlackBerry, put it in her lap, and played Free Cell until her eyes crossed and she got a headache.

After her headache came anger. These people took the whole afternoon to ask a simple question: Do we know where all our nukes are? Yes or no? After three hours, the answer was "Um, pretty much."

No wonder the big issues never got tackled; all anyone did was blather. If they tightened up their use of time, they might get around to more problems. And if a senior Senator kept a bill off the agenda at his whim, it did not exist, even if the problem was enormous. The Senate was supposed to deliberate, not to dawdle. No wonder Washington was in perpetual gridlock.

If I practiced medicine the way these people run the Senate, you could stack the dead bodies behind the hospital like so much firewood.

Poppy, Bob, and Abby grabbed a quick bite and then went into the Senate Studio at about thirty minutes before airtime. In the mirror off to the side, she added a little more blush and lip color, popped in some artificial tears, and checked her teeth. *No lipstick or spinach.*

The Senate studio was tiny, with a backdrop of bookshelves, the obligate standing flag, and a podium. Abby introduced herself to Sam, the floor director, and asked that he make her look as good as was humanly possible. He appeared to have the lighting similar to the Wicker studios, so that reassured Abby.

"Not hard with you, ma'am," he responded. He pointed to the monitor and Abby was shocked. She did look better than she felt.

He miked her, and she put in her IFB. When both were plugged in, she said, "Hi guys, I'm Abigail Adams. Is my sound okay?"

"You are looking and sounding fine," a reassuring voice in her ear said.

Abby rolled her shoulders, and made some silly faces so she wouldn't appear with a "frozen face," both tricks out of the Wicker Washington Media Manual.

Poppy paced, and Bob worked his BlackBerry, occasionally grunting or laughing.

"We're on in three minutes," the floor director, Sam, said. "Here's your live monitor." Sam pointed to a smallish floor monitor. "All audio from the host will come in your IFB, ditto for the other guests.

Abby took her place behind the lectern and thought she looked too tall on the monitor. So she slipped off her shoes and was pleased with the proportions. She remembered her cell phone was in her pocket, so she turned it off and placed it on the lectern.

"Poppy, get out of here," Abby said. "Your pacing is making me crazy. I can do this. It isn't brain surgery, and I've scrubbed in on that."

As Sam counted her down, she lasered her focus into the blank, black, rectangular face of the camera. In her mind, she was thinking of Michael Aston. *You and I are destined for each other, darling. Leave those Hollywood types and come to my bed.*

"In three…two…one…"

Abby was surprised that her heart rate did not jump as she heard the intro music. She could see the host and more importantly, hear him well. Then they cut to a two-shot of her and the head of the pro-life group. She definitely looked better. He was looking at his monitor, which of course meant he wasn't looking at the audience. She looked straight into the camera.

"Senator Adams, tell us why you voted against this bill," the host said.

"First of all, Tom, thank you for inviting me here. I voted No because the people of Texas were against it, and I represent them."

"But your party leader told you this was a critical bill for the party," the host followed up.

And, with all due respect, my bosses are the peo—"

The pro-lifer jumped in and began talking over her. She waited for him to take a breath and then jumped right back.

"Gentlemen!" she said smartly. Unthinking, she rapped her cell phone on the lectern. It was as if she banged a gavel. The men shut up out of shock. Then her voice turned back to honey. "I do *not* engage in verbal food fights. Either we speak in a civil manner, or I won't continue. Are we understood?" Then she smiled.

Both men on the monitor appeared stunned.

"Let me repeat. My bosses are the people of the State of Texas, and they were opposed. Now, Mr. Lafoote, what was it you wanted to say?"

Abby ceded the floor with another gracious smile and tilt of the head.

"How dare you accuse me of writing the bill. That is a flat-out lie."

"I didn't accuse you of anything, Mr. Lafoote. I don't even know you. All my staff did was look at your public website and compare it to a public bill and note the similarities. I believe that is called due diligence."

"Then why didn't you have the guts to come out and fight? Instead you sent your buddy, Peggy Mellon, to do your dirty work," he sneered. Abby kept her face pleasant.

"Ah, Mr. Lafoote, you're leaping to conclusions without looking. I am a member of a deliberative body. I deliberated with Senator Mellon. But I was as shocked as anyone to turn on my television yesterday morning and see her. She is her own person; I can assure you of that."

"Obviously, no one is in control in the U.S. Senate."

Abby noted the time clock for the entire broadcast was ticking down. She had maybe ten seconds, so she spoke a little more slowly.

"Mr. Lafoote, with all due respect, sir, the bill you wanted went down. These things happen. It's simply time to move on." Abby smiled a sympathetic smile and shrugged her shoulders.

The host jumped in.

"We're out of time. G'nite."

Bob Wicker was thrilled. "You took control of the interview away from the host. He'll get a major tongue-lashing for that. And you got the last word. How did you do it?"

"You forget I've worked with children."

CHAPTER TWENTY-THREE

THE BLOVIATOR

The next morning, Poppy brought in a stack of glowing clippings.

"I don't want to see them, thanks," Abby said.

"For crying out loud, why not?" Poppy asked.

"Believing your own PR is poisonous."

"You, lady, are a major pain in the ass," Poppy said, pouring herself another cup of coffee.

"Thanks. That's the kind of feedback I like. What's on my dance card today?" Abby asked. Poppy gave her the card.

"Elderly people lobbying for respite care for Alzheimer's families at nine."

"Then?"

"Armed Services Subcommittee at two.

"Can I see the briefing book after the Alzheimer's people leave?"

"Yes."

"Who's this Lafferty Weapons Systems at four?"

"He's a big donor, a defense contractor out of California," Poppy said flatly.

"I'm not running, and he's not from Texas. Why am I seeing him?"

"He's due face time. His jet took you home to Houston for Pris's funeral. Probably has a problem at DOD."

Abby was learning the alphabet soup of Washington. She didn't need to be told that DOD meant Department of Defense. She figured she was up to three percent of what she needed to know. Not adequate for a week.

"He only called yesterday, so here's his file." Poppy plopped it down. It included a bio put out by his website. Abby glanced through the file.

Self-made, easy on the eyes, big into philanthropy, owned a Gulfstream 650, and made state of the art weapons systems. *I can find a few minutes in my day for him.*

At nine thirty sharp, five elderly Texans came into her office. And at nine forty-five, all were charmed and out the door.

"I'll read the bill with you in mind. If it is as good a bill as you say, you'll get my vote. No promises, though."

Abby wished she had more time to listen. Old people have a lifetime of wisdom. But she needed time with that briefing book.

Abby unlocked the closet that held the Top Secret part of the Armed Services Committee materials. The book was roughly the size of the Manhattan phone book, but with bigger print. There were CDs in the back.

Abby started at the beginning. It was tedious material, but the question was simple. Did we know where all our shoulder-fired nukes were?

So Abby began hunting for numbers and locations.

There was one discrepancy she couldn't figure out on her own. She found the place on the second CD where the discrepancy occurred. She slipped the CD into her tote, made a copy of the two pages from the book, and was in the subcommittee with just moments to spare.

"Welcome, Senator," the chairman said. "Glad to know you passed your background check."

"Yes, they missed the late library books."

"This is where the real work is done. The other, the public hearings, are primarily senatorial theatre."

"I see." *It is bad theatre.*

The Extreme Bloviator, Patrick J. O'Neal, came in with a small retinue of staff, and appeared none too happy. He was paunchy, on the short side, maybe five foot eight, wore thick glasses and a ridiculous bow tie everywhere he went. He also had one of those turned-down smiles. Anyone who thought an exaggerated sneer was a smile struck Abby as arrogant. He also looked a little greasy or sweaty, like he had the day before. *Wipe your face.*

Abby sat and watched for a while. Without cameras, people weren't performing for them.

The droning, however, continued. A Senator would ask a simple question, and O'Neal would answer in as many words as possible. Buried in there might be a half-nugget of content.

Finally, in due turn, Abby decided to ask her one question.

"Mr. Secretary, my name is Abigail Adams, and I have been appointed to fill Priscilla Logan's seat until the election."

"I know who you are," he said abruptly.

"I have just one question. Do you want me to reference it by Bates numbers or by page numbers?"

He looked confused.

"Do you want to look up the answer on a CD or on hard copy, sir?"

"Hard copy." He spoke a little too loudly.

"On page seven eighty-three, paragraph three, there is a list."

One of his minions produced the page for him to see.

"How many Mockingbird missiles are listed on that page?"

"Seventy-eight."

"Now if you would turn to page eleven twenty-five, please?"

The minion produced that page.

"Yes. I'm there. So?" his voice lacked inflection and was still too loud.

"This is a table of Mockingbirds by locations. If I add the figures correctly, there are only a total of seventy-four."

Other members started to pay attention. The two who were playing hangman stopped. One got out a calculator and confirmed Abby's addition.

"I'm sure it is just a typo." The Secretary shrugged.

"It very well could be. I'm afraid I must insist that there be some reconciliation of these discrepancies." Abby was as sweet as she could be. "I doubt anyone is comfortable with a typo about small, shoulder-fired nuclear weapons."

There were a few titters from the committee that infuriated the Secretary.

"Miss Adams," he said, deliberately refusing to use either of her proper titles. "You have been in the Senate, what, a week? And you presume to ask me about whether there are typographical errors in a two-thousand-page document? I'm appalled."

"You may be appalled all you like, sir. However, yes, I do presume to ask you about this. I am a member of the Armed Services Committee, and oversight is part of my job description." Abby fixed him in her sights and would not look away.

He was about to blow a gasket. His face was red and he was starting to sweat.

The Secretary glared back at her. Finally, Abby decided to speak.

"I'd be content if you'd have someone research this and give us a timely reply."

The Chairman of the Committee, no fan of the Secretary's, jumped in.

"I think that is an excellent idea. May I have a motion to that effect?"

"So moved."

"Seconded."

"All in favor say 'aye?'"

All were in favor.

The Chairman said, "Motion passes. The Secretary of Defense is required to reconcile the discrepancy in numbers and locations of

Mockingbird Missiles within one month. Mr. Secretary, do you think you can do that?"

"You people," he fumed, his sneer deepening, "you people don't have any idea how hard we work over there at the DOD. You just sit around and nitpick numbers."

The Chairman banged the gavel. "We're in recess for fifteen minutes."

The Secretary stormed out.

He did not return after the recess. Without him, there was no reason to continue the meeting.

"Way to go," one Senator said as he gathered up his papers. "We won't get squat out of him now."

Cordelia Laurus glided up to Abby.

"You mustn't upset him, Abigail," she said in her grandiloquent voice. "He's very labile."

"Then, Senator, I suggest he either change his blood pressure medicine or get a lower stress job," Abby said.

She turned her back on Senator Laurus and strode briskly to her office. She could have taken the subway, but she needed the time to cool down.

"Don't." She held up her hand to Poppy as she came through the door into her office.

"Don't what?" Poppy said.

"Don't anything," Abby answered. She went into her office and closed the door. She soaked her handkerchief in ice water and sobbed into it for a full five minutes. Mikey and Poppy both heard her, but decided to leave her alone.

By five of four, her meltdown was over; she was re-groomed and ready to meet with a donor who happened to be a good-looking man. *I deserve something for this day.*

Lafferty entered at five past four. Lafferty looked rather like many businessmen. Well-groomed, pleasant to look at. No heartthrob, despite his extraordinary accomplishments. But he did possess vivid blue eyes.

Abby stood to greet him. "Abigail Adams."

His handshake was warm, firm, and not at all painful. "John Lafferty."

Abby pointed him toward the sofa and offered him a drink.

"Water, please."

She gave him that, and sat in the chair across from him, notepad in hand.

"Your sister is greatly missed," he said, shooting his cuffs. At least his nails weren't manicured. And he wasn't wearing a wedding ring.

"Thank you. And thank you for the use of your plane during the funeral," Abby said on auto pilot. "What can I do for you?"

"I am having problems getting an answer out of DOD on a bid we submitted sometime back."

"So why me? Shouldn't you be seeing your California Senator?"

"I have. She's working on it. They're both working on it. But Pris was a big supporter of Lafferty Systems. And we, of course, supported her campaigns."

"I doubt I can help. I just ticked off Secretary O'Neal." Abby laughed.

"He's rather prickly. Perhaps one of your staffers could call a counterpart at DOD?" he asked. "Poppy seems to know everyone."

"I'll look into it. Do you have the pertinent info?"

He gave her a file.

"No promises."

"I'll check in with you next week."

He was in and out in less than five minutes.

Abby could finally end her day. She read through every piece of snail mail that came from any official in Texas or the federal government and dealt with it. Her staff sent her a representative sample of constituent comments. She wrote a comment on each and sent them back. People liked being heard. By six, she was on the downside of the paperwork.

Poppy walked in carrying a pile of briefing books for the next day.

"Ugh." Abby leaned back in her chair and rubbed her eyes.

"Abs, you're working too hard."

"I gotta get up to speed."

"Pissing off the Secretary of Defense and demolishing a right to lifer is enough for one twenty-four hours."

"Poppy, all I did was do my job and shoot back. Okay, and have a meltdown. But I recovered."

"All you have to do for the next few months is enjoy the show. Think of it as a break."

"Pops, that'd be fine for anyone else. But I am a workhorse. Work is what I do. Giving any job less than one hundred percent isn't in my nature."

"So that's why Pris wanted you. I wondered."

Poppy shoved off, and Abby left by seven thirty. She was home by eight, in bed by eight thirty. There she read Mikey's clippings and hoped to finish *No Ordinary Time*.

The next thing she knew, the alarm was going off. She'd fallen asleep with the lights on. The Roosevelts were smushed in her lap.

Maybe Poppy was right. Maybe she did need to "enjoy the show." *Heck, maybe I need a week away over Easter Recess. No fun spending my birthday here alone.*

CHAPTER TWENTY-FOUR

FITTING IN

Abby got into the rhythms of the Senate fairly quickly. She was always going somewhere—a committee meeting, a floor vote, or a subcommittee meeting, then back to the office where hordes of schoolchildren appeared on their spring breaks. It was fun, if hard on her wallet and the staff who didn't like kids running everywhere. One kid was stopped just before he e-mailed his face to the President's personal e-mail.

She attended the signing of the Infants First Act in the East Room of the White House. Abby had never been to the White House and to go as a senator gave her goose bumps.

She presented herself and her ID at the Northwest Gate. Her name was on the list, so she was passed on to be wanded, scanned, and have her bag searched. Then she was escorted to the East Room of the White House. The Secret Service didn't let people wander around.

The White House had beautiful bouquets of fresh spring flowers everywhere. In what seemed like moments, she was in the East Room staring at a full-length portrait of George Washington. This must have been the Gilbert Stuart portrait that Dolley Madison saved in the War of 1812.

There were more reporters and photographers in the room than there were people participating in the ceremony.

The gathering was small, perhaps twenty people, but some were parents with babes in their arms. Abby recognized the House co-sponsor of the bill, Frances Lewis. Each was instructed by an aide where to stand behind the desk the President would use. Abby would stand just behind him and to his right.

The room popped to attention when the President and Mrs. Harrington came strolling into it holding hands.

"Abby," the President greeted her, folding her one hand into his two big warm ones. "I am so glad to see you in your sister's seat in the Senate."

"Thank you, Mr. President," Abigail said, blushing. There was no doubt the man had charisma.

Evangeline Harrington greeted her and told her, "It's about time the nation figured out that the first six years of life are the most important."

Harrington was never a fan of the bill, primarily because children didn't vote. However, he kept his word, signed it, and funded it. He would spin it to his own use, to show the nation how family-friendly his party was.

He took a seat at the desk and made a brief statement.

"The more we put into children, the more we'll get out of them as adults. They'll be productive people who pay taxes. Ignore them; they end up using tax money in one way or another. Not only does this bill help children, it has assessment tools to tell how well it is working. If we don't improve the lives of children, we'll know it, and we will be able to change the program or easily abolish it.

"As the late Senator Logan said, 'This is like having a kitchen that not only does all the cooking, it cleans up after itself.'"

The group laughed.

He picked up one of the pens and began the tedious process of signing his name with sixteen pens, one for each letter of his name. After he signed his name, Abby was given the first one in an embossed box that commemorated the occasion.

"Thank you, Mr. President," she said. *How wasteful and silly is this?*

At the short reception that followed, Mrs. Harrington took Abby aside.

"I am so sorry that your sister had to die to get Walter to sign this bill, but I am so glad he signed it. I'd been lobbying him for months on this one."

"Thank you. I've been looking for some meaning in Pris's death," Abby said, her eyes brimming with tears. Mrs. Harrington hugged her. Something had finally helped lighten the grief. The hug meant a lot more than the silly pen.

Fundraisers were in full swing for the primary elections and ultimately for the fall elections. Schwartz kept pestering her about Pris's war chest, and she finally got an accounting of it and all the people and entities from which it had come.

She returned it, pro rata, to each of the donors. It was tedious and time consuming, but ultimately, Abby felt it was the best use of the money.

More than one person wrote to say they'd never gotten a refund, and indeed there was a small squib in *The Wall Street Journal*. That morning, Schwartz came charging into her office.

Schwartz was livid, but Abby was calm.

"Do sit down, Senator. You look like you could use a cup of coffee."

"Only if you put Valium in it."

"Are you what Regina would call 'spitting mad'?" Abby inquired.

"That's putting it mildly." He did, however, accept the coffee.

"I thought long and hard. I did what I thought was right. It's a shame it's made you dyspeptic." Abby sipped her coffee.

"More like apoplectic," he said.

"With all due respect, I have made a sizeable donation to Lawson Gray's campaign. And lesser donations to other candidates. Those all came out of my pocket, though."

"Well, thank you for that."

"Unspent campaign money is not a slush fund or some sort of political jump ball. So I took this one out of play," Abby said sweetly.

Schwartz heaved himself up. Abby stood also.

"You could also stop picking on the Secretary of Defense," he said.

"I asked a simple and proper question. He went ballistic. He still hasn't accounted for all the nukes."

"You are so much like your sister, it's uncanny. I couldn't control that woman, no matter what I did."

"Why, thank you. That's a lovely compliment." Abby beamed.

He left shaking his head, but with a smile on his face.

Abby got more efficient and was able to leave the Senate most nights by seven. Without the need to campaign, she skipped morning and evening fundraisers. She spent her free time learning everything she could about the U.S Government and the problems it faced.

Mikey continued to "read" for her, and she was coming up to speed nicely on the nuts and bolts of the Armed Services Committee, the Foreign Affairs Committee, and the Judiciary Committee.

Mikey also had her reading basic economics. She was learning tons about economics, and how administration policy was a significant, but not determinant factor in the economy. For world affairs, she read Thomas Friedlander's books, Farouk Mazoon's work and taped his show. She recorded one right-wing talk show, as well as *Press Weekly* and one *Political Comedy* show a week and fast forwarded through the commercials.

Regina stayed in Houston and they talked every other day. Regina needed a serious rest and time with her own friends.

For her part, Abby was healing the only way she knew how: through work. Abby worked on Priscilla's estate, with the CPA and Marston Mills doing most of the work. Of course, at the fees they charged, they were delighted to do even the simplest of chores.

Still, Abby kept the door to Priscilla's room firmly closed. She would tackle it one day. There was no hurry. To recall her sister, she wore the Bulgari Green Tea, almost every day.

Abby wanted to travel during the Easter recess. How could she vote on Foreign Affairs if she'd never done anything except backpack in Europe one summer? Besides, she did not want to spend her birthday alone. Maybe Mikey would have an idea.

One Sunday afternoon in March, Mikey was due at her house for a tutorial session. Abby decided she'd put the Middle East on the agenda.

"Well, my dear, you do know how to choose the knottiest of problems."

"Mikey, I want to see it for myself. As a tourist, but with a twist. Not official, and off the beaten path."

"Well, of course, all that can be arranged, but you, my dear, are a 'high value target.' Your head would fetch a pretty penny for any kidnapper."

"Maybe I could wear the black robes?"

"You wouldn't last a minute. Your skin is so very white, your hands alone would give you away."

"Well, help me with this."

"But I am not at all sure this is a good idea. The security's better on a junket."

"And the party line stinks."

The next day at the office, Mikey sought her out. "I think I've found a way. I spoke with a journalist friend who travels extensively in the Middle East. He has a trip coming up and would be willing to let you come along for an interview at the end of the trip."

"I'd pay my own way, of course."

"Yes, but you'd have significant other expenses: security and a fixer. He can provide those."

"What's a fixer?"

"A native of the area who's plugged into everything. Part tour guide, part translator, part nanny."

"And would I be able to go off on my own?"

"No. You'd go where you wanted if the security man and the fixer agreed. The reporter's gotten wind of your independence. He doesn't want your blood on his hands."

"I'll behave."

"Here's his number." Mikey handed her a slip of paper. "Mind you, I'm not for this, but I think if you are going to do it, this is best. And do take both your passports."

"That's right. I have a diplomatic one as well as a regular one."

"Yes. You enter with the regular one, and you keep the other one in a pouch inside your panties."

Abby dialed the number.

"T.J.," a nice baritone answered.

"Hello, I'm looking for Thad Jackson?"

"That'd be me. Whatcha need?" He sounded rather secretive.

"Mikey Molloy gave me your card."

"Yep. Let's do this in person," he said curtly.

"You know my place? Seven?" Abby thought the cloak and dagger business was a bit silly. Everyone in America knew his face. He was a television babe of the first magnitude.

"See you there." He hung up.

Abby wore jeans and a sweater and answered the door in her bare feet when Thad Jackson arrived.

He couldn't help it that he looked like a dark-haired Ken Doll, so he deliberately selected the most dangerous assignments and wore faded black tee-shirts and cargo pants. Women ate him up. And men weren't threatened by him. Rumor had it the next anchor slot was his if he wanted it.

The stubble and grubby clothes were his uniform, but he was anything but dirty. His nails were clean and short, his hair clean and neat. His faded tee was fresh from the laundry, with starch, as were the cargo pants. He was slighter than he appeared on television, but still taller than she was. He wore a battered leather and shearling jacket for the D.C. chill. For shoes, he wore Doc Martens as he did on the air. Abby guessed he must have at least a dozen changes of the same clothes.

They exchanged greetings at the door and Abby invited him into the living room.

"This was my sister's place. I'm here just until I finish out her term. I'm starved. Here's the room service menu. Get whatever."

"Great. I forgot to eat." He read the menu with interest.

She poured them both a glass of a nice Meursault, and they settled in the living room to talk while they waited for their steaks to arrive.

"Why do you want to go to the Middle East?" T.J. asked.

"To see things for myself." Abby shrugged.

"Okay. Do you have any idea how dangerous it is?"

"No, but I'm an emergency physician in a major metropolitan area. I'm quite familiar with mayhem," Abby said, taking a sip of her weekly glass of wine.

"Ever seen somebody with their belly blown up?"

"Lots of times. A guy shot his pregnant girlfriend with a shotgun, and the baby had her hand waving in the air. We saved the baby, but lost the mom." Abby kept her voice deliberately flat.

"Jeez. Waving in the air?" T.J. recoiled. He looked a little green.

"God's truth." Abby said, still calm.

Their steaks arrived, and T.J. fell on his with zest.

"Ummm. Nothing beats a good steak," he said. "You can't imagine how awful some of the food I eat is."

"Um, can you say county hospital cafeteria?"

"Oh, okay. So you do know." He nodded his head as he patted his mouth with a napkin.

"Here's the deal," he said between bites. "We fly on the same flight, but not together. You travel alone. I'm with my crew: my photographer, my two producers, and my sound guy. One of my producers is really your security guy. I'll arrange to have you in the room next door."

"How?"

"Trade secrets." He winked.

"So you pay off the bellman?"

He ignored that comment.

"Your security guy is your 'husband' once we are in country. Your fixer is your guide. You go sightseeing. Take a few pictures."

"And if there's trouble?"

"We have local cell phones for use in country. Your fixer also has a sat phone."

"Sat phone?"

"Satellite phone. Looks like those brick cell phones from the eighties, but are more secure than a cell phone. Cost about three grand."

"Do I let the embassy know that I am coming?" Abigail asked.

"Not unless you want to get kidnapped. It's a sieve."

"How 'secure' is my security guy?"

"He'd like to be armed, but there are checkpoints everywhere, so he can't carry a weapon. He's pretty tough, though. Former Navy Seal."

"And what do you get?" Abby asked.

"You give me an exclusive interview at the end of the trip."

"What's going to be your angle?"

"The Israelis say they are letting in humanitarian aid to Gaza City. But they aren't. The Administration pretends they believe the line."

"And you'll want only my opinion of what I've seen directly?"

"Yes."

"So how much are we talking for the security guy and fixer, on top of regular expenses?"

T.J. named a high figure, but one Abby could live with.

"Downsides?" Abby asked.

"Aside from death and dismemberment?"

"Cute," Abby replied, one side of her mouth twitching upward.

"If you speak out against the Administration, you'll get in big trouble."

"So what?" Abby said. "I'm not running for anything."

"They'll label you a loose cannon, say ugly things about you."

"Sticks and stones."

"Are you sure you don't want to go into journalism?" he asked, his eyes narrowed.

"Quite."

They pulled out BlackBerries and fixed a date for their departure over the Easter recess. T.J. followed Abby into the study, where she booked her flight and room online. She printed out her itinerary for him. Her security guy would get her address from that and pencil it into his passport once in the country.

"See you in Jerusalem."

"Not 'next year in Jerusalem?'" she asked.

CHAPTER TWENTY-FIVE

TRIP OF A LIFETIME

"Poppy, you're right. I'm holding on too tight. I need a break." Abby announced as she went into the office a few days later.

"Finally, I can get some work done around here. Where are you off to?"

"Someplace warm and sandy. Over the Senate's Easter recess."

"Well, I might need a whereabouts memo. Let me check." Poppy pulled up the screen.

"Nope, you're cool. You're not President Pro Tem until November."

"Then you can just reach me on my cell."

"Do I smell a man in all of this?"

"Maybe," Abby said coyly. T.J. had shown no interest in her, but maybe something would develop. *A girl could do worse.*

El Al has the best safety record in the world, mostly because they have the best security. Just booking her ticket triggered a passport check Then Abby had to clear security twice: once in Washington and once again at JFK. There she changed dollars into a large sum of new shekels for the fixer. She had to arrive three hours before the flight and was interviewed at length, as was everyone. It was scant help that she was traveling business class. Luckily she'd made her reservations far enough in advance. Last-minute bookings were not welcome, unless of course you were a Jewish Israeli going home with a good excuse.

Abby stuck to her story. She was a physician traveling for pleasure to see the Holy Land and its sights. She was staying at the old, but high-dollar, King David Hotel in Jerusalem and would be taking day trips around to the tourist sites.

After being patted down, having her baggage searched and x-rayed, she was allowed to board the aircraft. She was nervous they would find her diplomatic passport, but they didn't. El Al even screens all cargo.

The man seated next to her was old enough to be her father. She asked to eat early, took a sleeping pill, and was fast asleep before the guy next to her started snoring. Her seat went to nearly flat, and she slept until reaching the turbulence over the mid-Atlantic. She took another half a pill, drank a half-liter of water, and awakened in time for meal service before landing.

Landing at Tel Aviv was uneventful, and she had no trouble with passport control or customs. Once El Al lets you on the plane, you're in Israel. Soon she was taking a long and expensive cab ride to Jerusalem. She might as well have been in the Southwest somewhere. The land was scrubby and rocky, but prosperous.

Everyone spoke English to her. Sure, there were a few *sabras*, native-born Israelis, who were redheads, but their hair was dark red and their eyes were brown. There was a handful of blondes in the country, so she really stood out. Her height only added to her conspicuousness.

About ten minutes after she got to her room, the phone rang. It was T.J. Would she come to his room two doors down?

There she met Marc, a dark guy from Boston who could pass as a Semite in a pinch, as well as Ari, her fixer. First she paid both guys.

Marc got U.S. dollars and Ari got new shekels. *Not your paper trail kind of guys.* Both men were pleasant, and Marc would be staying in the room adjacent to hers. He erased his Boston address and put in Abby's in Houston.

Abby wanted to get going, so Ari, Marc, and Abby headed out in Ari's car, a silver Mercedes that looked respectable enough to be allowed anywhere. Car bombers usually chose clunkers to explode. Besides, Ari occasionally worked for various non-governmental organizations, or NGOs, and had a UNICEF as well as an International Red Cross/Red Crescent sticker on his windshield.

They went to a checkpoint into Gaza. The wall itself was beyond hideous. It reminded Abby of supersized concrete freeway dividers that could be moved. These walls, though, weren't going anywhere.

The line to get through wasn't long. The three rehearsed their speech. Abby would tell the truth, mostly. She was a doctor, on her way to Al Shifa Hospital. Her hospital at home was thinking of sending medical supplies to the hospital, and she needed to know what they needed.

Why did her husband have a different name? That is common for U.S. women doctors. He came along because he didn't want her traveling alone. Ari was their driver and had been recommended by the King David Hotel, where they were staying.

They were waved through.

Abby felt she had left a first world country and entered a third. Children on the streets were barely dressed, filthy, and all had runny noses, usually with a fly or two perched in the mucus. Ari took them to Al Shifa, where Abby watched as patients arrived. Those who could walk in, did. Those who could not were often carried, sometimes on a litter, more often on a door. A pregnant woman in labor was borne by three men carrying the plastic armchair in which she sat, wailing with labor pains.

As the woman waited for care, Abby asked Ari to talk with her, find out when the baby was due and how she planned to deliver. After a few minutes, he reported that her name was Noor, this was her first baby, and she was not due for a month or more. The last doctor said the baby was sitting up. Abby pondered that and realized the baby was breech. *If they couldn't stop her labor, she would absolutely have to have a C-section.* Abby would be leery of drinking a glass of water from the "hospital," much less having surgery there.

At any first world hospital, the woman would be admitted, given drugs to stop her labor and mature the baby's lungs. Then, if she couldn't be prevented from delivering, a C-section would be done.

Suddenly a large gush of blood came from between Noor's legs, and Abby sent Ari in search of a doctor. Flies landed in the blood.

As Abby looked around at the people, she saw a child with untreated spina bifida, an open spine. The child should have died years ago of meningitis, but he drug himself along the streets, begging, his callused and useless legs dragging behind him.

Abby was glad she'd brought a big bottle of hand sanitizer.

Abby went to Noor who was pale and sweaty. Abby knew she was going into shock from blood loss.

"I am Dr. Abu Dalu," a tall, dark man said. "What is it you want?" He instinctively spoke English to Abigail.

"This woman is breech, likely with a placenta praevia or an abruption, and she's four plus weeks early. She needs a stat C-section."

"I can see that. I have no help. I have no IV fluids. I have no electricity. I barely have a clean scalpel. Do you propose to help me?" His shrug was a challenge.

"If I have to, I will. I've scrubbed on C-sections, but I'm really a Pediatric Emergency Specialist."

"Then, please, be my guest." He motioned her inside, a hint of optimism in his hooded eyes.

He shouted a few orders in a language she didn't understand, and Abby followed him down the hall. It stank of body odor. It looked more like a shooting gallery for heroin addicts than a hospital. People propped up against the walls, their eyes vacant with despair. The heat was stifling.

Marc, Ari, and the husband carried the moaning woman. *Moaning is good, her airway's open.* Noor dripped blood onto the floor.

"Put her in here."

Abu Dalu pointed to an empty operating suite without electricity. There were a few instruments on a single surgical tray, covered by a towel. A fat fly was sitting on the towel. There was no operating table, just a gurney, its black plastic pad ripped from overuse. It didn't even have a sheet on it.

It was unseasonably warm, and the room, lit and ventilated only by high open windows, felt like an oven. Abby had sweat running between her breasts.

The three men put the woman as gently as possible on the gurney.

Abu Dalu handed Abby the scissors from his back pocket. Abby began cutting off the woman's clothes. She cut straight up each pant leg and through the waistband. Then she cut the tunic up the middle.

Marc summoned T.J. via text. T.J. texted Marc to start shooting video from his cell phone.

While she cut off the woman's clothes, Abu Dalu emptied his pockets onto the surgical tray: two pair of sterile gloves, three packs of suture material, scalpel with a covered blade, a single hemostat. Then it hit her. Every resident she'd ever worked with had known to keep a personal stash of necessities on their person. She bet he was U.S. trained.

"I trained at Ben Taub," Abby said.

"Charity," he replied. "I came home after Katrina."

They were colleagues. They thought the same way.

"I have hand sanitizer and sanitizing wipes." Abby put both on the tray beside the hand full of instruments. "Oh, and a juice box and unopened water bottle."

"I'll operate, you assist." This simple sentence meant each knew where to stand and what to do. "We have no sponges, no drapes, so we must work fast."

Abby squirted hand sanitizer onto the parts of the equipment that needed to be sterile.

Abu Dalu felt the woman's pulse.

"Thready."

Abby told Ari to get the father out of the room. He left, mumbling prayers.

Abby noticed an old fetoscope hanging from a hook. She put the contraption onto her forehead and put the bell end onto the woman's belly. It took a few seconds to find the baby's heartbeat. She glanced at her watch for fifteen seconds. A healthy fetal heart rate was a hundred and forty.

"One hundred." Abby and Abu Dalu both knew the baby was teetering.

Abby squirted hand sanitizer into Abu Dalu's and her palms and both worked it in quickly. Abby helped Abu Dalu glove up.

Abu Dalu hollered something she couldn't understand. Abby squirted hand sanitizer all over the woman's belly. Then Abby gloved and rubbed the sanitizer outward in concentric circles.

Someone scuttled in and put a tea strainer over the mother's mouth, covered it with a handkerchief, and dropped some ether, or chloroform or God knows what, onto it. Anesthesia like that went out fifty years ago in the U.S.

Everything seemed to happen at once, but that is true of emergency C-sections. That baby would be out within a couple of minutes.

The doctor pricked the patient's skin with a scalpel.

There was no response. So he made a long slice through the top layer of skin down the middle of her belly, from the belly button to the pubic bone. A bright red V of blood followed in the wake of the scalpel. No time to do a bikini incision; besides, no Arab woman wears a bikini.

"Marc, Ari, grab me a towel, a gown anything," Abby called.

There was nothing, so Marc ripped off his shirt, his cell phone clattering to the floor.

"Put the shirt over my right shoulder," Abby said. Forget swaddling clothes, this baby would be delivered into a sweaty yellow polo shirt, probably the cleanest thing in the room. Marc at least had a tee shirt. He retrieved his cell phone and kept shooting.

Abby glanced at Marc and Ari, who were turning a little green. They couldn't be allowed to faint into this woman's belly, nor did Abby want them sitting on the filthy floor.

"Go stand up against the wall," she commanded. "And keep your damned hands in the air to keep them clean."

Marc chose a spot to give him the best angle. He'd shot lots of phone video.

Abu Dalu made another, faster cut through the thick gristle of the fibrous tissue that held the belly muscles together. Below it was the uterus. Abu Dalu identified the bladder, and Abby put her gloved left hand between it and the uterus, pushing the bladder out of the way. Without the proper retractor, her hand would have to do.

"Right uterine artery. Left uterine artery." It was important to identify them.

Abby nodded. "I agree."

They were huge wormy looking things. Nicking one would turn it into a fire hose of blood. The mother would die.

He made another cut through the body of the uterus. Without a mask, Abby remembered to keep her mouth closed. A fountain of amniotic fluid squirted out all over Abby's chest. She was soaked through to the skin. It wasn't the first time. At least there was no meconium in it. If the baby had pooped from stress in utero, he'd suck it into his lungs with his first breath and choke to death here.

Abby held her breath. Abu Dalu stuck one of his big gloved hands into the uterus and pulled out a small baby, managing to hook his thumb and index finger around the baby's neck, and another finger around an extremity. The baby came out with a sucking sound. Abby had to let go of the bladder to receive the baby into the polo shirt.

She held the baby just below the mother's abdomen for a few moments, and Abu Dalu realized he had only one hemostat, not two.

"Ari. Come. Open the packet of blue suture without touching anything inside."

Ari did. Abu Dalu grabbed at the sterile suture with two fingers and pulled out the length. He quickly tied the cord in two places. Abby grabbed the gelled scissors and cut between them.

"Time of birth?" Abby looked for the clock. There was not even a clock in the room. Her bloody gloves covered her watch.

"Four ten p.m." Marc said, looking at his watch. Abby was afraid someone would demand that Abu Dalu stop for prayers.

Abby took the baby in the polo shirt and put her on the counter. She used the shirt to wipe away the mucus from the baby's face. The baby, a girl, had not moved and was as limp as the polo shirt and still the deep purple blue of a fetus. She had some, but not a lot, of vernix, the white cheesy substance that makes the baby so slippery and moisturizes the baby's skin. That meant she was about five weeks early.

Abby pulled off her gloves and opened the juice box straw. She quickly sucked out the mucus in the baby's nose, and spit out the pittance clogging it. The baby recoiled a bit. Abby covered her index finger with an end of the shirt and swept her finger through the baby's mouth. Forget an Ambu bag and oxygen; there wasn't even a bulb syringe in this place.

Fifteen seconds, some stimulation, a clear airway, and the baby wasn't breathing. It was time for the "first puff." Just inflating the lungs a little stimulates many babies to start breathing on their own.

She put her mouth over the babe's mouth and nose and gave a quick small puff. The baby coughed and took in a deep breath. When she exhaled, she cried. Not much of a cry, but a cry.

Abby continued to stimulate the baby with vigorous drying, and the baby wailed louder with each breath. Each cry made her pinker and pinker. As she wailed, she began to move around.

Abby pinched the cord lightly and felt a nice strong pulse in it.

"Heart rate one forty and strong." She glanced toward the men.

Marc, Ari, and Abu Dalu all had tears running down their faces.

Abby wrapped the baby up and handed her to Marc. "Keep her near your heart so she can hear it. I have to help close the mom."

"A girl, little but tough," Abby said.

Abu Dalu wiped his eyes with his shirtsleeve.

"Let's hope we can save the mother. It was an abruption, so it was fairly easy to get the entire placenta out." Indeed there was a pink pulpy mass on the floor. He felt inside the uterus with his gloved fingers, and when he thought he'd gotten it all, he spoke to Abby.

"Chromic suture, please."

Abby gelled the hemostat and handed it, handle first, into the palm of his right hand. Then she opened the black suture package, and he clamped onto the curved needle, pulling out the suture. Abby dropped the empty pack on the floor

She gelled her bare hands again and picked up the scissors.

He rapidly put in interrupted sutures through the uterus. Abby snipped them without talking. Then he closed the fascia with the few remaining inches of dissolving suture. Again, each worked quickly and silently.

"What I wouldn't give for something to make the uterus contract," Abu Dalu said.

"How about a little help from Mother Nature?" Abby asked.

Abby instructed Marc to put the wailing baby to the mother's breast. Luckily the baby latched on. A nursing baby stimulates the uterus to contract down, clamping off its own unwanted bleeding.

Abu Dalu closed the skin rapidly. Abby cut sutures, and when all was done, squirted gel on top of it for good measure.

"If she doesn't die of shock, she'll die of sepsis. You know that." Abu Dalu said, taking off his gloves inside out by habit.

"Not if I can help it. Ari, get the car. We're taking her across to an Israeli hospital."

Abby turned to the pile of rags that had been the mother's pants. She ripped them into strips and put them in her bag. She went to the bottle the anesthesia person had used and doused a rag or two and put them in her pocket. The last thing this woman needed to do was wake up during the trip.

Within moments the mother, now loosely covered only by the remains of her long tunic, and still sedated, was put in the backseat. Abby knelt on the floor, beside the mother. She kept the baby to the mother's breast as much as possible.

Somehow, the husband crammed into the back seat. Abby signed that he should pick up his wife's feet, so he held them in the air. The flood of blood had decreased to an ooze between her legs. Abby put some of the plain fabric between her legs. This was progress.

Ari drove like devils were chasing them, and at the checkpoint, Abby yelled to the guard, "I'm a doctor and I have a dying woman and a newborn baby in here."

The Israeli guard spoke English and could see the gravity of the situation. He wanted to let them through, but could not.

"Get me your superior," Abby demanded.

He too nixed bringing three Palestinians across the checkpoint.

Reluctantly, they turned around, Abigail holding back a flood of furious tears.

Every time the woman moaned, Abby took a wad of chloroformed fabric and put it over her mouth and nose for a breath or two, and the moaning stopped. The baby would suck a little, and then drift off. Abby thumped her on the foot, she would start to cry, then soothe herself with another few sucks at the mother's breast. The baby had good lungs. The baby and mother helped each other, though neither knew it.

Everyone was quiet on the way back to the hospital.

T.J. showed up with tape running just before they pulled into the courtyard for Al Shifa. Abigail saw Abu Dalu was waiting for them with the dirty gurney. *He knew we'd be back.* The men put the woman on it while Abby held the baby, swaddled in Marc's shirt.

Since it was still daylight, the professional videographer had no need for lights. Abby was so wrapped up in what was going on, she didn't notice him doing his work. That he could blend into chaos was a testament to his skill.

Suddenly, there was another gush of blood from between the mother's legs, and her head rolled to one side. The video guy got a tight shot of the mother's face going from a sickly pale yellow to all but white as she lay dying.

Abu Dalu checked her pulse and shook his head. "Forty and weak."

Abby put the baby back to the mother's breast, hoping against reason that each would benefit. The baby would get valuable colostrum full of antibodies, which she would need to ward off the germs of the area. Perhaps the mother's bleeding would stop if the baby nursed enough.

In a few minutes, in the chaotic courtyard of the hospital, Abu Dalu pronounced the mother dead. The father mumbled something about Allah's will, and Abigail took the baby and held her close, weeping for her and for her mother.

Abby knew the baby needed some glucose, so she fished a juice box out of her bag and used the little straw to dribble it into the baby's sucking mouth. When she had given her about a half ounce, she stopped and burped the baby. She was unaware of the video guy doing his thing. She was focused on the baby.

Abby didn't know she had blood on her face and didn't care that she was soaked through with sweat, blood, and amniotic fluid. She was hungry and shaky from the adrenaline rush that always set in after a four-alarm emergency.

Smart in the ways of journalism, T.J. knew to interview Abby when her adrenaline was pumping. She wouldn't stop to think, she'd just react. Besides, with all that blood, she was a good visual, as was the baby wrapped in the polo shirt.

"So what was your impression of medical conditions in Gaza City?"

"They were abominable, atrocious, medieval. In the twenty-first century, in a first world country like Israel, it is a crime against humanity not to have soap. The doctor there knew what to do, he was U.S. trained, but had virtually nothing to work with. It's no wonder that mother died. It's a miracle the baby lived and she's not out of danger yet."

"So are humanitarian supplies getting through?"

"I saw nothing at Al Shifa. Nothing. They didn't even have power to turn on the lights. No IVs, no antibiotics, no oxygen, not even a bulb syringe. Not even simple operating tools or a way to sterilize them."

"Do you think you should have helped the surgeon deliver a baby in those circumstances?"

She recoiled. The baby squalled, so Abby stroked the baby's cheek with her manicured little finger. The baby began sucking it. The photog got a tight shot of that. *This is the money shot.*

"Would you jump into a river to save a drowning baby if you knew how to swim?" Abby asked, horrified.

"Do you have a message for the Israeli people?"

"I can't tell them what to do. It is their country. This part of the world should be a religious Switzerland. Religious wars are so medieval. Let's leave them behind. *Salam* and *Shalom* both mean *peace*. The words are so similar. Arabs and Jews are cousins. And it is time for this family feud to end. Right here. Right now. With this baby."

Then Abby burst into sobs and buried herself and the baby in Marc's shoulder.

T.J. could see his Emmy. It would fit nicely on the credenza behind his desk.

Poppy was doing her weekly pedicure. She was soaking her feet in a footbath and flipped on the news to see what her "babe" T.J. was up to.

Like many women in her demographic, she followed his reports keenly. She stood up and screamed at the television when she saw Abby, bloodied, proud, and then collapsing in tears in the footage.

Poppy called Mikey, who played dumb, and Mikey called Bob Wicker. Bob Wicker called the Senate Majority Leader, his next-door neighbor, who had missed the whole thing. Wicker called his office, and the night crew said they were taping all the feeds.

Never mind. It would run regularly for the next day. Schwartz thought seriously of expelling Abby from the Senate. Strangling her with his bare hands was probably an overreaction.

Meanwhile, Abby went back to the King David. She did more than unzip, she unplugged from the world. The amniotic fluid and blood had dried on her clothes and underwear, so she threw them in the trash. She shivered at the thought of another woman's vital fluids having soaked, forever, into her passport. Noor was dead, but Abby would carry her DNA around for years. She showered for a long, long time.

Then she ate everything in the mini-bar and drank everything that was nonalcoholic. She pulled the blackout curtains to shield her from the morning's light. Then she curled up in the fetal position and wept herself to sleep.

The next thing she remembered was her sister's voice. It was as clear as day.

Abby, go home. Your job's not finished.

Either she was going insane or her sister was right.

She packed her bags and made her flight.

When she arrived home at the apartment some twenty-five hours later, Regina was there. She'd seen Abby on television and knew she would need a soft place to fall. Regina would not let her come home to an empty house, not with what she'd been through.

"You did real good, Sweet Pea. Real good." Regina folded her in her arms. "And the television says that baby's going to make it."

"I am so grateful."

"You, girl, get a root beer float, then you take a shower and go to bed."

"Reege. I think Priscilla spoke to me when I was in Jerusalem."

"So?"

"She's dead, Regina."

"And you don't think that angels can talk?"

CHAPTER TWENTY-SIX

FALLOUT

Abigail called Poppy before she went to bed. Abby'd been off the grid for forty-eight hours. As usual, Poppy skipped saying "hello."

"There I was doing my pedicure, and who shows up on my television screen but you," Poppy said. "Why didn't you tell me what you were going to do?"

"I planned to do some sightseeing, and this just happened."

"T.J. doesn't 'just' happen," Poppy said. "If he did, I'd want him to 'just happen' to me."

"Well, all that happened between us was professional."

"Good, then you can introduce him to me." *This was going better than Abigail had hoped.*

"Poppy, do I have a press person?" Abigail asked.

"Pris did, but he wandered off as there was nothing to do. I've handled the press in the meantime. In the last few days, it's been a full-time job. Everyone and his dog are looking for you."

"So what did you tell them?"

"You're in transit and would get back to them ASAP. The list starts with Naomi, the President, and the Majority Leader, in that order, and goes through every press outlet in the free world. You are home, aren't you?

"No comment. Would Bob Wicker be available, at least short term, to do the press job? Then I promise to keep my mouth shut and behave."

"I think he would. And you'll behave when pigs fly."

"Okay, I'll call him. Can you be at my place at eight tomorrow morning?"

Abby got hold of Mikey and Bob to come the next morning.

Regina ordered up a good spread of breakfast nibbles for the dining room and kept an endless amount of coffee flowing. She wanted to help her baby girl through this time, and food was the best helper she knew in crisis. Regina folded up an antique Chinese screen, revealing a state of the art television and DVD player.

Abby was ready and dressed at seven thirty. Jet lag could be a good thing. She'd been up since five that morning.

Mikey arrived first and Abby gave him a big hug.

"I'll try to keep you out of this," Abby said.

"Why? It was my idea, dear girl. Let an old man have some fun, will you?" Mikey said.

Wicker brought a CD sampler of the coverage. They all four watched intently as they ate pastries and drank coffee with real cream. Regina didn't allow creamer in the house. She called it "paint."

"So, what does 'Doris from Dubuque' think?" Bob asked Abby.

"Doris is pretty darn proud of that girl," Abigail replied.

"Mikey? What are the politicos thinking?"

"They are Irish green with envy. They wish they'd delivered that baby themselves. No one could buy coverage this good in a midterm election year."

"And Poppy, what does the Washington leadership think?" Bob asked.

"The Administration is mightily ticked. Middle East peace is the Holy Grail of political legacies. They hate anything they see as grandstanding."

Wicker turned to Abby. "What do you think you should do now?"

"Go back to work and keep my mouth shut?" Abby floated her hopes.

"Not a possibility. First, you will have to return the President's phone call. He'll likely call you in for a dressing down."

"No good deed goes unpunished," Abigail opined.

"You are the hottest get in the country right now," Bob said.

"What's a 'get'?"

"You do need a media person. A 'get' is someone to be interviewed."

"Naomi's called me twice. Personally," Poppy said. Abby felt her throat go dry. She took a long swig from her bottle of water.

"Poppy, what about the Majority Leader?" Abby asked.

"He called and said, and I quote, 'I am looking into whether flogging is ever permissible for senators.'"

"So, Bob, what do I do?"

"One. Call the President and take your medicine. Ditto with Schwartz. Get both out of the way, hopefully today. Two. Do the major news shows as quickly as possible."

"Okay, that sounds fine," Abby said.

"But you know the President will surely try to make her a Middle East peace player," Mikey opined. "She's touched the problem, so she'll have to own it."

"Not interested. If they wanted peace, they'd already have it," Abigail said.

"You may want to rethink that," Wicker said. "You might save a lot more babies working from the inside of the problem. And you are on the Foreign Relations Committee."

"Can I just say I hate this friggin' job?" Abigail said.

"Don't blame us," Mikey said. "This was your sister's idea. She must have had some clue that you'd put your foot in things in a good way. You are doing well; you do know that, don't you?"

"Couldn't prove it by me," Abigail replied.

"You'll skip *Naomi*, too many chances to put your foot in your mouth," Bob said. "But you'll call her personally and thank her."

"Okay," Abby said. She did not want to be on *Naomi*.

"What about the Abby/T.J. connection?" Poppy asked.

Abby said nothing. Neither did Mikey. They looked like guilty children.

"What did you two do?" Poppy said.

"I introduced Abby to T.J. They took it from there," Mikey confessed.

"Why didn't you tell me?" Wicker jumped up and started pacing the room.

"Don't ask, don't tell?" Abby offered lamely.

Wicker stopped pacing and thought for a moment.

"Did you sleep with him?" Wicker demanded.

"Not no, but hell no," Abigail retorted.

"I would have," Poppy said.

Mikey filled them in on how he put them in touch.

"This is a media first. We just tell the truth," Wicker said. "Abigail wanted to see the Middle East, so Mikey introduced them. T.J. hooked her up with a security guy and a fixer. He told her he was going to be in the country at the same time. He showed up when the security guy notified him of the story," Bob said.

"I agreed to give him an interview if I had any interesting perspectives. No one could have anticipated Noor," Abigail said.

"Poppy, Mikey, you go on to the office. Wicker and I will work from here. I want to return the President's call. Bob, stay with me?" Abigail said.

"Groveling works," Bob said.

Abby called the White House and identified herself. She was put through to the President's secretary.

"Good morning. This is Senator Adams. I believe the President has been looking for me? I've just gotten back into the country," Abigail said as pleasantly as possible.

While on hold, Bob and Abigail talked about his fees and the duration of his services. Abby gulped at the price, but knew he would guide her through.

"Well, well, Abigail Adams, roving Senator," the President said with something of a smile in his voice. "I've been expecting to hear from you. You did clear immigration at, let's see, four-forty-three yesterday."

"Good morning, Mr. President. Yes I did, but I've had my phone off. Forgive me if I have breached protocol," Abigail said politely. The groveling had started. She wondered how long she'd have to do it.

"Are you available for lunch today?"

"Of course, sir."

"Good. Shall we say eleven thirty?"

"I look forward to it."

"I'm sure you do." He chuckled and hung up.

Next she called the Senate Majority Leader.

"Good morning," Abby said neutrally. "I understand you are looking to flog me?"

"Adams, I would strangle you barehanded if I thought I could get away with it."

"I assume the President gets first crack at me, so can we schedule the flogging for, say, around two thirty?" Abigail asked.

"My office. Two thirty." He hung up on her.

At least Naomi was polite when she called.

"I am disappointed, of course. I think a citizen Senator is a breath of fresh air," Naomi said.

"Thank you. What a lovely thing to say."

"Let's do keep in touch," Naomi said, giving her a semi-private number.

"That went well," Wicker said. 'Now you get to work, learning everything you can, recent events and players in the whole Gaza thing, while I set up your interviews. I want you out of the news cycle in a day. If you're lucky, something big will knock you off the front burner.

"My only hope is a plane crash? I think I'll take the flogging and be done with it."

CHAPTER TWENTY-SEVEN

THE REAMING

Bob dropped her off at the Northwest White House gate. The day was mild in the blush of spring.

She showed her identification, was scanned, wanded, her bag searched, and then she was escorted through the West Wing complex into the area outside the Oval Office. *Talk about being called to the principal's office.*

Laura Rowe told her that men are suckers for pink, so she wore a pink suit. And she wore her highest black patent heels. It's hard to intimidate a woman you look in the eye. Of course, her feet already hurt, but power can be painful.

As she waited, she noticed the hive-like activity of this place. She was glad she didn't work here. *It's a wonder the Fire Marshal didn't shut it down.*

"You may go in now." The President's secretary motioned to her.

Abigail stood up and waited while a Marine Sentry opened the door for her. Was it her imagination, or had he given her a thumbs up?

"Be with you in a sec. Have a seat or look around." Walter Harrington waved her toward the couches. He was in his shirtsleeves, his tie loosened. He was tapping away on his own computer. *Times had truly changed.*

In those few moments, Abby took in the room. She was awestruck, or perhaps power-struck was a better word. The desk was the famous "Resolute" desk, made from an English ship in Victorian times. From it, one man could unleash some terrible swift swords, or with more effort, bring forth the beauty of the lilies.

The art too was magnificent. Gilbert Stuart made a cottage industry of painting George Washington. He'd done over a hundred Washington portraits, and they'd become a national cliché in two hundred-plus years. Artistically, though, Stuart was a portraitist for all time. His subjects always fixed you in their gaze, no matter where you stood. All looked as if they were alive, just waiting to speak. She looked closely. There was wig powder on Washington's shoulder; what a masterful touch.

There was a Childe Hassam on one wall, a riot of American flags on parade. Flanking the fireplace were Houdon busts of Jefferson and Franklin. She wondered if some of Harrington's predecessors even knew who Houdon was. *Men like that did not deserve the presidency.*

"Senator Adams?" The President broke her reverie. He had greyed noticeably, even in the few months since she had last first met him.

"I'm sorry. I was absorbing the art."

"Welcome to my Golden Cell," he said, shaking her hand.

"Interesting perspective, Mr. President." Abigail again felt herself blush. His hands were so warm. "Please call me Abigail."

"I have a few other names for you today. Have a seat."

Abby perched on the front of one couch, ankles crossed, back completely straight. No relaxation for her. Harrington sat across from her, one arm thrown over the back of the sofa.

"Abigail, what you did was noble, not only about the baby, but in your desire to see the real situation. You spoke the truth and spoke it from the heart. Mikey Molloy called and confessed his aiding and abetting."

Abigail waited for the reaming out. *He can't eat you.*

"I assume you've heard of Tom Friedlander," Harrington said.

"I've read his work."

"All of it?"

"Yes, I think so."

"I'm impressed."

"Don't be," Abby said. "I'm a reader. I read like most people breathe. It's my addiction."

"Then you know this area is incredibly complex."

"I agree. The Middle East is politically, religiously, and morally the most complex real estate per square foot on the globe."

Harrington couldn't help himself, he laughed out loud.

"Well put. May I use the line?'

"Help yourself."

"Abigail, I and my Secretary of State must be the only people to enunciate U.S. foreign policy. Whenever anyone else in government offers an opinion abroad, it can be confusing to adversaries and allies alike."

"I've learned that recently. The hard way. I won't make that mistake again. I sincerely apologize. How can I make things right?" Abby inquired.

Harrington was momentarily speechless. She'd taken all the wind out of his sails. Abject apology rendered him mute.

"Your apology is accepted. I've asked the Secretary of State to join us for lunch."

"I'm not only flattered, I'm hungry."

"Tell me something, Abigail. Are all Texas women as plainspoken as you and your sister?"

"Well, Regina sure is. She taught us that it's important to think straight, to talk straight, and to shoot straight. In this situation, I think I should have kept my mouth shut."

"Shall we go into the private dining room?" the President asked. He rolled down his sleeves, slid up the knot on his tie, and put on his suit coat.

"You don't have to get gussied up on my account," Abigail said.

"I'm not. My photographer will be there. I swear the only place I get any privacy is in the bathroom. And there, I'm not so sure."

Marilyn Chernosky was already there, seated so Abby would have to look into the bright light of the window. She stood when the President entered.

"Marilyn, you don't have to do the jack-in-the-box thing all the time," Harrington said. Marilyn sat back down. Abby noticed she had on a navy sheath with her iconic three monkeys pin: hear no evil, see no evil, and speak no evil.

Rail thin and with abundant silver hair in a chignon, she had started as an academic in International Affairs at Georgetown, and she was a superb Secretary of State, according to Pris. Anyone who had overcome her adversities had the right stuff to be Secretary of State.

She was born in China to American missionaries just after Pearl Harbor. Her family fled to the safety of the British Fort Singapore early in January 1942. It was thought to be impregnable.

The Japanese took the entire island nation in seven days and interned them for the duration of the war. There, her father died of malaria, her mother died of dengue, and her sister of beriberi. It took months after the war to get her to her family in the States, and months more to overcome her own malnutrition. If she'd lost IQ points, then she'd gone from prodigy to mere genius level.

Recipient of scholarship after scholarship, Marilyn got a PhD in International Affairs from Stanford. She spoke seven languages, including Russian and Mandarin. She was the first female to be a full professor in International Affairs at Georgetown. She and her husband, a law professor, never had children so they traveled the world. He now had Alzheimer's, according to Poppy, but she never spoke of it. She merely added three shifts of male nurses to the household and kept on with her life. She cranked out an occasional best seller to finance her husband's care.

Marilyn's devotion to diplomacy was simple. People who are talking aren't shooting. She'd seen enough of the horrors of war as a small child.

She kept in constant contact with friends and adversaries alike. Like every recent Secretary of State, she hoped to solve the "Palestinian issue."

"Ah, Senator Adams. So very nice to meet you." She held out her very slim hand.

"Madame Secretary. I am truly honored. I understand you live down the street from Mikey Molloy."

"I have for nearly forty years. They don't come any better. Though his middle name should be 'Mischief,'" She laughed heartily. Abby thought a stiff breeze would blow her over.

A Navy steward came in with their plates, followed by the White House photographer. He quietly took a round of shots and disappeared before anything of substance had been said. *Gee, I'd hate to have a photographer following me around all day.*

"It's Monday, so I always have mac and cheese," the President explained, rubbing his hands together. "Childhood tradition. However, the White House Chef refuses flat out to make the kind in the blue box."

"I'd pull rank, sir," Abby said.

"I tried. He told me my wife had forbidden it. Even I have a boss."

This had hunks of lobster in it and was set off nicely by a salad. For dessert, lemon sorbet topped lemon squares. Abby noticed that the Secretary of State just picked at her food and left the dessert untouched. *Ah, guilt anorexia. Deprived of food for so long, she felt badly about eating at all. A decent meal would probably make her gut miserable.*

"Abby, you were right about the Middle East," Marilyn said. "And, I assume, you now know why you were also wrong about it."

"Yes, ma'am, I do."

"So, my question for you is this. How can we use this high-profile event to advance the cause of peace in the Middle East?"

"May I speak frankly?" Both nodded. "I don't think either side wants peace."

"We figured that out a while ago. But we have to keep trying," Marilyn said.

"Then I suggest you skip the leaders. Concentrate on those who haven't yet learned to hate. You know there are camps for teen leaders from both sides. I suggest ramping up things like that. Let's get more kids here for exchange students. Put them in prosperous Arab-American homes. Give them a better dream than terrorism."

"Would we end up recruiting our own terrorists?" the President asked.

"Smart kids, by definition, think for themselves. And the peer group would be Arab-Americans. We have to take a leap sometime."

"I do know the head of the Institute of International Education," Marilyn said. "Perhaps they could do something below the radar, of course."

The President nodded. "None of our fingerprints or the Palestinians would balk. Abigail, what about humanitarian aid?"

"We are hard-line allies of the Israelis, but we can also be hard-line humanitarians. Put U.S. hospital ships off the coast and tell the Israelis they are staying until the Israelis relent. Let Palestinian hospitals partner up with the ships. Funnel supplies that way. Treat them as colleagues, not as inferiors. Dr. Abu Dalu was an incredible surgeon, though he was U.S. trained.

"And please, take care of the kids. Remember the protein- and vitamin-enriched chocolates we gave out after World War II? The kids ended up loving us because of them. Oh my, look at the time. I've rambled on far too long."

"No, we like the freshness of the ideas," Harrington said. "Just don't *you* go telling the world about them."

"The press wants to talk to me. I have told Naomi no, but Bob Wicker, my press guy, thinks I have to do some. What are your preferences, Mr. President?"

"Talk. But emphasize private trip turned public, you don't speak for the Administration, et cetera." The President reverted to the half-speak of the busy Washingtonian.

"Will do."

"We talked, frank and open, always interested in fresh perspectives…"

"Will do."

"Oh, and Abby?" he said. "I'm really proud of you. You went out on a limb for that little girl and mother."

"Thank you." Abby gulped back tears. "Dr. Abu Dalu was the hero, though. You heard he trained at Charity in New Orleans and never left all through Katrina. When he had no place to practice, he went back home to help."

"Nevertheless, things turned out well," Marilyn put in. "Good stories always help peace."

The President stood. Both women did also.

"You two sit, have a cup of coffee," the President said, waving his hand in a vague circle. "Talk about shoes or purses or something."

"Actually, I am due at Senator Schwartz's office for a flogging at two-thirty."

The President put his hand on Abby's shoulder.

"I'll deal with Schwartz."

"I'll owe you. Big time," Abby replied, her voice full of relief.

And then he was gone.

"Oh, how I wish we could solve this problem," Marilyn said.

"Do you know how hard it is to change yourself, even when you want to?" Abby asked.

"Yes. I've been trying to give up cigarettes for thirty years."

"If it's hard to change yourself, it's impossible to change others."

"I think I'm too old for this job," Marilyn said.

"No you aren't. You just want peace, and since Cain slew Abel, we haven't had it."

"Yes, but the stakes get higher every year."

CHAPTER TWENTY-EIGHT

GOING NATIONAL

She went to Bob Wicker's office, weak-kneed with relief.

"You were so right," she told Bob. "Abject groveling does work."

"Here is your schedule for the morning shows," Bob said. "As well, T.J. wants a follow-up. I've arranged for Andre to do hair and makeup. Bring at least two different jackets with a black skirt."

"Why?"

"Some of the stuff airs in the morning. T.J. airs at night. The morning airings should have a different feel than the evening one."

Spared the wrath of the Senate Majority Leader, she felt up to anything. She and Bob went into the studio and did mock interviews for an hour or so, and then she headed home for the day. Her body thought it was midnight. She packed her outfits for the following day, checked in with Poppy, waved at Regina, and was asleep by seven.

The car service picked her up at four in the morning, which was fine with a still-jet-lagged Abby. She came downstairs showered, with clean, wet hair up in a banana clip. She wore sweats and clogs and carried her wardrobe choices. She clamped her hands onto the coffee her driver brought and thanked him profusely. As he drove to Wicker Washington, she held her face over the steaming cup to help her awaken. She inhaled its wonderful aroma, as she waited for it to cool. Then she drained it.

Bob had arranged to use his studio as the remote site. That way, traffic wouldn't be a problem. Each interview would take place in front of a Chroma Key green screen.

"How does that work?" Abby asked as they headed into the studio. Everyone was already there in the control room, including the floor director. Abby could mentally see the money meter spinning.

"See that wall over here?" He pointed to a lime green wall. "Every camera is tuned to filter out one wavelength. Most don't see this color, called a Chroma Key. So if you were to wear all that shade of green, all the camera would transmit would be your head and hands."

"Weird."

"Yes, but useful. All those times you see a weatherman with a map? He's standing in front of a lime green wall and looking at the map on a monitor. The electronics people add in the monitor feed."

"So what do I do?"

"Just answer questions. You did bring your IFB, didn't you?

"It's always in the makeup bag."

"Good girl. We are going to seat you in an armchair like you might have in your office. The background is various still shots of your office interior. That way, each show gets a slightly different picture of your office."

"How did you get the pictures of my office?"

"During your Presidential reaming, we were taking photos at the office."

Abby laughed.

"And how do the images merge?" Abby asked.

"Electronic magic."

"So what do I do?"

"Just sit up straight, and talk straight into the camera. Morning shows can be a bitch. The 'gets' are sleepy. So drink more coffee. Here, you can try it out. Tom, cue the backdrops," Wicker said.

She sat in the chair in front of the green screen and looked on the monitor. Sure enough, there she was sitting in her own office.

"Wow, I do need hair and makeup," Abby said.

Abby stumbled into the dressing room, draining her second large cup of coffee. Andre was set up, a bowl of iced, salted water on the ledge.

"Morning gigs are a bitch," he said. "Lots of ice water, darling. Sorry." He filled her eyes with artificial tears and put the icy towels on her face. She found the experience meditative.

"Let's go with something soft with your hair and makeup."

"Why soft?"

"You made a no-no, so soft looks make people root for you. If you needed to kick ass, we'd do hard hair and makeup."

Promptly at six forty-five, she was seated "in her office."

By 8:00 a.m. she was on her way to the real office, having done five "live" interviews "from her Senate Office."

In each interview, she answered questions simply and to the point, ticking things off her mental script: wanted to see behind the scenes, Noor's situation landed in her lap, moral imperative to act, remarks made after great stress, apologized for making foreign policy remarks abroad. That's clearly the job of the President and Secretary of State. "Both were gracious about my indiscretion."

One interviewer asked if she got reamed out at the White House. "I expected to be, I should have been, but the President was very gracious."

The only surprise was that ABC revealed that the father was going to name the baby Abigail.

"I am genuinely touched," Abby said, tears welling up, her hand going to her chest. "This is a first for me."

"Do you plan on going back to see her?"

"Maybe, for her first birthday party, who knows? But I'll clear it with the State Department first." Abby chuckled.

CHAPTER TWENTY-NINE

FIELD TRIPS

Abigail did not put her feet in any more cow patties. She enjoyed helping constituents battle the bureaucracy they paid to serve, not stymie, them. It was almost as much fun as making the nursing supervisor treat street people with respect.

Abby had a standing dinner with Duke every two weeks, and he was doing splendidly, planning on being a summer intern at one of the classier New York law firms. He was a desirable recruit. If there was a woman in his life, he didn't mention her.

She had dinner and tutoring with Mikey every week. He was a living history project.

Abigail finally had time to do normal things, like go to the grocery store, only to come home in disgust. She gave up counting when she got to twelve different kinds of milk. She ended up having her main meal at lunch, at the House Dining Room, often having a bowl of cereal for dinner, and getting most things at Tran's.

Mr. Tran still called her "Missy" and kept wondering why she hadn't found a man.

"I'm too picky." *No one had asked.*

"I'll keep my eye open for you," he said.

"Thanks," Abby said. *Fat chance. All the men she met were pompous, married, or gay. Some were all three.*

She read government and history every night, but beach lit on the weekend. Poppy had regrouped from her grumpy phase, and was pleasant a good ninety percent of the time.

One late spring Saturday afternoon, Kim brought Abby the gown she had ordered several months ago.

"I apologize for the delay," Kim said demurely. "There was a problem with the mill in Italy. I can adjust the price downward, if you like." She hoped Abigail still wanted the dress; otherwise, she was really out a lot of time and money.

"Oh, no, Kim, I'm sure it will be fine," Abby said. In fact, she'd forgotten about the dress, she'd been so busy.

Abigail opened the box and folded back the shroud of tissue.

The navy silk crepe dusted with the tiniest of silver sparkles was exquisite.

"Oh, Kim, this is beyond my wildest dreams," she said, extracting it from the box and holding it up.

"Please, never hang this dress; it is cut on the bias. Only fold in archival tissue," Kim said, giving her a package of it.

"Okay, may I try it on?" Abby asked.

"Of course. I have made you a special spandex undergarment for it, but you may try it with just your panties if you like."

Abby took it into Pris's dressing room and put it on. She called to Kim, who followed her.

Abby was standing up on tippy-toe as if she were wearing high heels. She was beaming as she looked at herself in the three-way mirror. The front soft cowl had a lovely drape. The back cowl was daring, dipping to just below her waist. The silver sparkles dusted the garment perfectly.

"I feel like Cinderella, just waiting for a ball," Abigail said with pure pleasure.

"Well, Senator Cinderella, I suggest silver shoes and a silver bag. And please, remember about the tissue."

As she wrote the check to Kim, she thought she saw a flicker, something Kim wanted to say. But she didn't, and Abigail let it slide.

"Thank you again for your business. I am always available to you."

The cherry blossoms were late that year, but were inordinately beautiful. Abby adored being a tourist in her own city. She figured out the Metro system, but preferred a car service. She read her Kindle while the car inched through traffic. She only drove on weekends out of the city.

At least one afternoon a week, she took a field trip. During the week, it was either to something near the Capitol or somewhere she oversaw in some capacity. She sat on the Foreign Relations Committee, the Judiciary Committee and of course, the Armed Services Committee. The weekends were devoted to more-distant tourist attractions.

She went to the Pentagon, but of course Secretary O'Neal was far, far too busy to meet with her, so he pawned her off onto the Chairman of the Joint Chiefs, General Cristoforo Salazar.

"Cristo Salazar, Senator," his handshake was firm. He had an air of casual authority, something Abigail found reassuring. He was trim and looked to be in excellent shape. His dark hair was peppered a bit with gray, and his black-brown eyes all but crackled with intelligence. He too wore a wedding ring. *Darn.*

"Abigail Adams, General. Thank you for giving me the tour."

"Do you want the quarter tour, or the nickel one?"

"Nickel. I'm sure you have real work to do."

He laughed.

"Walk or ride?"

"For the nickel tour, walk, please. I like to move."

And move they did.

"There are over seventeen miles of corridors in the Pentagon, but the design is so good, you can walk between the two most distant points in under eight minutes. Impressive, since you can put the entire Capitol along any one of the sides."

"I am impressed."

"If only the people were as efficient as the buildings," he said with a good-natured grin. "At least the days of triplicate carbon paper are over."

The walked and chatted, and she liked the man.

"So tell me, how did you end up here?" Abigail asked.

"Well, my parents are from Mexico. They crossed the border at Nogales to have me. They settled in, started a restaurant, and raised me, eventually becoming citizens. I was both incorrigible and scared to death of my mom's wrath. When I graduated from high school, there were no jobs in Nogales, so I joined the Army.

"Once in it, someone told me I'd make more money if I went to OCS. I didn't know what that was, but I applied. The rest is history."

"And you just happened to pick up a PhD in Middle Eastern Studies and learn most of the Middle Eastern Languages along the way?" Abby asked.

"Hey, the Army was paying, so I was learning." They came up to a bank of vending machines.

"Buy you a root beer?" he asked.

"Sure. A root beer float in our house is the reward for doing something well."

"At my house, it's homemade tortillas. My mom taught my Anglo wife to make them. But they aren't very good. Don't tell her, okay?"

"Your secrets are safe with me," Abby said.

They continued on their walk, and Abby asked about 9/11.

"They went in over there," he said, pointing to an area virtually indistinguishable from the rest of the building. "Straight into my office."

"How horrible. Where were you that day?" Abigail gasped in shock.

"I should have been here. My wife was visiting her mother, so I had to take the youngest, a freshman in high school, to school. He slipped and fell down the stairs, and broke his leg. I took him to the hospital. I've done four combat tours, only to escape death at a desk job because my kid broke his leg. I lost all my closest staff members."

"And I thought I had an awful loss with my sister," Abby said.

"Grief does with you what it will," Cristo said.

"Wise words."

They were back where they started, and it was time for Abby to go.

"Cristo, please, if you ever need me, call me?" Abby said, handing him her card. "I've enjoyed meeting you so very much."

They traded cards.

One Sunday in May, she read that the *U.S. Hospital Hope* would remain off the coast of Israel and provide medical support to any who needed it. By June, it was gone, as the Israelis allowed full supplies into the disputed territories. Abby felt a small glimmer of pride. *A whisper in the right ear could be important.*

She loved D.C., and went everywhere. Each was her favorite. The Library of Congress was her idea of Heaven. Originally created in 1802 as a research arm for Congress, the British burned it in the War of 1812. Jefferson, the nation's biggest bibliophile, donated all six thousand of his personal books to form the core collection.

The various museums of the Smithsonian were also a delight. So good to have so much stuff in the "nation's attic."

And the art enchanted her, from huge museums such as the National Gallery to small ones such as the Phillips Collection.

In June, she read that the IIE, a group that sponsors foreign exchange students, among its many programs, would actively recruit academically superior Palestinian kids to experience a year in an Arab-American family. *Another whisper, another chance at peace?*

Later that month, when the Supreme Court was not in session, she asked the Marshal of the Court for a tour, and he was happy to oblige one day during her lunch break.

"So what goes on over here at lunchtime when the Justices are here?" Abby asked.

"Well, the gentlemen play basketball, and the ladies have an exercise class. Justice O'Meara told us if any pictures of her in exercise gear appeared in the press, she would 'violate our civil rights in ways we couldn't imagine.'"

"My kind of woman."

In the room where oral arguments are heard, Abby asked the Marshal, "Have you ever sat in one of the chairs?"

"No. I'm too chicken."

"I think I am too."

Their pleasant visit over, they exchanged cards. Abby was enjoying getting to know the people who actually ran the government, not just the elected officials. She put all their cards in her sister's old-fashioned Rolodex.

On the weekends, she'd go further afield, out to Mr. Vernon or to some of the Civil War battlefields. The Senate was still technically in session, but a third of the members were home campaigning, so Abigail made sure she never missed a floor vote. If an employee in the private sector spent that kind of time schmoozing to keep his job, he'd be out of one.

One summer day, Abby took a tour of the Arlington National Cemetery with a group of tourists.

"President Lincoln needed more burial space for Union soldiers, so he told his quartermaster to find him an appropriate place," the tour guide said.

"How about Bobby Lee's place? the man replied. He's in charge of the Confederate Army. We'll plant the bodies in his front yard." Indeed, the Custis-Lee Mansion was just across the river into Virginia.

"That will do," Lincoln said.

"As fate would have it, the quartermaster's son was buried there after he was killed in the War Between the States," the guide continued.

She looked around at the tourists. They were all ages, all colors, too many of them were overweight, but many had brought either infants or their elderly relatives. She wondered how many had relatives here at Arlington. In American history, a hundred and fifty years is a long time. In the rest of the world, it is just yesterday.

We are such an adolescent country.

CHAPTER THIRTY

FOURTH OF JULY

Senator Adams was one of seventy-five people invited to the White House for the Fourth of July Fireworks Party. *Talk about the best seat in the city.* If the weather permitted, the group sometimes went to the roof of the White House. The Secret Service wasn't wild about this, but Walter Harrington pointed out that it was safer there, unseen by the crowd, than on the Truman Balcony.

After nearly six years in the White House, Mrs. Harrington was organized about rotating her invitations to make sure everyone felt welcome. Rumor had it that she put everyone's name in a hatbox and pulled out however many she needed. Then those names were unavailable for the next party. That way she got around to everyone.

Abby wasn't sure she believed that, but she was thrilled to be invited to the White House for something other than a dressing down. The guest list was always a splendid mix. Lobbyists were included, but only if they ponied up, big time, to Mrs. Harrington's favorite charities. As a result, charitable donations were enormous during the Harrington years.

Mrs. Harrington had only one rule at her parties. You may talk about religion, sex, or money, but you may not talk about politics. That was a heavy burden. There was a lot of talk about sports.

Abby had long since learned that everyone in Washington prepared for parties. They read all three papers that day—*The Washington Post*, *The New York Times*, and *The Wall Street Journal*. If they knew who was attending a party, or if there was a guest of honor, they'd Google them and were able to discuss their accomplishments with them. Parties were considered a part of work, not of entertainment, and exposure, not fun, was the objective.

Self-effacing charm was one's best bet at a good party. Once a South African doctor seated next to a female Justice of the Supreme Court asked "Sandy" what she did for a living.

"I do a little judging," she replied. At that point the penny dropped, and the man prayed the earth would open up and swallow him whole. He dined out on that story for years.

The invitation said casual attire, so Abigail called Laura Rowe, and she sent over an outfit. A long, white gauzy skirt with a cotton slip, a chambray shirt festooned with patriotic embroidery, and a Concho belt. She even included white sandals and a note that said, "Paint your toenails red." Abby did.

The day was sweltering, and Abby knew it would be miserable on top of the White House. Perhaps they would have fans, and the invitation wasn't until eight, so that helped some.

She arrived on time. One was not late to the White House. She went through security and walked up the stairs to the Family Quarters. To her surprise, the party was there.

Evangeline Harrington greeted Abby at the door. "We'll go up to the roof when the fireworks start."

"I've never been here before, and to come on the Fourth of July is a double honor. Thank you for inviting me."

"Please, get a drink and mix with the group. You'll notice we just have a big hall, no living room. Sort of awkward, except for parties."

Abby got a glass of iced tea and attempted to mingle. She saw a few people she knew, one of them Cristo Salazar. She chatted with him and his wife, Susan, a lithe woman her husband's age.

Another woman stumbled, and Abby reached out and caught her.

"Thank you," the woman said, embarrassed. Her face was familiar. "I don't want to do a face plant in the White House."

"I'm Abigail Adams. And you are…" Abby extended her hand, praying she wasn't someone she'd already met. The woman shook it.

"I'm Elizabeth Gehring. You're that Senator that delivered the baby, aren't you?"

"Guilty as charged." Abby said. *Gehring's husband was the biggest philanthropist in the world.*

"I admire your passion. Do you have a business card?"

They exchanged cards.

"May I call you? Let's have lunch one day. I'd like to pick your brain."

"I'd be delighted. As a pediatrician, I'm quite interested in the work your Foundation is doing."

Abby's horizon had just expanded. She would soon be leaving the Senate, and freed from the need to work, she might be able to help a world of children. *She who need not work must yet serve.*

Within a few minutes, little Margaret Harrington, aged four, had corralled Abby into reading her and her sleepover buddies a book. Children always sought her out.

For some reason, Margaret wanted to read *Goodnight Moon*. An addicting book, Margaret and her buddies knew it by heart. Margaret was dressed in red, white, and blue pajamas, and informed Abigail that she and her friends could stay up "until after the star works."

Since all the kids knew the book, Abby deliberately messed up the wording. Margaret and girlfriends were in giggles at this obvious stupidity. They adored "correcting" her.

Finally, President Harrington came to rescue Abby.

"Okay, guys, there's ice cream on the porch." The children thundered off.

"Thanks for entertaining them," he said.

"No, they entertain me."

Abby was quite surprised when John Lafferty tapped her on the shoulder a few minutes later.

"Happy Fourth of July, Senator," John said. "I was watching you with those kids. You're great with them."

"I often prefer them to adults, to be truthful. Do you have children?"

"Twin boys. They're three. Gone, I'm afraid. My wife took them and went back to England. Probably for good. We're getting a divorce."

"My condolences." Abby said. *What kind of millionaire doesn't fight for his kids?*

"Perhaps you will have dinner with me now?" he said.

"That might be possible. You'll have to check with Poppy. I'm not allowed to run my own life," Abby replied, smiling her best fake smile. "Oh, look, everyone's going up to the roof."

Everyone trooped up the two floors to the roof. The balustrades were almost six feet tall. Eisenhower used to grill out steaks up there in the privacy provided by them. Abby made it a point to be as far away from Lafferty as possible. She wanted to take it all in, alone. A small group from the Marine Band was playing patriotic music. And a breeze had come up to soften the heat.

The view was magnificent. All the unlit buildings were inky black, but the sky had a little blue left in it. The brightly lit Washington Monument looked close enough to touch, its two red lights like eyes caught by a camera. The White House South Lawn looked like a gentle slope up from the street. If memory served her correctly, Jefferson made it look that way. In fact, it was a series of berms to allow the President his privacy. *That would be right up his alley.*

Abby could see the Capitol Dome off to the east, the Lincoln Memorial to the West. In between was a calm crowd of people, enjoying their evening, celebrating together their national link, just as families celebrate any family holiday.

Just across the Potomac was the darkness of Arlington National Cemetery, broken only by Kennedy's eternal flame. A shiver ran down her back.

The fireworks were as spectacular as any she'd ever seen. When President Harrington stole a glance at Abby, he nudged his wife, and the two of them watched as Abigail Adams stood with tears running down her face. She made no attempt to stop the flow.

I want to remember this night for the rest of my life. Thank you, Pris, for giving me this.

CHAPTER THIRTY-ONE

CLOSING THE BOOK

Regina perked along in the equatorial heat of a Houston summer. Being with her friends was a great tonic to her. Her Mission Ladies met every Wednesday, and she also had a water exercise group she looked forward to three mornings a week at the Y.

By early August, the first stats were in on the Infants First Act. The first group was now three months old, and statistics were available for them.

Infant abuse was down by half compared with children born in the same zip code the previous year. Two visually impaired children were picked up and had gotten into care. Three children were showing signs of autism and were in therapy.

Parents were showing up for the classes and making friends. Post-partum depression was down over forty percent compared to the national average. Mothers with it were treated and supported. Other parents were pitching in to help them.

The Infants First Act was creating a community for new parents, something unexpected. One mother, a gifted singer, started a children's choir at the school. Three fathers, previously unemployed, found jobs.

Abigail was delighted that it would be expanded within three years to every school in the nation.

It was Abby's turn to host the Bookworms group, and with the help of Peggy Mellon, Abby was delighted. They had invited fifteen inner-city girls to the apartment. Abby was concerned the opulence of it would put them off.

"Get over it," Peggy said. "They come to my house, and I can see them literally memorizing their 'dream' sofa or painting. Bookworms is about books, but also about poise and dreaming big."

The group was a motley one: from short to tall, skinny to fat, and all shades of skin color. Pimples afflicted a lot of the girls. The girls who needed braces didn't have them. Most dressed in shorts, tee-shirts and flip-flops, the best of their summer wardrobe.

Each shook Abigail's hand and introduced herself. Every handshake was firm; every girl looked her straight in the eye.

Abigail served a "lady lunch" in the dining room. Chicken salad, fruit salad, and pimiento cheese, along with heaps of orange rolls that disappeared quickly. For dessert, she served pecan balls, and the girls wolfed everything down with perfect manners. She noticed that the girls watched Peggy and her for cues on manners.

Then everyone adjourned to the living room, where their adolescent bodies were all askew in chairs, on the floor, or draped over a sofa. *They've been grown up as long as they could stand it.*

Today's book was *The Diary of Anne Frank*. An African American girl named Shakira was the reviewer. The adults were there only if the discussion lagged.

Shakira summarized the book, showed some photos she had found online about the Anne Frank House in Amsterdam, as well as photos of the camp where Anne died.

"If goodness can live on, can hatred?" Shakira asked at the end of her review.

"I think the whole point of goodness is to eradicate the hatred," one girl said.

"My mother says we are supposed to forgive, but I cannot forget wrongs like these," said another. "Forgiving and forgetting are two different things."

"But if you harbor hatred in your heart, even for something as awful as the Holocaust, doesn't it eat at you from inside?" another girl asked. "I mean the Nazis deserved our hatred, but how long can you hate before it ruins you?"

Of course, there were no answers to these questions like these. The girls knew that, but would ponder them anyway. These girls were, quite simply, smart.

When it was time to go, Abby sent them each off with a bottle of water, an apple, and the book for the next time—*Stand the Storm* by Breena Clarke.

"Bye and thanks, Senator Adams," they all said cheerfully. Many hugged Peggy Mellon. Abby looked forward to getting their hugs.

"This looks good," one girl said, already opening her book. "Hey, it's set right here in the District."

As they waited for the elevator, many juggled their possessions to get into the new book. In them, she saw herself.

It was time.

"Regina, I'm ready to go through Pris's things," Abby said during one of their calls in early August. In fact, Abby had already bought the supplies: boxes, tape, and trash bags.

"Want me to come help?" Regina said.

"No, you can if you want to, but you can also just tell me things you want."

"Remember those Estee Lauder compacts I'd always give Pris?"

"Sure. You want those?"

"Yes, Sweet Pea. And thanks for not making me come. I'm healing over, and that would rip off the scab," Regina said.

She then called Poppy and asked what she would like. She volunteered to help.

"Your sister was part of my life for nearly two decades."

Duke also wanted to help. "I'll catch the shuttle Friday evening. We can get everything done over a weekend, don't you think?"

On Saturday morning, the three started in on Pris's things. Abby and Poppy made short work of choosing clothes they might want. Poppy got first dibs on anything red. "Kim will have some work to do," Poppy said.

"Remind me never to own this many clothes," Abigail said to Poppy.

"She was a major clotheshorse," Poppy said fondly.

They made other large boxes of clothes to donate. But what to do with fine couture that neither of them wanted was a problem.

"Hey, maybe that Kim girl would like to remake some of the clothes to sell. She remade some things for you, right?" Duke added.

Abigail and Poppy looked at each other and smiled.

"Great idea. She'd like the trim, if nothing else," Abby said.

So they made two boxes for Kim.

They tossed all Priscilla's high-end lingerie and underwear.

Memorabilia was more problematic. Duke made a pile for Regina and him. Abby put aside the compacts for Regina. Abigail and Poppy each kept some things, mostly pictures and gifts they'd given her. The rest went to a consignment shop. The proceeds would go to Bookworms.

Scarves were easy. A pile in Regina's palette, red ones for Poppy, and the rest for Abby. They were lovely in their orange Hermés boxes; a few still smelled of her sister's perfume.

Abby wanted all the Bulgari Green Tea, from the shower gel to the lotion to the Extreme *parfum*.

Shoes were also a problem. Abby kept the shoes that fit, the expensive Italian ones, and sent everything else to a consignment shop. Poppy counted over a hundred pair.

"Never, ever, will I own this many clothes," Abigail said. "I'd lose track of what I owned."

Then came Pris's library. Abby was grateful for her Kindle, she wouldn't need the books.

Any books appropriate for Bookworms went into boxes they could rummage through next time they were here. Duke suggested the rest go to a library for a used book sale. They fanned open each book upside down. Various bookmarks fell out. They found twenty-year-old receipts, even a love letter from Lawson Gray. She put that aside for him. Priscilla thought dog-earing a book was desecration.

There were twenty book boxes in the utility room by day's end.

Duke wanted the electronics. Abby would have the Senate IT guy scrub them.

The bathroom was easy. They pitched everything.

Poppy knew a place to take the wigs for women with cancer.

By six on Saturday, they were done. On Monday the cleaners came.

I can leave the door open now.

My sister no longer lives in the room in which she died.

CHAPTER THIRTY-TWO

MOCKINGBIRD

August 15

The Monday after they cleaned out Pris's closet, Abigail called Poppy into her office.

"Poppy, I need some advice."

"No, you don't need to lose any weight," she deadpanned.

"Thanks, but that's not the question. When I was at the White House over the Fourth of July, John Lafferty was there."

Poppy said nothing.

"He said his wife had taken the twins and gone to England. For good."

"And?" Poppy asked.

"He asked me out and I referred him to you."

"Good Senator," Poppy said as if Abigail had been a "good dog."

"Has he called?"

"No, haven't heard a word." Poppy seemed oddly stiff.

"My question is this. If he does call, do you think it would be okay for me to go out with him? He is a very attractive man."

"That would be a negative, Houston." Poppy sounded like Mission Control talking to astronauts.

"Was he involved with Pris?"

"No, she didn't do married men. Period."

"So what's your objection? I do value your input."

Poppy sighed. "Short version or long?"

"Whichever."

"Short: he's slime."

"I see."

"Abby, you are in a very powerful Senate seat. If a guy gets to your power via your panties, both of his heads are happy."

"Okay, that about covers it." Abigail had to laugh.

"Abigail? This is Lawson. You got a sec?" Gray called her on her back line.

Sure, what's up?"

"I'm doing a Labor Day campaign swing around Texas," he said. "I want you along. Rebecca Crocker's gaining on me. I need you to counter her."

"Fine. E-mail me details. Do I have to kiss any babies?"

"Oh, no."

"Phooey. I like kissing babies."

Lawson laughed. "You're the only one who does. Hey, are you having any fun?"

"Define 'fun'."

"You know, anyone special?"

"Nah. I think a good book beats a bad date any day."

"Well, hell. That's one reason Pris wanted you in the Senate. Swim in a bigger pond and all that."

"Lawson, I'm looking. But I won't date colleagues or lobbyists. Throw out ugly, dumb, or mean, and that leaves the gay guys."

Lawson laughed.

"Your time will come. Someone's going to snatch you up. You mark my words."

August 31

By the next Armed Services subcommittee meeting, O'Neal had still not produced the numbers on the Mockingbird missiles.

"Mr. Chairman, the Secretary of Defense does not have the right to ignore the United States Senate," Abigail said.

"He has more important things on his mind, like the ongoing hostilities in Afghanistan," Cordelia Laurus said from her internal mountain on high.

"I do not think he has the power to ignore us," Abby said. "At least that's how I read my copy of the Constitution. I'll be happy to cite Article and Section if you like."

The chairman knew Abigail was right, but he also knew the Secretary of Defense was, at heart, both mean and smart. The country didn't get one without the other. Right now, it was more important that they have a smart Secretary than a nice one.

"I make a motion that P.J. O'Neal, Secretary of Defense, be cited for contempt of Congress for failure to produce documentation as ordered," Abby said.

"Do I have a second?" The Chairman looked around at the committee. No one said a word.

"For lack of a second, the motion fails." The Chairman banged his gavel.

The rest of the business was also concerning top-secret weapons and other matters pertaining to the troops in Afghanistan. At the end of the meeting, the Chairman said, "As everything we discussed here today is Top Secret, if I hear one word of the failed motion, there will be hell to pay. Do I make myself clear?"

Abby knew The Extreme Bloviator would know about her frontal assault before she was back in her office. She'd launched it for a reason. Principle. If the Senate asked how many jellybeans were in the Pentagon vending machines, they had a right to know that.

Abby didn't worry too much, she had a plane to catch.

She was packing up to leave the office when the IT guy for the Senate returned Pris's scrubbed computer and BlackBerry. He also gave her a few CDs of the material he'd swept off them.

"Hey, thanks. You sure they are clean? I want to give them to my nephew."

"Pure as driven snow. All new everything."

"Great. What do I owe you?"

"Nothing. The Senate wants old equipment scrubbed."

Abby crammed them into her tote. She was meeting Duke at the airport. She'd hardly seen him all summer, and was eager to hear how he liked his New York clerkship.

Abby would campaign and Duke would visit Regina. She found him at their boarding gate. His big strong arms hugged her as gently as if she were a porcelain doll. He might be a hotshot New York corporate law clerk, but he was still her sweet Duke, who relieved her of her heavy bags, allowing her to carry her handbag.

Once airborne, she handed him the electronics, and he was thrilled.

"This is great," he said, going on about gigs, rams, and speed.

"All I know is they're as good as new," Abby said.

He set about configuring the computer.

"What are these CDs?" he asked.

"Oh, stuff that came off Pris's computer."

"Can I use them to transfer some files?"

"Let me see what's on them first, okay?"

Abby loaded the CDs into her laptop and scanned through them. One file jumped out at her. Mockingbird.

It was password protected. Abby had, at one point, written down all her sister's passwords somewhere, but knew that if she put the matter aside, it would come to her.

She read her Kindle for a while, then it hit her. Pris's ultimate password was Regina's childhood address in Houston.

She typed it in and the file opened.

It was a memo from Priscilla to the Secretary of Defense, the selfsame O'Neal, dated fifteen months earlier. In it, she asked for a reconciliation of a discrepancy in the numbers of Mockingbird missiles in virtually the exact situation as Abby had figured out.

The man had been stonewalling for nearly two years. But why?

Abby studied the rest of the CDs and could find nothing. She should have gone through Pris's computer earlier. *Damn.*

The plane touched down at Hobby Airport. Abigail knew she was home when she stepped into the jetway. Heat and humidity rolled over her. Her lip was sweaty in seconds.

Abigail and Duke separated at the airport, as Abby was going on to Austin.

"Give Regina my love," she said, hugging Duke and kissing him on the cheek.

Abigail was met by a guy from MillionAir at baggage claim and driven to the private jet hangar, where Lawson waited for her. When you crisscross Texas, you're going virtually eight hundred miles in each direction. If you want to hit most big towns in a weekend, a private jet makes sense.

Lawson was at the hangar and they took off within minutes. Funny, in a big jet, there is little sensation of speed, but Abby really felt the ground whiz under her as they took off from Hobby's washboard runway.

"So, what's the drill?" Abby asked.

"Bad food, worse hotels, and hot weather."

"If you'd told me that earlier, I'd a-skipped it."

Abby was a good sport and was glad she'd brought only washable white and navy knits, as well as two red, white, and blue scarves. The first night by the time they stopped, she'd been wringing wet for hours. She put her clothes in the hotel's self-serve washer and headed to her room for a shower. She came back in her flip-flops and a lightweight bathrobe and put the stuff in the dryer. She sat there, wet-headed, reading a biography of Jefferson and watching her clothes go around.

They campaigned all Saturday, hitting Abilene, Big Spring, Odessa, Midland, and ending up in Amarillo, where she did the same laundry run. Sunday, they greeted Baptists going into early church in Marfa, and Methodists coming out of late services in Alpine. By the time she got to Houston, she was so tired, her eyeballs hurt. *If I ever think of running for public office, I should be committed.*

Somewhere high over Texas, she found the time to give him the love letter. He read it and sipped at his bourbon.

"I 'preciate this, Abby. Every day I kick myself for letting her get away. I know it's been thirty years, and I love my life with Lorena, but I was put here on earth for your sister. I let her down. When you find that person, grab him and don't let go," he said, finishing his drink.

Fat chance of me finding anyone. And with this inheritance, how would I know whether he wanted me or the money?

She checked in with Poppy each night. The Secretary of Defense called Mikey the afternoon Abby left. He bellowed at Mikey and accused Abby of leaving town because she was "running scared."

Mikey, for his part, told the Secretary, "You are a rude and arrogant man. You have no idea with whom you are dealing. The Senator knows far, far more than she is revealing. If you have any sense at all, you'd cease this puerile behavior at once. Not that you know what 'puerile' means." Then Mikey hung up on the gasbag.

On Monday evening, Abigail returned to Washington with Duke, who was eager to start his third, and final, year of law school.

CHAPTER THIRTY-THREE

THE LIGHT AT THE END OF THE TUNNEL

October 12

Abby could see the light at the end of the tunnel. She'd be out of D.C. by the end of the year. That was fine with her. She had to get her sister's office cleaned out after twenty-five years, but first, she had a Judiciary Committee meeting to attend.

The Judiciary Committee is Payback Central in the Senate. The minority party deliberately blocks appointments to federal benches just because they can. The price for unblocking the nomination can be steep, usually a piece of pork the size of the Space Shuttle.

Harrington wanted to elevate William Hirsch from the federal bench to the Ninth Circuit Court of Appeals. He was frankly apolitical, seldom was reversed on appeal and had even been an Eagle Scout. By chance, he'd been in junior high with Walter Harrington, but then they'd lost touch.

Harrington had to play ball with Senator Whitman, the ranking member from the other party. Whitman was the Senator with the most cosmetic surgery and dentistry. He even had regular laser skin treatments of his face, neck, hands and arms to erase signs of age. He wore so much fake tanner that Abby could smell him coming from twenty feet.

In person, he looked like a caricature of a male face lift addict, but he photographed handsomely.

Whitman was blocking the nomination because Harrington didn't want to build a dam across a river in Whitman's state. Why not? With the drought in the West, the "river" was a seasonal creek at best.

Whitman's people were furiously looking for dirt on Hirsch. Meanwhile, Hirsch answered the committee's interminable questions with variants on, "I just call balls and strikes," or "I can't speak to hypotheticals," or "that case is still pending, so I can't comment."

Abby's rear was numb and she was outraged at the waste of time and of talent. The man was a superb jurist. *Confirm him or don't, but stop with the droning.*

A vote was due that afternoon at five. Period. Harrington had the votes, but only by one. At ten minutes to five, an aide to Whitman came running in, looking like the cat that just ate a cage full of canaries. Whitman placed the large photo so the cameras could see it.

There was a young Judge Hirsch dressed as Hitler, in front of a Nazi flag, complete with a 'Heil Hitler' salute.

The gasp was audible and the committee chairman had to bang the gavel to settle everyone down. Hirsch was momentarily puzzled, and then produced a resigned smile.

"Do you have an explanation for this, Mister Justice?" Whitman's voice dripped with sarcasm.

"Yes, I do," he said equably. "In seventh grade, we were to dress up as someone from history, whether someone good or evil. My father had fought in the war and brought back all that stuff. In fact, he helped liberate Birkenau where my maternal grandparents perished."

The crowd gasped. Whitman would've gone white, but he wore so much self-tanner, he turned orange and began to sweat orange bullets.

"The kid who came in second was Walter Harrington. He came as Rasputin."

Whitman faked a coughing spell and left the room.

THE LIGHT AT THE END OF THE TUNNEL

The justice was confirmed unanimously.

Abby was ashamed to be a member of the U.S. Senate. She was glad she was leaving. *I cannot get out of here fast enough.*

Abby had only a few months left in her sister's term before the new Senator from Texas would be sworn on January third. Luckily, Lawson Gray was ahead in the polls, and mercifully, she didn't have to campaign anymore.

The Infants First Act was growing and results were better than expected. Abigail felt some sense of accomplishment in that, but mostly the Senate was a waste of her talents and time.

Abby had only a vague idea on her life after the Senate. She knew it would never include politics. She had to do something about the ranch. Right now the only thing she knew about ranching was to wear boots. Rattlesnakes can't bite you through a good pair of boots.

But her life? She hadn't the foggiest idea what to do with that.

Mother Nature did her beautiful striptease of the leaves around Washington in early November, but no one except Abby seemed to notice the greens going to everything from yellow to orange, red, and purple. Everyone was absorbed with the election. Abby of course, was hoping Lawson Gray would win, but she just wanted out of the Senate.

"You're traveling days are over," Poppy said to Abigail on November first.

"Why's that?"

"You're President Pro Tem until the end of the year."

"What exactly does that mean?" Abigail asked.

"*Pro tem* in Latin means 'for now' or 'for the time being.' So you are, for now, President of the Senate. If the President, Vice President, and Speaker of the House die, you're President. And any day the VP is gone, and that's a lot, you are at the beck and call of Barbara Lansky to do ceremonial things."

Abby pulled up the people behind her in line for the Presidency. Surprisingly, they weren't in the Constitution, but in the Presidential Succession Act of 1947. Then she got down to the real work at hand: getting her sister's office of twenty-five years cleaned out.

"I'm not sure I have time for Barbara from Jersey with the green sequined glasses."

"Don't forget her matching nails."

Every morning at eight, Barbara Lansky sashayed into Abby's office. Barbara could have e-mailed her a marked-up copy of the Senate schedule, but since only Barbara could decipher exactly where and when Abby's presence was required, she came in person.

"You're a credit to the Senate," Barbara said. "Of course, that's not hard, as most of these guys are just blowhards with two-hundred-dollar haircuts."

Then she'd cackle and toddle off. She thought nothing of telling off anyone who got in her way.

On the Hill, real estate is everything. Lawson won Pris's seat handily, but he hadn't a prayer he'd get her office. Senior Senators were looking at Abby's office the way a hungry man looks at steak. And Lawson was a junior Senator now.

Getting an office cleaned out of nearly twenty-five years of a Senator's "stuff" is hard enough for the Senator. For the Senator's sister, it was an incredible task.

It was while going through the Top Secret files on the computer that she again came across the Mockingbird files. *When did I first see these?* She thought back. It was Labor Day weekend. She rummaged through her tote, and the CDs from Pris's laptop were still in there.

For the better part of the Saturday after Election Day, she pored through files, but only one thing piqued her interest.

John Lafferty of Lafferty Weapons Systems made the Mockingbird, the shoulder-fired nuclear weapon that O'Neal blustered about.

She could find no correspondence between Pris and Lafferty. And only the one letter from Pris to the Secretary of Defense. Not long after it, Priscilla's health cratered.

She sat and pondered. Poppy had called Lafferty "slime." Maybe Poppy was the link.

Abby called her at home.

"Hey, what are you up to?" Abigail asked.

"Working on my resume, what do you think I'm doing?" Poppy laughed. "I'm going to be out of a job come the first of January."

"Not if I can help it," Abigail said honestly.

"Thanks. What's up?"

"Can I come by? I need a glass of wine," Abigail said.

"Sure. Come on."

Abigail shut things down and was at Poppy's place within a half hour.

Poppy had all the curtains in her third floor apartment open, and some of the leaves outside were as red as Poppy's hair. Others were yellow, orange and even a purple one here and there.

"This is like living in a tree house," Abigail said, delighting in the leaf show outside. Poppy had a bouquet of red carnations and eucalyptus that perfumed the room.

"That's why I chose it. I hope I don't have to move."

"Pops, anyone with a lick of sense would want you. Besides, I'm Pris's executor, and when the estate is settled, you'll have a nice nest egg." Abby gave her a large, round number. "Unfortunately, I don't know when it will come through. But the National Bank of Abigail is available for an interim loan if you need one."

"Oh, wow. Thanks. I was over the moon with the mink coat, but this is mind-bending."

Poppy uncorked a Sauvignon Blanc, poured it, and raised her glass to Abigail.

"Here's to Pris." Poppy had a smile on her face.

"I'll drink to that." Abigail touched her glass to Poppy's.

"So what do you need to know? You don't make social calls," Poppy said.

"Why do you think John Lafferty is slime?" Abigail knew Poppy did not tolerate verbosity.

"Because he is," Poppy sipped her wine and looked blank.

"Would you elaborate on that?" Abigail asked softly.

"Remember when you came back from Pris's funeral, and I disappeared for a few days?"

"Yes." *It was odd you went to a spa and came back pale.*

"I was off nursing hurt feelings." Poppy's voice was flat, her stare almost confrontational. "We'd been sleeping together for some time, and when he announced Jemima was leaving him, I thought that meant we would be together.

"He set me straight. 'Poppy, I sleep with women like you; I marry women like Jemima or Priscilla.' The guy even had an indulgent smile on his face. Like I should have known better."

"Oh, Poppy, how awful," Abigail wanted to comfort her, but Poppy, with her arms crossed and feet tucked beneath her, was in another place.

"Okay. What was his relationship with Pris like?" Abigail asked.

"Strictly business, though he obviously was interested in Pris. He was a defense contractor, which meant he courted all the members of the Armed Services Committee."

"So what did he do for her?"

"Mostly, he had his plane fly her back and forth from Texas. Remember his plane was the one we used for the funeral?"

"Now that you mention it, yes."

"And remember when she went to Wimbledon? She stayed in his company flat in Knightsbridge."

"And what would he get for his generosity?"

"From Pris? Not much. She scrupulously avoided being seen alone with married men. She always took his calls, and if he asked for an appointment, he got one on the day of his choice."

"Did she support his business on the Hill?"

"Hard to say. A lot of it, I wasn't privy to." Poppy was relaxing a bit, her arms uncrossed; she took another sip of wine.

"Is there anything else you can think of that I need to know about him?"

"Not really. You're leaving office, so it's moot anyway."

"Yeah, I guess you're right. Something just doesn't smell right, though."

"Welcome to D.C. It started as a stinky swamp and it still is one."

CHAPTER THIRTY-FOUR

LOOKING FORWARD

November 8

The midterm elections went as predicted. The party in power, the one to which Abigail theoretically belonged, kept its majority in both houses, but lost the odd seat here and there.

Lawson Gray won. Abigail's campaigning had evidently helped. With the election out of the way, Abigail could turn her thoughts to her remaining two months in Washington.

"I want us all together here in Washington for Thanksgiving," Abigail said to Regina the day after the election. "I can't leave, as I'm President Pro Tem, and Duke is here, so you've got to come, Reege."

"I hate traveling over Thanksgiving," Regina said.

"Then come the week before. Besides, when my term is up, we have to think about what to do with this apartment."

"Oh, okay. But don't you go thinking I'm going to let you cook the turkey. I've made that mistake once, and I'm not making it again. Drier than the Sahara desert, it was. And tough as cowhide." The perfectly adequate, if somewhat bland, turkey got worse with every telling.

"All right. I'll confine myself to opening the cans of cranberry sauce," Abigail said, glad to hear Regina was her old self.

"Now get a pencil and paper and get this ordered." Abigail made and edited a shopping list that would feed a family of ten for a week. Twenty minutes on the computer, and Thanksgiving necessities were ordered, including the wines. Even the flowers were ordered and would arrive Wednesday afternoon.

Duke was happy that the three of them would be together. He'd been up to his eyes with Law Review as well as interviewing. He could use some downtime, not to mention some of his aunt's cooking. What that woman could do to a turkey was divine. He'd have to arm wrestle Abby for the dark meat, but it was his year to win.

When the food and wine arrived, it took Abby nearly an hour to put everything away in the right place, in part because she hadn't been in the kitchen more than a couple of times while Regina was gone.

Regina was already at the apartment when Abigail arrived late on that Thursday evening, a week before Thanksgiving.

"Oh, Reege," Abby said, hugging her hard. "You look wonderful." She was rested and calm, still supreme commander in charge of all things domestic.

"Thank you, Sweet Pea. You look good to these old eyes. And you've even kept the place nice while I was gone."

"I tried," Abigail lied. She'd let it go to ruin, and then called in the cleaners, twice, in the last week. If she'd cooked anything more difficult than French toast, she couldn't remember it. She subsisted on food from Tran's and room service.

"Where's my baby Duke?" Regina asked.

"He'll be around this weekend sometime to say 'hey.' He's got some last-minute stuff for school before the holiday."

"And I wonder what her name is," Regina huffed.

Duke showed up for lunch on Saturday, and the little family was happy just being together. Regina made his favorite oatmeal molasses cookies, some party mix for Abby, and a big pot of Community Coffee for herself. The apartment smelled right, a mix of fresh coffee and something sweet in the oven. Life was good, except for the empty chair at the kitchen table.

Duke was trying to decide whether to clerk for a Supreme Court justice (he wouldn't say which one) or whether to go to New York and enter a boutique firm that specialized in corporate securities litigation.

"They have a six year partner track. Better than a lot of places," Duke added.

"But do you want to live in New York City?" Regina asked, as if she'd smelled a dead rat.

Perhaps now was the time to bring up Priscilla's estate, which was all but finished. The accountant was just waiting for January first to file the final tax returns. How the country could be strapped for money was beyond Abby, not with the size of the estate tax bill.

"Guys, we need to talk about the future," Abigail said. Both Duke and Regina looked at her, stricken. Was something wrong with Abby?

"No, wait. Back up. Nothing's wrong," Abigail said, laughing. "I'm fine, really. We need to talk about Priscilla's gifts to us."

"Oh, for a moment there, you had us worried," Duke said.

Abby had a pretty good handle on what the final taxes would be, and gave each of them their ballpark "number" with silence. Finally, Regina spoke.

"What am I going to do with all that? I already have a roof over my head and a chair under my bottom," Regina said.

"As the executor, I have to give it to you as soon as things are finalized. What you do with it is up to you." Abby said.

"I'll be generous, but real quiet about it," Regina said.

"Duke, you know how trusts work. You'll get the income off your money quarterly until you are thirty-five, then you get it all. I also have the ability to give you more at my discretion if you want to buy a house or something," Abby said.

Duke was thoughtful for a moment.

"What are you going to do about the ranch?"

"Well, I don't know. I thought we'd think about that after I leave the Senate. I'm going at a dead run to get things cleaned up there."

Then Abigail brightened. "Speaking of the Senate, I'd like to give you guys a super VIP tour on Wednesday morning, the day before Thanksgiving. Everybody and their uncle will be gone already. Barbara Lansky, who 'runs the joint,' is a real character. I thought we might meet up with her about ten at my office. What about it? I'll show you Sam Houston's desk. It's mine now."

"You're on." Duke's eyes brightened. School was already out for the Thanksgiving break.

"I have to make the cornbread for the stuffing, but I guess I could come," Regina said.

Over at the White House, Walter Harrington was finishing his Saturday work. He'd done the radio broadcast, antique that it was. He was anxious to pack for the ski trip on Tuesday morning. He had some new gear and wanted to check the fit. Early ski conditions at Beaver Creek were unbelievably good. He couldn't wait to hit the back bowls via heli-skiing. Sure, Evangeline would carp at him about it, but he flew in helicopters all the time.

If she wanted to worry about something, let her worry about whether the kids would get along. One of the three always had some grudge to air. Plus, Margaret wasn't bringing any friends, so she'd have to be entertained. Heaven knew Margaret's mother wasn't going to do it. The First Lady would have to be Babysitter-in-Chief.

The Vice President was at the Admiral's House fretting about her physical on Wednesday. She was tired of being lectured about her weight, her smoking, her drinking. If the doctor wanted her to have less stress, he could start by skipping all the lectures.

Even Jane, her partner of twenty years, was kvetching at her to at least get out and take a walk. Plus, her parents were coming for Thanksgiving, and they were heading firmly into their dotage. She had to watch them like toddlers. Neither could remember anything, so every conversation was a virtual repeat of the last one. This would probably be their last year at the Admiral's House, even though she wouldn't leave office for two more years.

The Speaker of the House was in rare form. He'd just won at tennis at Burning Tree, and since he had won, his opponent was paying. Normally, he'd have a burger, but the head of the biggest pharmaceutical lobby was paying, so he had a humongous steak, and they shared a bottle of ridiculously expensive Clos de Vougeot, a *grand cru* Burgundy.

Franklin Chariton heard stories of the Speaker's table manners, so he decided to watch them closely. He could not believe the way the Speaker ate. He cut his steak into huge bites, popped one in his mouth, perhaps chewed it once or twice, and then swallowed. Immediately he did it again. He polished off a fourteen-ounce rib eye in, according to Chariton's count, fourteen bites. His watch clocked him at under forty seconds. He doubted an underfed junkyard Doberman could do any faster.

It put him completely off his meal. He picked at a Maryland Crab Cake and ate a little fruit. He took a sip of the two-hundred-dollar-a-bottle wine, and the Speaker finished the rest himself.

It was no wonder the man always looked as if his tie and belt were strangling him. He was exploding inside his clothes.

"Great lunch," the Speaker said, barely stifling a loud belch.

"Glad you enjoyed it. Next time, though, I'm winning." Chariton said. He meant it too. It was demeaning enough throwing games to the politicos. No matter how much he got paid, nothing was worth having to watch crap like this.

CHAPTER THIRTY-FIVE

THE CATAPULT

Wednesday, November 22

Abby never felt comfortable wearing pants in the Senate. Perhaps it was because so few were long enough. So she dressed for a regular day, wearing a navy wool crepe suit with a shawl collar. She wore her sister's Seal of the United States pin and slightly pink baroque pearl earrings. As always, she was groomed to perfection. Andre had taught her well. As well, she knew Regina and Duke would be well-groomed and well-dressed to visit the U.S. Senate.

Barbara Lansky told great Senate stories as she showed Abigail, Duke, and Regina around the Senate. They were almost finished about ten thirty. Duke was impressed that Abigail sat at Sam Houston's desk, and he insisted that she carve her name in the wood.

"May I, Barbara?"

"Suit yourself. I sure would. And the original Abigail Adams damn sure would have."

Regina had a metal nail file with a sharp point. Feeling a little sheepish, Abigail carved in "A Adams." She wanted to cry, but settled for just tearing up as Duke whipped out his camera and took a picture of her.

They were heading back to Abigail's office when someone ran up to them in the corridor and said, "The President's been in an avalanche."

The few people in Abigail's office were glued to CNN.

Poppy pulled up some more chairs, and Barbara, Abigail, Duke, and Regina joined in the watching.

"Details are sketchy, but this morning the President, an avid skier, appears to have fallen victim to an avalanche outside Beaver Creek, Colorado. Accompanied by two local guides, and two Secret Service agents, none of the men has been heard from. They had gone by helicopter to some of the back areas.

"The President's exact location is known from his GPS device. Rescue workers are working as rapidly as unstable avalanche terrain allows."

Abigail looked at her watch. It was 10:32 a.m.

Abigail calculated his odds as slim to none. If he wasn't head injured, the sheer pressure of the snow mass would not allow his chest to expand, even if he had that rarest of things, an air pocket.

Every network had the same information.

The work of the entire nation appeared to stop.

While Abby had been vandalizing her Senate desk, the Vice President was at the Admiral's House. She would show the doctor a thing or two. She set out for a brisk walk on the grounds, accompanied by two Secret Service agents. She walked for a while, but it was boring, and she decided to jog.

Her jog was that of a pygmy elephant's: slow, cumbersome, and short in stride. Within a few yards, she was sweating like someone in a bikram yoga class in a 105-degree room.

The agents eyed her.

"I'm fine, dammit," she wheezed.

And she was, for a few yards. Then she stopped, put her hands on her knees, and gulped for breath. It was at that time that the Secret Service learned of the avalanche in their earpieces. Each took an arm and began trying to haul her inside.

She didn't like being grabbed by each arm.

"Let go of me. Tell me what is going on." She was still short of breath, and her color was gray.

"The President's been in an avalanche. Things don't look good, ma'am."

She made a fist with her right hand, put it to her chest as if something in her chest was squeezing too tightly. Her face contorted in pain. She turned the color of old asphalt and pitched to the ground.

🇺🇸

The television showed the same footage over and over, but no one could turn away. People did not want to be alone, they wanted to be in a group, and Abby was glad Regina and Duke were with her.

At eleven fifteen, another reporter broke in, visibly nervous.

"We've just gotten word that the Vice President has collapsed at her home while on a walk. I have no firm verification on this and no word on her condition," she said.

The concern level ratcheted up to near panic in the office. Was this the Second Tower being hit?

Abby took Poppy into her private office. Abigail's entire professional life had been about emergencies. She reacted almost robotically, and then melted down on her own time. It was a system she had honed for years. This was no different.

Manage the crisis.

Anticipate.

Do not waver.

"Poppy. Things that happen in twos, happen in threes. I need to know the exact whereabouts of the Speaker of the House."

Poppy tried her landline. It didn't work. She tried her cell. It didn't work.

"Everything seems to have crashed."

"Okay, we're out of here," Abby said. "Regina and Duke, Barbara Lansky, as well as you and I are going to the Supreme Court before anything else happens."

"Why?"

"I have to plan ahead. If the Speaker falls, I'm next. I must be able to take the oath in a secure location, and the person to administer it should be one of the Supreme Court Justices."

"Got your ID?" Poppy asked.

Abby whipped it out of her bra.

"I'll walk out with Regina and Duke," Abigail said.

"I'll follow with Barbara," Poppy said.

"Tell the staff I've been called to a secure location," Abigail said. "We'll head to the Supreme Court together."

Within moments the five of them walked out of the Russell Office Building. Security was just starting to ban people from coming in, but no one thought to stop anyone from leaving. They strode across Constitution Avenue and then turned left across First Street SE in the brisk fall air. The streets were virtually deserted.

At the door of the Supreme Court, they were stopped by security.

"I'm Senator Abigail Adams, and I wish to see the Chief Justice." Abigail showed her ID.

"I'm sorry, ma'am, we're on lockdown."

"Then please get the Marshal up here. Tell him Senator Adams is here. He knows me."

"With all due respect, I don't take my orders from you," the beefy man said.

Duke stepped in front of Abby. He made two of any man.

"The Senator asked nicely. Surely the Marshal is able to spare a moment for the President Pro Tem of the Senate. She will be the President of the United States if anything happens to the Speaker of the House. You wouldn't want to go down in history as the MO-ron who sent her out into the dangerous streets, now would you?" Duke asked sweetly.

The Marshal was summoned and immediately recognized Abby.

"Senator. What an awful morning."

"Yes, Busby, especially since I'm President Pro Tem of the Senate and do not know the whereabouts of the Speaker of the House."

"Come with me, please."

All five followed Busby Learner to the back of the building. Everyone there was glued to televisions. The Marshal summoned the Chief Justice, who escorted his guests into his office. It also had a television.

Abigail made the introductions.

Barbara Lansky whipped out her ID and verified that Abigail was the President Pro Tem.

Chief Justice Duncan Jacobs tried to get into the government's website, but it too had crashed. They were out phone service as well.

"I guess we wait and watch television," he harrumphed.

"We'd be happy to wait with the others," Abigail offered. "Perhaps you'd like some privacy?"

"No. I don't want you out of my sight, young woman."

The Speaker of the House was invited to brunch that morning by the Black Angus Beef Growers of America. Turkey was their enemy, especially this time of year, so they always had a morning meeting. Then everyone left for whichever football game they would attend the next day.

The brunch was at a private club, the Franklin Potomac Club, inside Franklin Towers. It was as clubby as could be. Pre-worn leather chairs and sofas, antique oriental rugs, every newspaper known to man, and a quiet and courteous staff that served nothing but the finest. The wine list was so extensive, it was indexed.

The Speaker required a five star meal and a five figure honorarium to give a canned speech. He was taking a sip of water during his speech when the manager burst into the room. "The President's been in an avalanche."

The Speaker choked on his water, and his face turned red, but he managed to step aside, coughing, as they lowered a flat-screen television for everyone to watch.

The chef didn't know what to do with the meal he was readying for service in a few minutes, so he did nothing.

The group watched for a while. As nothing was happening, the Speaker suggested to his hosts that if he was getting hungry, surely others were. The command went to the chef, who hastily finished his preparations. The Speaker looked forward to the tournedos with Béarnaise. He also loved the potatoes they made at the Potomac Club, as well as their Death by Chocolate. He'd been known to eat two in a day.

He wished he could afford to join, but he couldn't. And being Speaker of the House didn't qualify him for an *ex officio* membership. The only *ex officio* member was the President.

The Speaker dug in when the food came. The tournedos were slightly smaller than filet mignons, and thickly napped with sauce. He cut one into thirds and popped a piece into his mouth. He chewed it once or twice. Just as he started to swallow, the television announced the collapse of the Vice President.

The Speaker inhaled in shock, and the bite of meat, lubricated nicely by the sauce, flew into his windpipe. It was a perfect fit. Everyone stared at the television. By the time people noticed that he was in silent trouble, his face was a deep blue.

People called nine-one-one only to find their phones dead.

Several people tried the Heimlich maneuver on him, but with his sheer bulk, it was completely ineffective.

Another person suggested putting him on the ground and sitting on him to bring up the piece of meat. That too was useless.

A third person suggested they cut a hole in his windpipe with a steak knife, but no one knew how.

He died on the floor, his last thoughts of the Presidency slipping through his fingers, and of missing the Death by Chocolate.

CHAPTER THIRTY-SIX

THE PRESIDENCY

Wednesday, November 22, noon

"This is Andrea Kendall. We have confirmation that the Vice President is dead. Time of death was 11:33 a.m. Preliminary cause of death is cardiac arrest."

The anchor, still on the air from the morning show, thanked her and pitched it to the correspondent covering the President.

"Any news for us?"

"No good news. Multiple flyovers have revealed no debris associated with skiers: no poles, no hats, nothing. The latest attempt is a hover directly over the President's GPS signal. People are on the ground digging furiously. As well, the crew will attempt to push a tube through the snowpack in an attempt to listen for signs of life and to simultaneously administer oxygen. Back to you."

At this point, the anchor stuck his finger in his ear and unwittingly said aloud to the nation, "Holy crap."

Then he recovered and went on as if nothing had happened. "We just have word that the Speaker of the House is dead at the exclusive Franklin Potomac Club. He appears to have choked on a piece of meat. We are going via sat phone to Congressional Correspondent Jake Agerton. Jake, tell us what you saw and heard."

"I was there covering the Speaker's talk to the Black Angus Beef Growers of America. The Speaker finished his speech when we got word of the President's situation. While waiting further word, everyone had lunch. He apparently choked on a piece of meat when he heard about the Vice President. No one noticed him silently turning blue until he fell onto the table.

"People tried the Heimlich maneuver on him, but as you know, he is a large man. I would time his death at about eleven forty-five."

"Jake, how close were you to him?"

"I was sitting at the next table, not three feet away. I didn't see him put the meat into his mouth, but I can tell you that no one approached him in any way. I got out my phone to get a picture of him, a reaction shot, on becoming President, and he was a deep purple blue. His head hit the table with a thud. I have photos in my phone, but the system's crashed."

At that point, the Chief Justice clicked off the television.

"The time has come. I am going to administer the oath of office. Should the President be found alive and competent, you will give him back his job."

"Yes, I agree," Abigail said.

She asked for a ladies room, and the Chief Justice gave her the use of his private facilities. She looked at herself in the mirror, put her hands on the chilly sink.

This is my Constitutional duty.

She added more makeup. She must not only take the Oath of Office, she must take ownership of the Presidency. What was it Wicker said? You not only were a Senator, you had to play one every day. Now she was going to be the President. She had to play that role. She could not falter. Not in today's world. She breathed in deeply and let the breath flow out gently.

She stepped back into the room, her eyes bright, and her spine straight. The Chief Justice had put on his robe. The other four justices in the building were robed and standing behind him.

The Court's videographer was setting up, as was a still photographer. Duke too had his camera out.

Regina produced her Bible from her capacious purse. Barbara Lansky would be the witness from the Senate and the Marshal of the Court the other witness.

At the last minute, Abby put her sister's copy of the Constitution on the Bible. She took a moment to center herself. *Head up, shoulders back, pleasant, serious neutral face. Duty. Honor. Country.*

"You're good to go, sir," the video guy said. The Chief Justice paused for a few beats, then began to speak.

"My name is Duncan Jacobs, and I am the Chief Justice of the Supreme Court. The time is noon, and the date is Wednesday, November twenty-second.

"Being apprised of the incapacity of the President, and the demise of the Vice President and the Speaker of the House, I am going to administer the Presidential Oath of Office to Senator Abigail Adams, who is President Pro Tem of the Senate. Should the President be able to resume his duties, she will, of course, cede powers back to him. If other reports are erroneous, she will cede power to the Vice President or Speaker of the House.

"Witnesses are Barbara Lansky, a chief administrative officer with the Secretary of the Senate, and Busby Learner, the Marshal of the Court.

"Ms. Lansky, in your administrative capacity in the Secretary of the Senate's office, can you vouch for the fact that Senator Adams is a native-born American?"

"I can. I verified her place of birth as Texas upon entering the Senate."

"And is she President Pro Tem of the Senate?"

"Yes, according to the rotational schedule, she assumed that duty on November 1 through the end of this calendar year."

"Senator Adams, have you attained the age of thirty-five years?

Abigail produced her driver's license. "I am thirty-seven."

"Who is going to hold the Bible and Constitution for you?"

"Regina Temple, my childhood guardian.

"I understand you wish to add the Constitution to the Bible for your swearing-in?

"Yes, sir, I do."

"Then please place your left hand on the Bible and the Constitution. Raise your right hand."

"I do solemnly swear…"

Abigail felt her heart slow, felt the words left her mouth clearly and with purpose.

When the oath was over, he shook her hand, holding it for longer than necessary. Shutters clicked, and Abigail hugged Regina, who looked as if she was going to faint. Abby had her sit down.

"Duke, get her home, will you, please? And later today get her to put an outfit together for me for tomorrow. Please bring it to the Northwest Gate." Abby's mouth was suddenly dry. "Of the White House."

The Chief Justice interrupted.

"Now, I'd best get you to the White House," the Chief Justice said. "Tell my driver we're on our way down to the car. Make copies of that video. Get it to the closest media outlets. Walk it if you have to. Most communications are useless. Release it immediately."

There was no going back now.

Abigail and Poppy followed the Chief Justice through the maze of the building. They entered the back of a black armored SUV, and the double gates of the garage opened. Next to the driver in the front seat was a man who introduced himself as the Chief Justice's primary Secret Service agent. He would be part of her escort into the White House. When the first gate had closed behind them, the second gate slid open, and they exited onto Constitution Avenue.

It took less than ten minutes to arrive at the White House, which was ringed by police in black riot gear. A few people milled around the area.

The Chief Justice was known on sight, which was good, as was the Secret Service Agent in the front seat.

That was good. The computers were down, and no one could verify the car as "safe" in the database.

The Chief Justice and Abigail exited the SUV beneath the West Wing.

Jacobs explained things to the Secret Service, who escorted all of them to the Situation Room. Abby was thoroughly lost. She did, however, recognize the guards outside the door as Marines in dress uniform. *They look vaguely like Christmas nutcrackers.*

Everyone stood as the Chief Justice entered the room. He was definitely an anomaly there, especially in his robe.

"Ladies and gentleman, I have just administered the oath of office to Abigail Adams, who until a few minutes ago was President Pro Tem of the Senate. She is now President of the United States, unless of course, the President, Vice President, or Speaker of the House are found alive."

And with that, he turned and left.

Everyone remained standing.

"This is my Chief of Staff, Poppy McElroy," Abigail said. Someone pointed to the President's empty chair for Abigail and a chair at the periphery of the room for Poppy. If there were another chair she could occupy, she would have. There wasn't. She strode to the President's chair and sat down.

Logan Chaffee, the President's Chief of Staff, looked stricken when Abby sat in it.

"Please. Everyone sit." Abigail took control of the meeting away from Logan Chaffee.

At that moment, the video of the swearing-in lit up one of the screens. Someone turned up the audio. Everyone stood and watched in silence.

"Okay, we've seen that. Please turn it off." Abby said to the person with a remote. "Please take your seats."

Abigail knew Cristo Salazar, the Chairman of the Joint Chiefs, and Marilyn Chernosky, the Secretary of State, and her Senate nemesis, P.J. O'Neal, the Secretary of Defense. Other faces were familiar from the news, but she didn't know them personally.

Everyone sat except for the Secretary of Defense, who was midway down the conference table.

Before Abigail could even open her mouth, he jumped in.

"Now Abby, you and I, as well as most of the people in this room, know that you are in way, way over your head here. I'm sure you were a perfectly good little baby doctor, but this is the biggest of the big leagues. Having a novice in the job is dangerous."

That SOB, he's gunning for me before I have a chance to say a word. No nice way to do this, so do it fast. And hard. Play POTUS. Hell, play Stalin.

He started to sit down.

"Please remain standing, Mr. Secretary." Abigail's voice was icy.

He did, but he stared at her.

"Our system provides for the removal of the President via impeachment in Article II, Section Four of the Constitution. We do not have the British vote of no confidence. You know perfectly well that if I resign, the Presidential Succession Act of 1947 mandates the job go to the Secretary of State. However, Secretary Chernosky cannot serve, as she is foreign born. Neither can the Secretary of the Treasury as he is too young. So that would leave you."

She noticed a jaw or two drop open. She forged ahead; glad she'd memorized the Constitution before beginning in the Senate.

"You have served your country well and long, and the nation thanks you for your service. However, you do serve at the pleasure of the President. And your outburst displeases me greatly. You are relieved of your duties. Your termination is immediate."

The room was deathly quiet. O'Neal was turning purple with rage.

"General Salazar, I would appreciate it if you would step in as Secretary of Defense, effective immediately," Abigail said neutrally.

"Yes ma'am," Salazar replied crisply.

O'Neal gathered his things and was turning to go.

"Mr. O'Neal. You are not yet dismissed. Poppy, get the Marine Sentries in here, please."

Within moments, the men were in the room. She wished they wore sabers that rattled. Abigail addressed the two young men.

"As you may know, I am Abigail Adams, and I am now President. I'm ordering you to take former Secretary O'Neal to remove his personal effects from his office at the Pentagon. Get the officer on duty to get him locked out of computer access."

The two Marines cut their eyes to General Salazar. He gave a small nod of approval.

"Go to General Cambridge's office, I'll radio ahead the President's order," Salazar said.

"Yes, ma'am," the two Marines said in unison to Abigail. They bookended O'Neal.

O'Neal looked around the room, visually beseeching someone, anyone, to come to his assistance. No one did.

In a moment he was gone. The only noise was General Salazar stepping to another part of the room and speaking quietly into a headset.

"Now," Abigail looked around the room pleasantly. "Does anyone else wish to join the private sector today? No? Then someone show me how our nuclear capability works."

The President had the real nuclear "football" with him in Colorado, while a backup stayed in the Situation Room. Capt. Tom Hitchcock was in charge of the backup one.

Either of the two "footballs" allowed the President to make war from any place on the planet, or even in the skies above it. A large laptop computer, it sat on a foam egg crate in a bulletproof briefcase.

Hitchcock opened it, logged Abigail into it, with General Salazar's verification of Abigail. Then Hitchcock gave her a card on which she wrote her password sequence. They easily made her a thumb drive and gave it to her so she could access the equipment.

"Cristo, what about the football with the President?" Abigail asked.

"I'll have to find out," he replied and headed back toward the communications area.

"Keep them on you at all times, ma'am," Hitchcock said of the launch codes and thumb drive.

"And you, Hitchcock, you stay in my line of sight until I say otherwise," Abigail said.

"Yes, ma'am."

Abby put the card and the thumb drive down the front of her suit jacket and into her bra.

CHAPTER THIRTY-SEVEN

MOVING FORWARD

"Please get the head of the NYSE for me," Abby said to Chaffee. Within moments, the man's voice appeared. *At least some of the White House phones worked.*

"Madam President, what may I do for you?" he said.

"I assume you've ceased trading for the rest of the day as well as Friday," she said.

"I closed everything down at the first word of the President. Our plan is to stay closed until Monday."

"Excellent. I'll try to get everything taken care of this weekend. I hope all exchanges will close until Monday, though I don't get a vote. Communication is spotty, so please pass the word."

"Yes, ma'am."

"Keep in touch." Abby rang off. "At least we don't have to worry about the markets tanking between now and Monday."

"Now, Salazar and Secretary Chernosky, do we have any indication that any hostiles are up to anything?"

"No, ma'am, but our military readiness is up a notch. As is airport security."

"Well, I won't undercut the TSA at this point. These appear to be a series of unrelated events. Does anyone have any other thoughts?"

Everyone in the room shook his head no, including the spy people.

"Chaffee, thanks for being here. I sincerely hope the President's able to return. In the meantime, I need you desperately, as does the country. I hope you and Poppy will work together."

"Yes, ma'am." He was ashen.

"What about the football?" Abby asked Cristo.

"It was aboard the helicopter hovering over the president as he skied. The guy carrying it wasn't skiing. Of course, the codes to it are buried in the avalanche."

"Order the aide with the football to Air Force One. The last thing I want is to leave it behind, accidentally. And void the President's codes immediately. Ditto for the VP's. We can always make him new ones."

"Yes ma'am."

"I want to talk to families and heads of state, please. With the phones a mess, I'll talk to who is available first."

There were serious telephone meltdowns in Washington. CNN was asking everyone to refrain from making unnecessary calls.

Even the way she placed a phone call was now different. She simply said who she wanted to talk to, and they appeared on her phone with a White House-generated caller ID.

"Ma'am," Secretary Chernosky said, "it's important that you not keep heads of state waiting."

"Thank you."

Abigail spoke with the First Lady, who was in Colorado "hopeless one minute and optimistic the next." Abby reassured her everyone was doing their best to find the President alive. "Everyone here sends you their love."

There were similar calls to the Vice President's partner and parents at the Admiral's House for a Thanksgiving weekend. Abigail put the partner on hold for a moment. The elderly parents had actively hated their daughter's lesbian partner for twenty years.

"Someone see if the Barkers can be moved into Blair House," Abigail said.

"I'll call O.T.," Chaffee said.

"I'm going to try to move the Barkers to Blair House, Jane," Abigail said.

Thank you so much, Madam President," the partner said.

Abby was stunned at the use of her new title.

The Speaker of the House's wife was still livid with him, even in her grief.

"If I've told that man once, I've told him a thousand times to slow down and chew his food."

"I hear you," Abigail said. At least the woman had some anger. That was a good sign.

The wives of the Secret Service agents were grateful for her call, but one, Todd Wilson's widow, had a four-year-old daughter and was due to deliver a son any day. *No one should have let him go skiing.*

"Do you have anyone with you?" Abigail asked.

"No, ma'am. My parents should be here tomorrow."

"I'll send someone over," she said and rang off.

"Get the Secret Service to send someone she knows to sit with her. She does not need to go into labor home alone with a four-year-old."

She even managed a few brief words with the local guide's families. They were impressed, but Abigail felt it was the least she could do.

The calls to heads of state were easier. Marilyn Chernosky not only knew who to call, but when. Some wanted to be awakened, others would be annoyed. Many cared only that Adams was calling them, reinforcing their self-importance. CNN had already told the world.

CNN reported the NYSE, NASDAQ, and Chicago Board of Trade ceased trading early and would be closed until Monday.

It had not escaped her that all this happened on the anniversary of the assassination of JFK.

Captain Hitchcock stayed in the room with her, as did Secretary Chernosky and Salazar, the Chairman of the Joint Chiefs turned Secretary of Defense. Someone might be able to pull the wool over her novice eyes, but no one could get past those two.

The room was windowless, and with all the activity, the room was also stuffy.

"I need to talk to the nation," Abby said. "Someone get me air time, and get Bob Wicker over here."

The President's Assistant Press Secretary, Billy Duggles, slipped away and returned ten minutes later, confirming she had airtime at 8:00 p.m. The Press Secretary was out indefinitely with an infection following a hip replacement.

"Chaffee, show Poppy how to get someone into the building, please. Wicker and Duke will need unfettered access, and Duke is coming to the Northwest Gate with clothes for me."

She called Duke. Somehow her call went through.

"How are you holding up, Auntie Abby? Need me over there for a little muscle?"

CHAPTER THIRTY-EIGHT

THE GOLDEN CELL

November 22, afternoon

"I think it's time I went upstairs," Abby said. "Someone show me to the Oval Office, please?" She took a deep breath and let it out. She vowed to slow down.

She followed Cristo through the labyrinth up to the Oval Office.

"Give me a moment, please?" Abigail said to the group behind her.

She stepped across the threshold, alone, to a new life. Everyone stayed outside the door. The White House photographer quietly shot pictures without Abby's notice. This was history. Recording it was his job.

The first thing she noticed were family pictures on the credenza behind the President's desk. They made her incredibly sad. She picked them up and touched them. She looked around the room. It had not changed since she was last there. The butter-yellow walls, the navy rug with the Presidential Seal and the WH in the center were exactly as she remembered from her reaming out in the spring. Now the trees were bare. The Washington Monument loomed as if just out of reach.

I'm President and I've been in this room exactly once. For about fifteen minutes. Well, if Harry Truman did it during a war, I guess I'll have to also. I don't have any other choice. Maybe Harrington will be found alive.

One of the doors in the office wall led into a small study and a private bath. She could live out of there for now. There was a loveseat in there, but alas, it wasn't a sofa bed. Above it was a small painting, likely a Mary Cassatt, of a mother reading to her little girl. A masterpiece for the President's eyes only. *Did the child remind him of Margaret?*

The bath was tiny, the shower the size one might find in a French hotel bathroom, but it would do. Everything except the toilet paper was graced with the Presidential Seal: towels, soap dish, even the hand soap.

She walked back into the office.

Sooner or later, she had to sit in the chair. She tried it out. It was too big for her, but not by much. She found a throw pillow and put it in the seat. The chair was perfect. A shorter woman would look like a child behind the desk.

George Washington stared at her from across the room, and a monument to him was at her back.

I'll do you a good job, sir.

The Houdon busts of Jefferson and Franklin flanked the fireplace. *Oh, for an ounce of their wisdom.*

Once again, she heard her sister's voice.

Relax. You are standing on the shoulders of giants.

She beckoned in Salazar, Marilyn, and Hitchcock.

"If you two would work on my call list, I'd appreciate it. I'll be back in a second." She stepped outside to find Poppy, who had camped at the secretary's desk. Harrington's secretary was out of town.

"Poppy, how are you holding up?" Abigail asked.

"I'm making my lists of lists and trying to find people to do them."

"Would you ask the guy in charge of the building to come up here for a few minutes? I don't know if he is the curator or what. Chaffee should know."

"Yes, first I want to introduce you to the White House photographer."

Abby realized this too would be an unwelcome addition. She would, however, do her duty with as much grace as possible. Abby strode over to the man with a camera around his neck.

"I'm Abigail Adams." Abby stuck her hand out.

"Ken Clutter, ma'am." *Clutter, like Shutter. Luckily everyone wears badges.*

"Tell me the drill, Ken," Abigail said.

He gave her the short version. "Ignore me. I know to leave when secret things come up."

"Please signal me if my makeup needs work. The country doesn't need a hag. Pull on your ear or something."

He pulled on his ear.

"Yes, like that."

"No, ma'am. That wasn't a test."

Abby chuckled. She went into the office, dug out her makeup bag, and touched up her concealer and lip color. He followed her.

"This okay?" she asked.

"Yes, ma'am."

"And please, never let a picture of my rear end see the light of day."

"Yes, ma'am." He laughed. "You're not the first person to tell me that."

Ken started his camera clicking away as Marilyn and Salazar worked the phones. Hitch sat, Buddha-like, at the end of the room, the nuclear "football" in his lap.

"I made the list and gave it to the White House operators while you were out of the room,"

Marilyn said. "As soon as each person is on the line, you'll be notified by a tone and flashing caller ID."

"Got it."

Abby sat down at the desk. She remembered one other person to talk to. She dialed "0."

"Yes, ma'am?" the operator answered.

"Would you please get me the lead agent for President Harrington in Colorado?"

"Yes, ma'am," the voice said.

The phone trilled again. No ID.

"This is Abigail Adams."

"Tom Adamsen. SAC with President Harrington. I'm told you need a sit rep." His tone was condescending. He was clearly angry that someone else was answering his boss's phone.

Abby had watched enough television to know that a SAC was Special Agent in Charge and a sit rep was a situation report.

"Yes, please. I'm so very sorry for all of you, but can you update me? I'm putting you on speaker. I have the Secretary of State and General Salazar in with me. Bottom line please, at least right now?"

"There's not a snowball's chance in hell that he's alive. Oh, my God, that came out wrong."

"We're all stressed. Go ahead, please, sir."

"The base powder there was almost fifty inches, enormous for this time of year. Relatively low risk, except for some freeze/thaw cycles this time of year. We have video of the avalanche from the chopper as it happened. They were nearly at the bottom of the mountain, when the avalanche started. They heard it before they saw it, so they turned ninety degrees to get away from it. Unfortunately, they turned the wrong way. Sound is weird out in the mountains. They turned directly into the path of the greatest mass. Our best guess is that they are under at least a hundred feet of snow, rocks, and trees. It's been five hours; the likelihood of any survival approaches zero. For all of them."

"How about recovery?" Abby asked gently.

"We know where he is, based on his GPS signal. The problem is access."

"Is there equipment you want?" General Salazar asked.

"If I could get snow dozers airlifted into here, that would help. We can maybe go in from the sides."

"I'll get started on that. Give me your GPS coordinates." Salazar wrote them down.

"And your number?" Salazar wrote that down as well. "I'll be back with you."

"Agent Adamsen, can you send me the video over a secure line?" Abigail asked.

"No, ma'am. It'd go over the Web." Abby looked around the room. Salazar shook his head.

"We'll see it later, then. Do not release it to anyone in the meantime."

"Yes, ma'am."

Abby spoke with Majority Leader Schwartz, as well as other Hill leaders. Her message to each was the same platitude. I need you with me, lest our adversaries sense weakness. All agreed. She wondered how long that would last. *Hopefully till the end of the year.*

The phone trilled again.

It was the Queen.

"Good evening, Your Majesty," Abigail felt her throat drying out. She made a gesture for water, and Marilyn found her some, put a bottle on a coaster on the desk, and nodded her approval to Abby.

"We are so sorry. Is there any news about President Harrington?" The Queen sounded exactly as she did on television, though more animated.

"None. But we have several more hours of daylight in Colorado, so perhaps we'll have some news soon."

"This happened to friends of Arthur a few years back. It was devastating. One feels so helpless."

"Yes, I remember. Now I'm trying to emulate the 'Keep Calm and Carry On' mentality your mother personified during the War. And please, ma'am, do call me Abigail."

"My mother carried on with liberal quantities of gin, Abigail. I don't recommend it."

"I'll bear that in mind, ma'am."

"Do keep in touch," she said, then she was gone.

The French President Latour was lugubrious, but he was not known for any other personality trait.

Chancellor Vronsky of Russia was a wily old coot, but could not have been nicer to Abigail.

"Harrington is a good man. I assure you Russia will not take any advantage from this situation."

"Thank you, sir."

"And I don't know you, but you've nothing to fear from me. At least not now." Then he chuckled. "You call me if you have problem."

"Thank you, sir. I will."

As Abby made calls, she sent out notes of things to be done: get Duke in with clothes for tomorrow. Does he have a permanent pass yet? Gather entire building's staff after broadcast.

The curator showed up. He was a distinguished African-American gentleman somewhere in his older years. He wore rimless glasses that were spotless. His shoulders drooped a bit, and he had something of a paunch, but he was immaculately groomed in a dress shirt and tie and a cardigan sweater. He extended his hand.

"O.T. Wagner, curator."

"Abigail Adams. I need some help, and I was wondering if you were the person to call."

"If it has to do with these buildings, yes, ma'am. I've been here since well before you were born." His voice was warm and slow like molasses, his avuncular presence reassuring.

She told him what she needed. Within minutes after he left, the loveseat left the little study. Then a rollaway bed and rolling garment rack, cheval mirror, and floor lamp were installed. A housekeeper appeared with a pile of linens and left soundlessly a few minutes later. Another man appeared with an iron and ironing board. O.T. returned to check on things.

"Seeing as how you are a lady, I thought you would need more of a mirror than that little one in the bathroom. And the lamp is better for reading."

"Why, thank you, Mr. Wagner, that's quite thoughtful of you."

"Thinking is a critical part of my job," he said.

"This isn't your job, but I'd like to speak with everyone in the building after the speech at eight with refreshments. Can you set that up?"

"Of course."

"If the kitchen can't manage on such short notice, I'll be happy to spring for the refreshments." Abby dug into her purse and pulled out an AmEx.

O.T. laughed. "You are a breath of fresh air, that you are. Put that thing away, ma'am."

"What about alcohol?" Abigail asked. "I'm inclined against it."

"I agree. Too much sorrow to start drinking. And too much work ahead to get these people laid to rest."

"Speaking of that, are you also the House's historian? What about the protocol officer?"

"Close enough. We have one of each, but they report to me, and both are away for the holiday."

"If you need to call them back, please do."

"I already have."

"Good. You'll be in charge of the funeral arrangements, and dealing with the families, if you don't mind."

"It is the least I can do. Do you think the President is alive?" O.T. asked.

Abby spoke softly, with a hand on O.T.'s arm. "I hope so, but we should plan anyway." O.T. noticed she was shaking her head.

Duke appeared with her clothes on a hanger and a shopping bag of accessories. He hung them in the little study and Abby followed him in.

"How's Regina?" Abby asked.

"She's fine, waiting for you to give her some chores. Pretty fancy office you got here. Anyone ever tell you it was out of round?" Duke said, looking out into the Oval Office.

Abby rolled her eyes.

They went into the Oval Office, and she introduced him.

"This is Duke Temple, my nephew, and the apple of my eye," Abigail said.

If anyone thought it odd that he was six five and African American, no one said anything.

"How do you do?" he said, with a firm handshake to Marilyn, Cristo, and Capt. Hitchcock. Then she walked him to the door.

"Poppy, get Duke a permanent pass. I'm going to need all the help I can get over the next few days."

Poppy nodded.

"Duke, you may be Phi Beta Kappa and Law Review, but what I need right now is a gofer. And you're it, okay?" Abby said.

"Sure. I'm all yours. Regina says for you to eat."

"It's getting to be about that time."

"You scared?" he asked.

"Witless."

"Don't be." He put his big hands on her shoulders and looked down into her blue eyes. "You're smarter than the average President and a you are a fine human being. You'd get my vote, Madame President."

"Thank you, darling man, but don't you 'Madame President' me, Duke. Someone's gotta keep me in my place. Oh, here's the back line number." Abby scribbled it on a sticky note with the obligatory Presidential Seal on it. He immediately put it in his phone.

"I'll call in the middle of your speech, tell you how you are doing."

"Okay, Mr. Mouth, get outta here." Abby stood on tiptoe, bussed him on the cheek, and he left.

CHAPTER THIRTY-NINE

REASSURANCE

Abigail asked Poppy to send up dinner for all: Chernosky, Salazar, Cristo, Poppy, Chaffee, and Hitchcock. Everyone had to eat, they might as well do it together.

In the meantime, she did a rough draft of her speech on her mini.

By the time dinner came, she had a second draft. She timed it at less than five minutes. She hadn't a clue how to get it printed or to a teleprompter. Bob Wicker was due at six thirty—with Andre—thank goodness.

She'd polish the text with Wicker, and by seven they could set up.

Navy stewards served dinner for all in the President's dining room. Everyone was famished. They fell on their food like linebackers who'd missed the previous meal. For once, even Marilyn ate.

About halfway through the meal, Abby began to laugh.

"What's so funny?" Hitchcock asked, looking around.

"No one has said a word," Abby said. "We were all too hungry."

"You've got that right," Poppy replied, putting a big forkful of mashed potatoes into her mouth.

Abby slowed in her eating, wondering at the strangeness of a day.

"Just think, Hitch, I didn't know you this morning. Now you all but go to the bathroom with me."

"I'm used to waiting for women outside of ladies' rooms. My wife is pregnant, and she can't pass a ladies room without going in."

Everyone chatted for a while, and normal conversation was calming to Abby.

Dessert was chocolate mousse, and Abby was definitely a fan.

"I'd like this with every meal," Abby said.

"You'd hate it after a month straight," Poppy said.

Their thirty minutes of civility was over and all were back to work.

Salazar reported he had a dozer on the ground well away from the GPS signal, but close enough to start in, as well as generators and night lighting. They could work all night.

"Excellent, Cristo. Would you call Mrs. Harrington and tell her that? I will include that in the speech."

Abby added the phrase to the speech in her mini-computer. She asked Logan Chaffee how her Dell mini could be synced with the teleprompter.

"I'll call Charley. He knows everything electronic," Chaffee said.

"Oh, no. He'll take it away, along with my BlackBerry and Kindle, too."

"You'll get them back quickly."

"Okay, I guess."

"Goes with the territory. If you get the launch codes, you have to let them tinker with your toys," Chaffee said.

In about five minutes, a guy appeared who looked about twelve, except for his goatee.

"Hi, I'm Charley. You want your mini to talk to the teleprompter?"

"Yes, please." Abby was hoping this wouldn't take long. She had to polish the speech and get herself ready.

He fiddled with Abby's computer and talked into his headset.

"Is it up yet?" he asked of someone out in cyberspace. "Good."

"Ma'am? You're good to go. When you hit Print, choose Teleprompter and it will be there."

Abby was impressed.

"I assume you'll want my BlackBerry too?"

"'Fraid so." He held out his hand. She handed it to him.

"I don't want a tacky ringtone."

"You'll like it, I promise."

"Do you want my Kindle too?" Abby asked.

"Yes, but it'll still work just fine."

"Good. Otherwise I get cranky."

Each moment there was no news from the Situation Room, Abby felt safer. No hostiles were acting up anywhere. Yet.

Bob Wicker appeared in time to review her speech. Abby could tell he was in deadline mode. She conferred briefly with him about how she wanted it shot.

"I think you should speak from the White House briefing room," Wicker opined.

"No. I must be more Presidential. I will use the Oval Office."

"But it's too soon to sit behind the desk. You'll look like an interloper."

"I agree. I'll stand in front of Washington's portrait. Flank me with the busts of Jefferson and Franklin. I'll stand behind the lectern with the Presidential seal. If that doesn't project POTUS, I don't know what does," Abigail said.

While Wicker was setting up the broadcast, Andre set up his equipment. If Capt. Hitchcock was slightly startled at Andre's flamboyant appearance, he said nothing.

"Ooooh, Madam President, you have had a long, long day," Andre said as he set up his lighted mirror on the desk in the Oval Office. "I couldn't see my hand in front of my face in that bathroom."

"Don't you dare mess this desk up. It's priceless," Abby chided him.

"As is your image. So pipe down and let me work." He leaned her back in the chair, put a smock over her clothes and a shower cap on her head. Then he wrapped her in iced cloths. Abby hoped Clutter wasn't shooting this.

Andre unpacked his tackle boxes and chose his colors for her. Then he set out the hair products he would use.

"MmmKKkTkkk," Abby mumbled.

"Yes, I know you can't talk. That's why I did it that way. You know they do have a beauty salon over in the White House itself. Let's use that next time, okay?"

"MMMmm."

Andre unwrapped the cold towels. Five minutes later her makeup was done. Hair took another five.

"Shiny, shiny for the hair, so wash it tonight, okay?" Andre said, spraying hair spray all over. He pulled off the smock.

"Twirl, slowly."

She did. He took a lint roller to the part of the suit that would be in the shot.

"Perfect. Straws for the lipstick." He put a few in her hand, packed up, and was gone in under two minutes. "See you in a few." He blew her a kiss.

It was seven fifteen. Wicker approached her, and Abby stood to meet the White House floor director. He was a large slab of black granite and would have been more at home on the football field.

"Ma'am, I'm Samson. Mr. Wicker tells me you know how this works."

"Sort of."

"That's better than a lot of the Presidents I've worked with," he chuckled.

"All I ask is that you light me well. Light me badly, and I'll have to hunt you down," Abby said with mock anger.

"Yes, ma'am. I do not want a President mad at me."

Abby slipped in her IFB and miked herself.

"How is this for sound, magic guys in the control booth?" Abby asked. She hadn't the vaguest idea where in the White House complex they were.

"You look and sound fine," someone said into her earpiece.

The fire had been lit and would be burning gently in the background.

"Are you picking up any of the nat sound?" Abby asked. Background, or natural sound, enhances video.

"Yes, ma'am."

"Where is my monitor?" Abby asked. Sam pointed to it.

"Ooh, I need some eyedrops. Bob, can you hand me my bag, please?"

She deftly placed one drop in each eye to make them sparkle, then looked into the monitor again. Everything looked good.

The camera had the prompter on it.

She took a sip of water from a straw in a bottle, and then Wicker took it out of the shot.

"Ten minutes, everyone."

Abby asked for a run through in part so the person running the teleprompter could pick up her phrasing. Of course, she had written in the phrasing with her spacing, just like they taught her at Wicker. If it was good enough for Churchill, it was good enough for her.

"Bob, time me, please?"

At the end, he said, "Four fifty."

That was a little long for Abby's tastes, but compared to the droning most politicos did, it was downright brief. Any less would be rude.

Abby repositioned herself in front of the lectern. She kept her back ramrod straight. She leaned into the camera and put on her serious, but pleasant, neutral face. She imagined talking to just one person, to Regina, as she looked into the face of the camera, where the teleprompter put the words visible only to her.

"We're on in three…two…one…" Samson then pointed a finger to her.

She paused for half a beat to give re-broadcasters an edit point.

"Hello, everyone. My name is Abigail Adams.

"Through a bizarre and tragic series of events, I am now in the Oval Office as President of the United States. As of now, we think today's events, however tragic, are unrelated. We will, however, follow the evidence to a sound, and unbiased, conclusion.

"Acting Secretary of Defense Cristo Salazar just reported to me that heavy equipment, generators, and night lighting arrived by air near the site of President Harrington's GPS signal. Work will continue… night and day…to find President Harrington and his skiing companions.

"We all hope they are found alive, though the odds are against them. It does not escape me that this all happened on the day John F. Kennedy was lost to the nation in 1963."

Abigail briefly detailed the deaths of the Vice President and the Speaker of the House.

"So how does a Pediatric Emergency Doctor you've never heard of end up President? It's a little confusing, so bear with me."

She detailed the circumstances of her becoming President Pro Tem of the Senate.

"This morning, I started out giving family members a tour of the Senate. We got word of the President's tragic accident on television. Then we heard about the Vice President's collapse.

"Something…call it intuition…made me leave the Senate and cross the street to the Supreme Court. If something evil was afoot, no one would look for me there. I was with the Chief Justice when we learned about the Speaker's death. The rest you know from video the Court released.

"Long story, short? In a horrible and chaotic situation, the Constitution worked, just as it was designed to do. There has been an orderly transfer of power, and the country is as safe tonight as it is any other night. The business of government will continue as seamlessly as possible.

"We did have overuse problems with communications. We'll address this problem in the coming weeks.

"I am here, on duty to my country, until either the President returns or his term expires. As an emergency doctor, I am used to watching over people at night. It's one of the things I do.

"I cannot promise you perfection, but I do promise you my absolute best. Your safety and well-being are my first priority.

"Tomorrow is Thanksgiving Day. For millions of us, it's not only about giving thanks for our blessings, it's also about turkey and football. As you gather your loved ones, please remember not only our missing and lost leaders and their companions, but the families they leave to mourn.

"We enjoy the blessings of freedom because some two-point-two million Americans serve their country. Many are far away and in harm's way. They too deserve your thanks and prayers.

"We'll talk more over the next few days about how and when we will honor those who perished today. For now, their families join me in urging you to go on with your holiday plans.

"Good night, and God bless."

CHAPTER FORTY

BEDTIME

Abigail waited for Samson to tell her she was clear. She knew to wait for that signal. Otherwise, she'd say or do something the world would see and hear.

"We're clear," he said. "Great job."

She exhaled into a slump, unplugged her IFB and mike. She wasn't sure if she could stand. She sat down hard on the sofa. She had been on auto-pilot during the talk, picturing herself talking to Regina and Duke, who were watching at home.

She was fine with that fantasy. Reality was millions, maybe billions, around the world saw her.

She started to get the shakes.

Wicker appeared at her side with a glass of lemonade from the little fridge.

"Here, drink this. You need some sugar."

Abby's hands were shaking, but she drank it through the straw Andre had left her.

Wicker squatted in front of her and made her look into his eyes.

"Home run, bases loaded, last game of the World Series," he said.

"Really?" Abby was near tears.

"Don't you dare cry, you have to talk with the people in the building."

Mikey Molloy, whom Poppy had summoned, appeared with his arms open. Abigail walked into them for a hug. She was surprised her legs supported her.

"My dear, you have made an old man very proud," Mikey said.

She noticed that George Washington was still looking at her from his portrait on the wall. She was going to have to get used to that. Then Hitch walked in with the football to add his congratulations.

"Where is the meeting?" Abby asked.

"The East Room of the White House," Poppy answered. "Only room big enough for everyone."

Ken Clutter came in, snapping away. Secret Service agents appeared to walk her east. Since the West Wing sits lower than the White House itself, they walked from the first floor of the West Wing into the basement of the White House. The red carpeting was cheerful, but Abby thought the underground walkway cavernous and chilly.

They took an elevator up to the State Floor of the White House and walked down a short hall into the East Room.

The room was filled to capacity, and everyone stood as Abby walked in. Many were somber, most were very tired. She shook as many hands as she could, whether it was a busboy's or a Cabinet member's, as all had gotten her through this day of days.

She spoke from a lectern just at the entrance to the room. This configuration, she would learn later, allows for the most people to be in the room. If she were to speak from the traditional East end of the room, not everyone could be accommodated.

"Please, please, everyone take a seat. We've all had a long, horrible day. We just need a few minutes together, to share a glass of something. What is it we are having?"

"Spiced cider," the chef boomed from the back of the room. "Und gingerbread." Everyone laughed at his thick German accent.

"Today has been a horribly tragic day for our country. All of you did your duty with honor. You kept this country going, even if you didn't know that's what you were doing. Thank you from the bottom of my heart. Everyone, please, get something to eat and drink. Something to fuel your prayers for the Harrington family. And help you through the days ahead."

Abby mingled with the crowd of staff, but declined pictures. It wasn't the time for pictures. It was nearly ten by the time she finished. The staff's energy buoyed her along, but she knew she was going to go face down if she didn't get to bed.

She said a brief good night in the White House to Poppy and Mikey.

"I'll see you at seven for the PDB," Poppy said. Abby hadn't the vaguest what a PDB was, but she'd be dressed and ready. Mikey's man was coming to get him and Poppy.

Abigail, Hitch, and her agents trudged back to the West Wing.

Her feet felt leaden and swollen. Each step seemed a greater effort. She pictured the bed made up. She imagined a good shower, her nightgown, some socks, and a face plant into the bed.

Sufficient unto the day was the evil thereof.

Hitch's relief was outside the door to the Oval Office.

"Captain Shad Dabaghi, ma'am. I'm here to babysit the football," he said, extending his hand. His name might be foreign, but his accent was pure New Orleans.

"So nice to meet you. Do you stay awake all night?"

"Yes, ma'am. I telecommute to the Pentagon while on duty."

"I don't know why they let him into West Point," Hitch said. "He was the worst tight end in West Point history."

"As long as he keeps hold of this football, I'm happy. Good night, gentlemen."

Two Marine Sentries flanked her door.

"Night, guys," Abby said, trudging through the doors.

"Good night, ma'am," they said in unison.

Abby undid her suit jacket and unzipped her skirt as she crossed the Oval Office. As soon as she was in the little study, she hung up her suit, peeled off her panty hose and undergarments and threw them in a pile in the corner. She unpinned her hair and headed naked into the little bathroom, her makeup bag in hand. She rummaged through it. There was no shampoo, but at least she had extra contacts for tomorrow.

She took out her contacts and cleaned the layers of makeup off her face with the wipes she always carried. She brushed out her hair before she stepped into the shower.

The water was furiously strong and beat the kinks out of her shoulders. There was s hotel-sized bottle of shampoo with the Presidential seal on it. Washing off the day's grime was essential to her sleep. She washed her hair first, then vigorously scrubbed herself with a rough washcloth from her face to between her toes. *I might make it as far as the bed after all.*

She rinsed off and wrapped a hand towel around her wet hair, then patted herself dry with the bath towel. She reached for her robe, but it was not on the hook.

Damn.

She wrapped herself in the towel, brushed her teeth, slicked her face with moisturizer, and slathered lotion on her still-damp skin. She padded out into the study.

In the shopping bag were underwear and accessories for tomorrow. There was nothing for her to sleep in.

Double damn.

She could not sleep naked in the Oval Office study. What if there was an emergency? She wouldn't sleep in dirty underwear. She'd never fall asleep in a suit.

She needed something, anything, even a...

She flicked on the lights in the Oval Office and streaked across the room.

She opened the door and stuck her toweled head around the edge.

The Marine Sentries snapped to attention, and at the glimpse of Presidential skin put their eyes forward.

"Uh, guys. I have a problem. I need a tee-shirt. To sleep in. Please?"

They tried not to smile. They tried harder not to laugh. Even Shad was amused.

"I know, I know, but can I have one of yours, please? I'll return it clean, I promise," she said. "I don't care who donates, just one of you please help me out."

The taller one looked at the other, and they shrugged.

The taller Marine said, "Certainly, ma'am. After all, you are the Commander-in-Chief, and if you order me to give you the shirt off my back, I'll give it to you."

"It is not an order, it is a request." Abigail realized dignity dissolved in the face of near nakedness. *They were enjoying this, all three of them.*

As he began to unbutton, she quickly shut the door. She was also suddenly scared someone would see her through the undraped Oval Office windows. Transparency was great for government, but lousy for a woman wearing two towels in the Oval Office.

There was a rap on the door. She opened it a crack. A male hand put his tee-shirt through the door.

"What's your name and rank, Marine?"

"Thompson, Mark. Sergeant, ma'am."

"Thanks, Sgt. Thompson. I'll return it."

She shut the door, streaked across the room, and shut herself into her study. She jotted his name and rank onto a sticky note.

She put on the tee-shirt and smelled the pleasant fragrance of pure male. *Oooh, it had been a long time since she'd smelled any man up close and personal.*

She sat down on the bed and went to set her BlackBerry, forgetting that Charley still had it. She picked up the phone and gave her wakeup call to the operator.

"Sleep well, ma'am."

"Thank you. Thank you very much."

"If I may say so, we all thought your talk was wonderful. Our switchboard lit up, and ninety-nine percent of the calls were favorable."

"And your name is?"

"I'm Mabel, ma'am. I've been the head operator on the night shift for nearly fifteen years."

"Thank you, Mabel." *Mabel was biased, and as for the speech, it was likely beginner's luck.*

The bed was made up and turned down for her. There was a mint on her pillow. Even it had the Presidential Seal on it. *Oh, good grief.*

Abby ate it anyway as it was dark chocolate.

She unloosed her hair and towel dried it as much as she could. She called Regina and Duke, who were together.

"Hi, guys, I'm sorry I'm not going to be there tomorrow for Thanksgiving," Abby said, nearing tears.

"Girl, you got other rows to hoe," Regina said. "You did a real good job on your speech. The phone's been ringing off the hook here."

"Thanks. Oh, when you send Duke in the morning, would you pack me enough stuff for a week? Including stuff to sleep in. Also I'll need more contact lenses and my hair dryer."

"Oh, I am so sorry," Regina said. "What are you sleeping in?"

"Oh, I rummaged around and found a tee-shirt," Abby sort of lied. Duke told her good night, that he'd be there in the morning about ten.

Then she crawled into bed.

As soon as she stretched out, she felt the dig of the cross bar. She could have sworn this was the same damned bed she had in her sister's apartment. Oh, well, she was so tired, she could sleep on a bed of nails.

Then the tears started. At first it was a trickle, then a flow, finally a torrent. She knew they were tears of fear, sheer unadulterated fear. *What was I thinking? Why didn't I just let O'Neal have the damn job? Who do I think I am, Superwoman?*

Then the tears slowed from a torrent to a flow, back to a trickle, and she was asleep.

The phone jangled once. At 3:00 a.m. She did not bother to lift her head. She simply turned her face toward the phone and put it to her ear, as she had countless times in hospital on-call rooms.

"Thisdoctoradams," she said, sound asleep. She would awaken only if necessary.

"President Adams. Cristo Salazar. In the Situation Room. Sorry to disturb."

Abby was immediately awake.

"Yes, Cristo, what is it?" *Please, please, let this be something I can handle.* She sat up and flipped on the light.

"The President's body has just been recovered."

Abby felt the world drop out from underneath her.

TO BE CONTINUED

EXCERPT
THE ACCIDENTAL PRESIDENT

The third Saturday in January

Abby gave herself extra time to get ready for the State Dinner. As President, she got dressed at a dead run most of the time. Regina was downstairs tending to something, so she had peace and quiet.

Winter always gave her lizard skin. So after her shower, she slathered baby oil onto her damp skin. She was practically glistening from so much extra moisture. She patted herself dry and fished out the spandex, backless slip from the accessories bag. Her sparkly red toenails were supposed to be seen, so she did not need panty hose. *Yes!*

Andre was due momentarily for hair and makeup, so Abby pulled the slip over her head. Well, she tried to, anyway. Somehow, it wouldn't go down. She contorted herself and one arm shot out through an armhole, like a stone from a slingshot. She was starting to sweat. *I must look like a perfect idiot.*

She wrestled the other arm into its armhole, but it was even harder. She'd try for a while, then rest and try again. By now, sweat was streaming down between her breasts.

The spandex monster took on a life of its own and settled in the real estate between her breasts and her armpits. She could barely breathe. The underwires poked her, and one pointed ominously toward an eye.

Don't panic. Just push the panic button. Help will appear.

She was not going to summon armed men to see her naked, sweaty, and being squeezed to death by an overgrown rubber band. There was no female agent on today. There had to be a better way.

I'll cut this off. Where were the scissors? Regina had them downstairs. *Okay. What about a knife?*

Don't be ridiculous. She couldn't walk across to the kitchen to get that chainsaw thing for the turkey. *Besides, what if I cut myself?*

She sat down on the bed and got control of her emotions. She wasn't blue. She could breathe. Sort of. This thing had to go back up over her head, or it had to go down.

At first, she tried to pull it down. That didn't work.

Judging from the discrepancy between the small size of the tube and the relatively larger size of her body, back over the head was the most likely way to extract herself.

She crossed her arms, her right hand grabbing the wad under her left arm and vice versa. She exhaled to make her chest as small as possible and she pulled with all of her might.

Nothing.

She tried it again.

Nothing, still. She was sweatier, but that didn't count as progress.

She would rest and try a third time. If that didn't work, she'd wrap herself in a robe and call her agents. She'd do whatever it took to silence them. *Probably a case of some rare, single malt Scotch for each. Cads. They'd blab anyway. She'd make Secret Service history.*

The third time, the garment came off with a giant plopping sound. Abigail inhaled lungs full of nice, sweet oxygen. She looked at herself in the mirror. Her face looked like a wet beet, her hair was in full frizz.

At least I didn't break a fingernail.

Andre knocked at the door.

"Just a second," she said, hastily throwing on her robe.

"Madam President, baby, what on earth have you been doing? You look horrible." Andre gasped and put his hand to his mouth.

"Oh, well, you know." Abigail waved her hand vaguely. "I'll pop into the shower and be out in a sec. Just start setting up."

Andre was suspicious until he saw the garment snake on the bed.

"Ah-hah! You tried to put a spandex slip on over your head, didn't you?" he all but cackled.

"No comment!" Abigail yelled from the bathroom. She showered quickly and did a quick rinse of her sweat-laden hair. She didn't want to smell like the workout she'd just had.

Andre worked in record time.

Abby wore her hair in a loose French twist, with "charming escapees."

Just as Andre finished, Kim knocked softly on the door.

"Aunt Abby, would you like me to help you with your outfit?" she said sweetly. "If you have dusting powder, it will make things go more easily. I tried to bring some in, but the Secret Service would not let me."

"That would be lovely, Kim." Abby tried to channel Kim's calmness.

Andre blew her a kiss and stole away.

"First you must be completely dry, no oils or anything. Then put on a lot of dusting powder. Then you step into the slip and pull it up. You may wear a thong, but the dress works best with just the undergarment," Kim said, demurely turning her back for Abby's privacy.

Great. Now she tells me.

Abby considered putting on a thong, but with her luck and this thing, she'd likely have the Mother of all Wedgies at a State Dinner

Abby skipped the underwear and dusted herself with scented powder. She stepped into the spandex creature. It behaved perfectly. Abby fiddled with the underwires and straps for a moment, and then all was well. She put the launch codes and thumb drive into the bra part.

"I think I am ready for the dress now, Kim," Abigail said, looking into the mirror.

Kim helped her into the dress and zipped up the side zipper. The side slit went nearly to the bottom of the zipper. The dress felt like a liquid silk, and Abby gasped at herself in the mirror.

I feel like the most beautiful woman in the world.

The midnight-blue silk crepe, with the tiniest of silver sparkles, draped beautifully at the neckline, a cross between a small cowl and a bateau neck. If the neckline were an inch wider, it would fall off Abigail's shoulders. The dress was all but backless, with a true back cowl. Kim took out the double-sided tape.

"This way, nothing will show," she said, putting the double-stick tape in strategic locations.

Abigail put on her late sister's Edwardian diamond and sapphire shoulder-duster earrings. Pris loved antique jewelry, she called it sparkling history. She wore her watch and signet ring, both also from Pris. *I miss you so much, Sissy.*

Perhaps, just perhaps, I can forget the Spandex Strangler and enjoy myself.

"You are very lovely," Kim said sweetly. "Mr. Aston will be amazed."

"You made me lovely. The talent is all yours. And who is Mr. Aston?"

"He's your escort? Michael Aston? I met him on my way up. He is even handsomer than in his movies."

Abby's heart all but stopped beating. Was Michael Aston really Mikey Molloy's "nephew with the U.N.?"

Mikey Molloy, I swear I will get you for this one. Only you would send me on a blind date to a State Dinner with this year's Sexiest Man Alive.

CPSIA information can be obtained at www.ICGtesting.com
Printed in the USA
LVOW081556260612

287746LV00012B/166/P